IN SEARCH OF HEER

Manjul Bajaj worked in the field of environment and rural development before she became a writer. She is the author of *Come, Before Evening Falls* (shortlisted for the Hindu Literary Prize in 2010) and *Another Man's Wife* (shortlisted for the Hindu Literary Prize in 2013). She has also written two books for children —*Elbie's Quest* and *Nargisa's Adventures*.

IN SEARCH OF HEER

MANJUL BAJAJ

First published by Tranquebar, an imprint of Westland Publications Private Limited in 2019
1st Floor, A Block, East Wing, Plot No. 40, SP Infocity, Dr MGR Salai, Perungudi, Kandanchavadi, Chennai 600096

This edition independently published by Manjul Bajaj, 2019

ISBN: 9781692671778

'The future has an ancient heart.'
– Carlo Levi

Contents

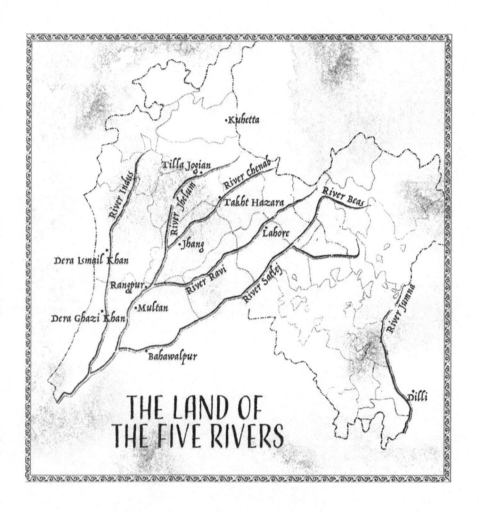

THE LAND OF
THE FIVE RIVERS

I

LEAVING HOME

1

Deedho No More

EVEN WITH A BLINDFOLD on me, I would know Takht Hazara in
an instant. I would know it from the sound of the Chenab as it
rushes and rolls over the boulders congregated like a gathering of
ruminating old men on the bend in the river. From the fluttering of
the terns winging their way to their nests in the sandbanks at dusk.
And from the smell of the winter fog on the riverbank as it gets
smoky with the smell of burning cowdung patties. But most of all
from the soft caress of the river breeze on my face, its touch as gentle
as my father's hands as they wiped away my tears when I was a boy.

But Takht Hazara was not for me.

You could say that it was ordained from birth that I should
leave my father's village one day. What parents would name their
son Deedho and expect him to stay the course? Dee-dho, dee-dho,
dee-dho. Like a donkey braying down a dirt path protesting the
too-heavy load on its feckless back. One could make excuses for
them, I suppose. You could blame it on my mother's exhaustion.
The nine successful deliveries that preceded my birth—seven sons
and two daughters—must have left her with very little imagination
and originality when it came to baby names. Or, perhaps, it could be
attributed to the overprotective and intense love that my father felt
for his youngest son and how it coalesced into this weak, squeaky

sound for a name. Like something that's knobbly at the knees, green behind the ears, entirely without spine. What stature could anyone hope to grow into with a name like that? Youthful rebellion was a given from the first time that misguided moniker left my fond parents' lips. You could say that my departure from Takht Hazara began with the giving of that ridiculous name at my birth.

In contrast, my family name was a proud one, one becoming of the best of men. But I needed to cross the river and enter the world as a stranger before I could stake my claim to it. In my village there were hundreds of Ranjhas. My seven brothers, my scores of cousins, their combined progeny. All ruddy-skinned, bright-eyed, long-limbed, narrow-hipped, broad-shouldered, full of male shine and swagger, or getting there. I could never have become Ranjha, living peaceably amidst all those Ranjhas. I had to leave Takht Hazara to repossess and claim the name of my clan and make it truly my own—to relegate into oblivion the brothers, the cousins, the nephews, all—and stand poised across the vast, undulating deserts of time, the sole bearer of that name.

After I left Takht Hazara, I heard some stories circulating of my being a rake of sorts. Not true. I was nothing more than an average scorer at the rough and tumble in the haystacks game. What ladykiller could go around making amorous conquests being called Deedho all the while? I was just a lad. Easy bantering, getting a laugh out of the ladies, playing Krishna with my flute to the gaggle of cowgirls on the riverbank—it came naturally to me. Charm ran freely in our bloodline. But in Takht Hazara I was and always would be a tail-ender. Pampered, indulged, favoured by my father, but the runt of the litter all the same. The youngest born don't get to grow into their illustrious fathers' shoes. It's not scripted that way. Unless you're not squeamish about fratricide.

My father, Chaudhary Mauzzudin or Mauju Chaudhary as he was more commonly known, was a benign banyan tree of a man. While he lived, rebellion was not an option. Everything prospered under his shade. Like the fretting of the black ants, the stinging nastiness of the bees, the scurrying diligence of the squirrels, the raucous shrieking of the parrots, the reckless swinging of the long-tailed monkeys and the night-time grumbling of the grey owls know a hospitable home and an easy co-existence in the spreading branches and aerial roots of the grand ficus, all of us brothers, sisters, uncles, aunts, cousins, elders and youngsters knew not our own warring natures and varying proclivities while we were contained in the expansive, all accepting goodness of my father's heart.

When I was barely a young lad of eight or nine summers, some premonition of my future careers as a legendary lover and wandering fakir must have rippled through me.

'I don't want a haircut,' I said, running away from the monthly tonsuring ritual.

Father, my seven older brothers and I were sitting in a neat row on the raised platform running along the front of the house, being ministered to with scissors and scalpels by the village barber and his two grown-up sons. I simply stood up and started walking away. My curly brown locks were too beautiful to be messed with by these thick-wristed, heavy-handed, coarse-fingered men. The barber's sons scurried after me trying to persuade me back to my place. Father stalled them with a gently held up palm.

'Let the child do as he pleases,' he said. 'There are worse crimes in this world than keeping long hair.'

My eldest brother's wife hunted through her vanity box and mockingly made a present of her arsi to me. It amused me to wear that mirrored ring she gave me for many days. When she passed by, I made it a point to gaze at my reflection in the ring and sigh in mock admiration. To crack jokes at one's own expense is not entirely without danger. The incident left me saddled with the reputation of being a dandy.

Father, having conferred the right of self-determination to me on matters tonsorial, did not once get swayed into decreeing otherwise.

I wore it long, I teased it into a mass of curls, I oiled it and perfumed it with the finest fragrances. I had it cut to a manageable length whenever I tired of its excessive drama and grew it back again a few months later. When the mood took me, I stuck a peacock feather in my tresses and played my flute on the riverbank like the infidel god. I was the Chanan river's own Kanhaiya, silhouetted every dusk against a sky burnished in the red-gold hues of the drowning sun, every grain of sand on the riverbank drenched in my music, every reed swaying softly to my tune.

'Father, this sweating and slaving in the fields like a beast of burden is not for me,' I told him, when the time came for me to start farming my portion.

'So be it,' he said.

I was made the chief cowherd of the clan, our hundred and twenty head of cattle my sole responsibility. My buffaloes, my flute, my cowherd's staff, the banks of the silvery Chanan—this was the life I was content to lead. A staff in my hand, strong thongs on my feet, a bamboo flute to my lips, a coarse shawl over my shoulders, a robust packed lunch in my bag. I would leave home at dawn with the herd and return only after dusk.

Every morning began with a bath in the cool river water. Leaving my clothes on the riverbank, I would plunge in for a swift swim, the river's strong current a challenge to my limbs. That done, I walked around till I found the finest bits of pasture for the herd to graze upon. While the cattle grazed, I would sit under the shade of some tree and eat my morning meal of stale bread with raw onions and green chillies, glugging down the accompanying pitcher of buttermilk in a few quick gulps. As morning turned to noon, and the coolness of water began to call out to the cattle, we headed back to the river. The buffaloes would sit about in the shallows, caked in wet mud, their bellies swollen and sated, their breath rising and ebbing, their bodies in communion with the spirit of the earth. On some afternoons I would search out conversation

with a boatman or with the occasional wise man who may have
come down from the snow-clad Himalayan peaks for a short respite
in the plains before disappearing again into his pristine cave. On
others I would stretch out for a nap. My brothers' wives complained
that I was unmindful of saying the five prayers that should ritually
interrupt every man's day. But, in truth, my entire day passed like
an unbroken prayer.

My music was the purest form of worship. I searched for the
perfect bamboo reed and fashioned it into a flute. Placing my lips
sideways against the wood, my breath blowing through its hollow
length, my fingers lightly moving across it, my mind poised at the
edge of existence, I pulled out the day's tune from the sky of all
possibilities. I played with all my heart and for all I was worth, each
time, every time. The buffaloes would fall into stillness, only their
limpid black eyes alive to the music, glittering, sentient. The cows,
the goats, the stray curs, the wandering mendicants, the boatmen
on the river, the girls come to fill water, all of them would be drawn
into the umbra of the music and become still. The trees, the birds
nesting inside them, the clouds, the river rushes and reeds, all at
rapt attention, listening to Ranjha on the riverbank playing his flute.

However, my growing reputation as a flautist in the surrounding
villages disturbed my mother deeply. It wasn't a man's work, she
despaired. Her disapproval burnt into me softly, with its steady, dull
heat, like the ashes from the coal oven on which she cooked our
meals. The ashes looked innocuous but I, who was inside their folds,
felt their burn reaching my heart and singeing it.

'Let the boy follow his heart,' Father said.

'It is not without reason that the head and shoulders are placed
above the heart in the human body. If you permit him to continue
like this, mindless and irresponsible of life's demands, who will feed
him once we are gone?' countered Mother.

'The All Seeing, Almighty Allah who feeds us all,' Father
responded, his face wreathed in his customary smile, his gaze

conciliatory. He did not wish for this to become another reason for Mother's growing displeasure with me.

Mother's quiet anger could rage like the summer west wind, the hot and dry loo breeze, relentless and sapping when it was in season, reaching into the cool depths of the heart and leaving it dried out and shrivelled at the edges.

'What woman will take him for a husband?' she fumed.

'The very finest in the land. One who is noble enough to know that there is more to life than just the growing and eating of bread,' Father replied.

'Your leniency is spoiling him,' said Mother, banging the door behind her as she stormed out of the room.

'Better spoilt than ruined completely,' said Father softly into the settling dust of her departure.

Mauju Chaudhary was a man way ahead of his time and amongst all of us who called him Father, I was certainly the proudest to do so. He knew so well the art of letting be, letting things prosper and flourish. He was all gentle rain, no threatening thunder or flashing lightning to his persona. There was not a single illiberal bone in his mighty frame.

However, destiny deploys life and death to play the game on its behalf. One sullen evening it rolled the dice of death without warning. The dove of father's soul rose up into the sky and became a tint of blue in the vast infinitude. Something ruptured in my heart and I felt that sad, moist evening's weight settle on my shoulders, never to leave again.

My time to leave Takht Hazara was approaching.

It could not be otherwise. I do not bemoan my mother's meagre love for me. I do not blame my brothers for their cupidity or their wives for their grasping greed. Kindness on their part would have only delayed the unfolding of my destiny. I needed to leave. How else would I have met Heer?

Better a hundred deaths for Heer than a life without her.

The world hates those who do not conform. It is easier to forgive liars and cheaters, thieves and murderers than to tolerate someone who does not aspire to the same things as others. To be loved and respected by his brothers, a man must want what his brothers want— ample land to his name, rich food on his table and a comely wife in his bed. To be indifferent to these is to cast a slur on their lives.

No story of brotherly discord can be complete without the treachery of women. Without my brothers' wives there might have been no departure from Takht Hazara. Men only fight to become heroes in their women's eyes. They only seek the trophies of land and gold to proffer them as offerings to their women. And women, what do they want? If only we knew that, all of our lives would be simpler.

To come into manhood in a large family full of women was no easy thing. Seven older brothers. Their seven wives (not to mention the occasional visits of the two married sisters and their husbands). Seven different couplings to break the silence of the nights I slept in. And in the day, seven pairs of breasts to keep my eyes from straying inadvertently. It was far simpler really to be the clan's cowherd than to hang around at home playing youngest brother. To leave at dawn and to return so dog tired at dusk as to be insensible to the snogging sounds that filled the night. I stayed clear of my sisters-in-law instinctively. I avoided both, the ones who sought to mother me and the ones who sought to make eyes at me from behind the dupattas they asked me to help them dry out in the courtyard.

Only with Sahiba, the seventh one, I erred. She was the nearest to me in age and I mistook her for a friend.

A favourite thing for my brothers' wives to do was to sit at the spinning parties with their friends, night after night, talking about my waywardness. The spinning circle is the bane of village life. It's not all love songs and raunchy jokes that the women sing and share, as they sit together spinning yarn. Nor is it just exchanges of sisterly sympathy about menstrual cramps and mothers-in-law, though that too happens. Gossip is what keeps those wheels spinning well into the night.

Deedho has an extra serving of rice or buttermilk and he becomes a man of insatiable appetite. He throws a few coins at a beggar and he is profligate. He shares a quiet chillum with a sadhu on the riverbank and he is an addict without a future. He smiles and chats up a girl for a few minutes and he is a philanderer. A random woman, entranced by his music, sends him a love note written in her blood, her husband wallops her when he finds out and Deedho, who had nothing to do with the entire sequence of events, becomes a homewrecker.

Sahiba would come running to me with these freshly spun tales of my perfidy. And young and stupid that I was, I sat there mulling over them, trying to sift the lies from the truth.

Vain.

Flirt.

Wastrel.

That was the main thrust of the spinning circle's accusations against me.

Vain. Yes, I admired the fineness of my features, the bounce of my curls, the lightness of my gait, the dexterity and fluidity of my music, the vastness of my mind. What good is false humility? He who shuts his eyes to his own beauty becomes blind to the rest of the world's magnificence too.

Flirt. Not true. Many silly girls had feigned the act of fainting on the riverbank in the hope of being carried back home by me, but to hold me responsible for their dramas was ridiculous in the extreme.

Wastrel. Yes and no. Yes, if the only definition of work is ploughing the land, if the only tenable measure of a man's worth is the number of bushels of grain that he can extract from the earth's rough surface. Yes, if the jingling of coins in a pocket is considered more musical than the notes of sweet melody that rise out of a flute and into the air.

Egged on by their wives, and silently supported by my mother, my brothers went to great lengths to cheat me out of my fair share of our father's inheritance. Strange, when you consider that my part of the land was all theirs to cultivate anyway. All I ever asked in exchange was a bellyful of rice, some coarse bread and buttermilk, with a few slices of onion on the side. I was not asking for the food as alms either, for I looked after their cattle in its stead.

Yet, the qazi was called and bribed to measure out our lands and I was given the most inhospitable tracts to cultivate, land so hard that a bull would refuse to defecate on it. But the man of justice saw it fit to risk his eternal soul to cheat me of my rightful share. The village elders sagely sided with him and my brothers. The whole village lined up against a young man of twenty-odd summers. Why?

History would have you believe it was jealousy, sibling rivalry come to a head, for was not Deedho his father's favourite? But I don't think it was jealousy at all. It was fear. Raw, naked, frightened-out-of-its-silly-skin fear. That everything they were striving for was perhaps worth nothing. That they had got it all wrong and happiness wasn't fine clothes and many servants and pots of gold but notes of music teased out of the air and blown adrift again into the passing breeze. And thus gripped by this fear, they struck.

Sahiba dealt the final blow. A homely woman is more dangerous than an outright beauty. Her queenly ego, I was to find out, was no less lethal for being camouflaged by her scrawny figure and buck teeth. A woman should not be plain. It fools a man into dropping his guard.

'My friends tease me saying I must be in love with you. They say that's why I bring you hot food every day,' she said to me, one desultory noon as we sat beneath the reeds on the cool riverbank, a lone white cloud shaped like a headless horse floating aimlessly above us in the measureless blue of the sky. Fetching food for me was a practice she had begun when she came into the family. I had been happy to go along. I thought it was her ruse to get away for a bit from my mother's dour disapproval.

'Well, if the gossip upsets you, just stop coming. That will shut them up real quick,' I said, taking one last gulp of the cool buttermilk before handing the urn back to her.

'You mean it's nothing to you that I have been bringing food for you, day after day, for the past two years? Just stop, he says. Just like that. Hired today. Fired tomorrow. Like I'm some kind of servant girl,' she spat out fiercely, standing with her hands on her hips, her nostrils flared in anger.

'Wait a minute before you flash those eyes at me!' I said. 'I'm not ungrateful but if it's getting you into trouble or spoiling your reputation, it clearly must stop, mustn't it?'

It would be silly for Sahiba not to heed the warnings being thrown her way, while they were still couched as jokes and harmless leg pulling. Gossip is society's watchman, wall and whip, all at once. Tale by malicious tale, rumour by rumour, the wall of society's narrow morality is erected. Inside it is the cosy warmth of belonging. Outside, it is brutally cold and lonely. Sahiba was better off on the right side of the divide.

'Oh, don't you worry, my beautiful brother-in-law, I've found an effective way of shutting them up. I told them you are to marry Habiba,' she laughed. 'I told them I'm just keeping an eye on my little sister's prospective groom till she comes to take charge of his lunch.'

I blanched at the thought of her little sister. She had been a freckled, straggly twig of a girl with a slight limp during the time of my brother's wedding two years ago. I was aware, of course, that time did magical things to scrawny teenaged girls, making them all curvaceous and comely, but in Habiba's case, time could try every trick and it would still fail. Besides, she giggled annoyingly and excessively. I was certainly not going to be brother-in-law twice over to Sahiba, whatever fond hopes she might nurse.

'You must not tell such lies. It will be worse for you when you are found out,' I said sternly.

'But it's all fixed,' she said airily. 'Your mother has agreed. She is happy with the terms my parents are offering.'

Oh, so that was it! I was being sold off for a fat dowry.

'How dare you plot and plan behind my back,' I said angrily. 'Why would I marry some chit of a girl with more freckles on her nose than cells in her brain?'

That was a bit reckless and rude, I must admit. I saw Sahiba's face heating up, the small red spots on her cheeks suddenly raging like a blistering noon, her face a summer storm.

'My sister is not good enough for you, is it?' she said. 'Who are you going to marry then? Heer Syal?'

It was held in our parts that the women of Jhang were unrivalled in their beauty—light-eyed, fair-skinned, ruby-lipped, lissom and graceful—veritable fairies from heaven walking on earth. The finest amongst the Jhang women were the daughters of the proud Syals. Raised in the lap of luxury, they bathed from childhood in rosewater and milk; pastes of sandalwood and almonds, mudpacks from Multan, crushed saffron and sweet honey from the mountains of Kashmir and perfumes from Arabia made up their toilet. Only the finest silks and muslins touched their lovely bodies. The very finest, the most legendary beauty amongst these magnificent daughters of the Syals was Heer, the diamond among women.

My father's words ran through my head. Only the finest woman in the land would do for me. If Heer was the finest, then Heer it would be.

'A wastrel like you should be glad of whatever you can get,' said Sahiba sourly, her lips curled into a sneer to underline what a worthless creature I was regarded to be, all around.

It hurt. I had thought of her as my best friend till then.

'Yes,' I said to her through gritted teeth. 'Heer Syal shall be my wife. Tell my mother that, and my brothers too. Tell that to your gossiping friends in the spinning room. I will come back to Takht Hazara with Heer as my bride, or I will not return again to see their faces.'

Saying that, I left.

'Deedho,' she called after me frantically.

But I was hell-bent on being Deedho no more.

2

Feet and Flute

IF I WERE TO do it again, I would not leave home with only the clothes on my back, my staff and my flute. Food, any food, even puffed rice and roasted gram, would have come in handy. As would have an axe, a small knife, a heavy blanket, a comb, and perhaps my sister-in-law Lali's mirrored ring. Don't laugh about the comb and ring. That altercation with the mullah at the mosque in Lalian could definitely have been avoided had I been better groomed. These men of power, these chieftains and clerics, they panic from somewhere deep inside of themselves and start frothing at the mouth when they encounter the uncombed and the unwashed. It is like a throwback into primeval times when institutions and hierarchies counted for nothing.

But I run ahead of my story. The Lalian mosque episode came later. First, there were the wolves, the hyenas, the wild hogs and the wild cats. All eager for a nick off a lad with a coarse wool blanket across his shoulders, out alone in the wild world, in search of a sweetheart who did not yet know that he existed. A house with seven ministering women (eight if you count Mother, overlooking her sparse interest in cosseting her youngest offspring) is pretty much the last place you would look to prepare a boy for a life on the road. How sorely I ached for home in the first few days after my

departure—for the particles of dust dancing on the first rays of the
sun slanting in through my window and warming my slumbering
body, for the cauldrons of water being heated for bathing, for the
crackling sound of firewood leaping into a flame as the preparations
for the morning meal began, for the churning of vats of butter in
the sun-drenched courtyard, for the early morning tête-à-tête of the
broom with the floor. Only the image of a woman's face imprinted
on my mind kept me moving.

Not Heer's—she was nothing more than a notion to me then.
Sahiba. The memory of her curled lips would not leave me. I could
not turn back and give her the pleasure of sneering some more.
Every bone in my body ached from the long hours of walking and
from sleeping on hard, unfriendly surfaces. Though my arms and
legs were scratchy from the thorn and bramble of the rough road,
though my stomach was wracked by spasms of hunger, I willed
myself to keep going.

As for the wild creatures of the forest, my flute was my defence.

Before there was life, there was sound. We are all, creatures big
and small, birthed of the same seven notes. He who has complete
mastery of the seven notes can communicate with the soul of all
things. The cattle of Takht Hazara had taught me this. All I needed
now was control over myself. I had to steel myself and hold still
against the panic and subdue the instinct to run, as dark animal eyes
glittered at me from behind the surrounding bushes. Each successive
night was better than the last, as I learnt to breathe deeply and
ignore the trembling of the leaves in the branches above my head,
the shifting patterns of shadows in the surrounding darkness and
the sudden sounds of something snapping in the dry undergrowth.
Stilling the drumbeat in my heart to a dull, even murmuring, I would
begin my concert under the stars. It takes a great deal of dexterity
as a flautist to put a jungle full of antagonistic creatures into the
dream state, for the wild cats respond to low notes and wolves and
hyenas to higher pitches, and the snakes and scorpions to a rapid

switching of scales. I was stretched to my limits, or perhaps, I learnt to venture beyond them.

The terrain through which I walked south-west towards the fiefdom of the Syals was bleak and challenging. The villages were few and far between, surrounded by date palm groves. Along the river, the saltworts and the tamarisks prevailed, their thorny leaves and bristles reprimanding the traveller for having ventured so far from home. A route through the uplands would have been less marshy, easier to traverse, but the Sandal Bar is no place for a stranger. The nomads who herd cattle, sheep and camels through those wilds are untamed and unfriendly, and not above looting and leaving a lone traveller dead, without any compunction, just for the blanket on his back. So I stuck to the marshes.

My road took me across time, the centuries past crunching underfoot in the soil of the earth as I walked upon it, floating and howling in the air surrounding my head, playing out in melancholic tunes from my flute. This was the land Alexander had coveted, it was here that the fierce Malloi tribesmen had pursued and ambushed the retreating Greek army, shooting a near fatal arrow through their godlike hero and demoralising the invaders completely. It was here that the White Huns had struck repeatedly in the hope of bringing the land under their heels. However, disarmed by the beauty of the Gujjar girls, they had stayed on to become householders: the Hunas now a sub-clan of the Gujjar tribe. The light eyes and the fleck of gold in the dark hair of the children running barefoot in the fields were the only remaining traces of the conquests their forefathers had made in this land.

I moved through the land, gathering and sifting its stories. In familiar surroundings the mind grows lazy. Travelling gave me brighter eyes and keener ears, jolting my senses to a fine alert. Arriving at dusk in unknown settlements, a stranger among strangers, I understood the fellowship of man, of how the things that separate us are lesser than the things that we have in common.

Leave behind your land, your gold and the minions at your service and you come face to face with your essential self. Before I left home, I had been equally a stranger to the fear in my belly and the strength in my sinews. As I walked the road to Heer's village I came to discover myself, my vulnerability and my invincibility.

The path from Takht Hazara joins the road from Sarghoda towards Jhang near Lalian. I was deadbeat and tired but determined to walk the remaining two kos to the mosque there. After six—or was it seven nights, I lose count—of sleeping under trees and inside smelly cattle barns, I craved four walls and a solid roof. Not any walls but the walls of God's own house, not any roof but the roof of God's own kindness. I sought to belong somewhere, if only for a night or two. And isn't faith our home away from home? I wished to wake up to the sound of the morning azaan, the muezzin's call to prayer, as familiar to me as the deep, quieting timbre of Father's voice. I wished to soothe my eyes with the sight of the sunken doorway of the mihrab pointing me in the direction of the qiblah as surely as Mother's finger pointed out the moon to me when I was a toddler and she hadn't yet begun to despise me. I craved familiarity.

At last I reached the mosque, but passed out cold on the steps. One minute I was standing there awestruck by the beauty of its perfect dome and tall minarets silhouetted against the star-spangled night sky, staring at the intricate wooden trellis work on the raised minbar platform from which the call to prayer was announced, the next minute I had collapsed senseless from exhaustion.

I was woken rudely by a kick in my side and angry hands shaking me by the shoulder. I looked up to see who it was.

A mullah's shadow fell on me like an evil omen.

'Get up, you filthy fakir,' he shouted, a spray of spit leaving his mouth as he spoke. His voice had a strange, rasping quality to it.

'How dare you defile Allah's house like this? Get up this instance and be gone before I have you beaten to pulp for your insolence!'

'God's house is open to the least of his fellows,' said I, turning my face to look up at him. 'Who are you to deny me entrance?'

A look of disbelief sent his eyebrows shooting up towards his skull cap. I don't think he was used to being answered back.

'Who am I! I am Allah's representative, the guardian of this sacred space. I cannot allow beggars and dogs to dirty it,' he intoned, raising his arms high and wide to tower even more ominously over my crouching form. The sleeves of his long robe flapped noisily as if to join in the admonishment.

I shifted myself out of his looming shadow's fold. The shade of a sanctimonious man can kill the blooms of joy that live in the heart.

'I am no beggar or thief. I am a Ranjha from Takht Hazara. The son of Mauju Chaudhary, none less,' I said. Peace be to Father's soul, it wasn't in vain that I invoked his name. The further I moved from my family, clan and village, the more I needed to remind myself of who I was. My identity anchored me in the blur of ever changing names and places I encountered each day, gave me something to hold on to in the continuously shifting geography of my nights. Without it, this fire-breathing Mullah's blast of hot words would have simply swept me out of reckoning.

'Don't try and deceive me with stories. Your long, matted hair, your tattered clothes and worn-out apology for a blanket are all the introduction I need from you. I have your measure, lad. You are a fool to think you will be welcomed here. Look at this fine mosque. The finest masons from across the river have fashioned it. Ustads from Chiniot were hired to carve the wooden trellises of this minbar. The lacquer work on these minarets is the work of master craftsmen. Boatmen on the river find their way home on the darkest nights guided only by the sheen of these lofty minars. A finer mosque than this is not to be found for a hundred miles around. Not in all of Multan or Sialkot or Gujjranwala even,' said the mullah.

'What good is this beauty if it is used to distance Allah's followers from Him?' I challenged. 'You think God cares more for your stone and wood, for carvings and masonry work, than for the heartfelt prayers of an honest man?'

For a moment he was completely silent, as if stunned speechless. Then he erupted again into an angry hiss of words, the spray from his mouth flying in all eight directions.

'How dare you talk to me of prayers? I know the verses of the Quran by heart and the ninety-nine names of Allah are always on my lips. I recite the Kalima continuously and none in these parts will you find more pious than me,' raged the mullah. His eyes bulged red under his darkening brows, his cheeks puffed out, his lips blanched. In that moment he reminded me of a puppet with a grossly painted face, dangling on the string of his own emotions, jumping up and down jerkily.

I straightened my body to my full height and wrapped my frayed blanket around me firmly, preparing to leave. I had had enough of this narrow-minded bigot and his ugliness. Better the wolves and hyenas than this piece of self-serving grandiosity.

'What good is piety that makes you proud instead of humble?' I asked him, as I prepared to leave. 'If you truly understood God's greatness, you would not be so arrogant as to turn the faithful away from God's house.'

'You dirty, unkempt fiddler of the flute, you presume to teach me about faith! Do you not know that a mosque is no place for music?'

At that I lost my temper. For him to belittle me was okay. But I couldn't let him berate music. Music is the soul of the world. The thirty-six ragas and their raginis are parents to all of creation. The sun, the moon and the planets, the seas, mountains and rivers, the animal and plant kingdoms, the seasons, the weather, the diurnal rhythms are all encoded with the seven notes. It was impossible to be a representative of God and not recognise his signature on all things. It was time to teach this mullah something.

I settled down on the steps of the mosque and wiped my flute lovingly and placed it against my lips, my fingers curling upon its length.

As I began to play, I was unable to speak of God at first. My flute, its heart full of hunger pangs, cold floors, the sorrow of leaving my childhood home and parting from kith and kin, wept tunes of its own destitution. Hearing me play, one by one, the miserable of the village gathered around the steps of the mosque—the stray curs and alley cats, the landless peasants, the scavengers of night soil, the maimed and the abandoned, the abused wives and the cuckolded husbands, the old and the ailing—for sorrow calls to sorrow.

The mullah stood nonplussed, staring at the gathering crowds.

Having wept its heart out, the flute began to change its tune. Stories of small joys spilled from it—the moon's face peeping from behind the date palms, a perfectly round marble in a boy's balled fist, the colour of the blue jay's wings, carrots being dipped in vats of freshly made gur, the blooming of the dhak trees in spring, the setting up of monsoon swings under hoary old trees at the first smell of rain, bird song and frog choir in the village pond, a comet streaking through the night sky ...

This brought the children from their homes—first in ones and twos and threes and then by the dozens and scores—followed soon by their sleepy-eyed and confused parents.

The mullah stood rigid against the entrance to the mosque, watching the gathering of villagers at his door at that late hour.

Finally, my flute began to extoll the glory of God. His power and His magnificence. His laws and His perfect justice. His mercy and His infinite kindness. Soon the village began to empty of people and the maidan around the mosque began to fill up as farmers, tradesmen, carpenters, ironsmiths, potters and barbers, good wives, good mothers, wise grandmothers and beloved grandfathers, all came out in search of the source of the music that called to the blood flowing through their arteries. A growing whisper rustled through the still night air, fanning through it a soft breeze of gentle regard flowing toward me.

'Who is he?'

'Who is this magician?'

'Who is this beautiful lad?'

'Who are you, young man?'

'Who are you, brother?'

'Who are you, son?'

I told them I was Ranjha from Takht Hazara, a wanderer seeking a night's refuge in their mosque, but not allowed in by their imam.

The crowd lifted me on its shoulders and carried me into the mosque, past the mullah standing there like a stone statue. I hoped he would move soon. An idol has no place in the precincts of a mosque.

Later, as they were plying me with food and blankets, he came up to me and said, 'You played very well.'

I wondered whether he meant the flute or the game of one-upmanship or both.

'I thank you for your hospitality,' I replied.

'It's God's house. I am a mere servant,' he said.

These men of power and pelf are all the same. They understand only shows of strength. Show them your muscle and they begin to talk politely that instant. It was hard to believe this man had been shouting at me only moments earlier. His entire artillery of fine words was now out on display for the crowd surrounding me.

'Please stay for as long as you need to,' he said.

'Yes, why only for a night? Stay here with us awhile,' the crowd around me urged.

'Stay, brother, rest your limbs a while.'

'Stay, son, let your cheeks fill out a bit.'

'Tell us your story, sweet-faced wanderer. How did you come so far away from home?'

I told them the story of my departure from Takht Hazara (oh, the joy of taking my village's name again) and my determination to wed Heer. The whole world loves a lover. The more impossible his quest for love seems to them, the more they love him for it. They took me to their hearts and plied me with useful information on how to approach my goal.

The woman I sought to make my bride, I gathered from the stories they told me, wasn't exactly the kind of girl you took home to your mother. She hadn't been taught to cook or sew. Instead, she rode horses with her band of girlfriends and was something of a warrior princess. Rich, spoilt and beautiful beyond imagination. It seemed she was also quite the rescuer of hapless men. A boatman called Luddan had been thrown out by his employer, a nobleman by the name of Noora. Heer Syal had apparently challenged Noora to a duel on the banks of the Chenab and taken his wronged boatman under her protection. Good, I made a mental note to myself, no need to shave. I would go with the grunge look, appear as if I'd had a rough time, and inspire her to take me under her wing.

I also gathered that Luddan now plied his boat as a floating resort for Heer and her friends, from this shore of the Chenab to the other. She allowed him to take passengers for fare on some parts of it when she was not using the boat, so that he could make a living.

It would be Luddan's boat and none other that would take me across the river to my bride.

3

Boat and Beauties

I STOOD ON A high white cliff, staring across the river, the wind roaring and whistling past my ears, the waters a turbid, swirling grey below me. My eyes were fixed on the neatly set out fiefdom of the Syals on the distant shore. Like others are farmers, herdsmen, potters and shoemakers by profession, my prospective in-laws were rulers by occupation. They considered lording over others their calling. Jhang Syal was a relatively new Syal settlement. From the stories I had gathered, these Syals were warriors of Rajput descent. An ancestor named Rai Shankar, spurred by the lack of satisfactory lording-it-over opportunities in his native Daranagar, in the doab of the Ganga and the Yamuna, moved to Jaunpur in the east. However, the waters of Jaunpur were not to the liking of his son, Sial. Tales of how the north-west lay shaken and rudderless after successive Mongol invasions made Sial head westwards in the hope of carving out a leg of land to rule over.

Sial wandered long and hard in these parts before he met the great Sufi saint Baba Farid of Pakpattan and, with his blessings and grace, set up base in Sialkot. It was good, I reckoned, that Baba Farid had inspired the Syals to convert to Islam, otherwise there would be more than the river and the famed Syal pride standing in the way of this Ranjha from Takht Hazara and his bride.

In the century since Sial built the fort at Sialkot, his descendants had spread along the Chenab, appropriating larger tracts under their landlord-ship, building a town here, a settlement there. Jhang Syal was the latest of these, the pet project of Mal Khan, sixth in the line of descent from the first Sial. His cousin Mir Chuchak was my Heer's father and currently the most important Syal chief of Jhang. The Syals were lords and masters of all the land they surveyed, the taxes paid by poor peasants and cultivators their main source of income. In addition to this, they kept mighty herds of cattle. And of course, they kept standing armies.

It was for the favour of being able to cultivate unmolested by the Mongols and Turks that the Syals collected levies from the peasants. That the Syals had armies in place to enforce their writ would, of course, be factored into the local peasantry's calculation of how quickly to pay up the taxes. It was all a matter of scale. Deprive a peasant of his harvest with a flash of the sword once and it is called robbery. Do it at random intervals and it's described as banditry. Do it systematically, year after year, backed by swordsmen in uniforms, and it is called governance.

As I stood on the cliff, I pondered long and hard about my desire for Heer Syal. What was I? A wounded ego out looking for the best salve on offer? A macho fool out on a silly dare? A man besotted by an impossible dream of love? A philosopher in search of the meaning of life? A musician in search of the perfect composition? Why do explorers set out in search of new worlds? Why do astronomers look for new stars? Why do the Sufis seek fanaa? What takes a yogi to a remote mountain cave? Is it the restlessness in their hearts or does their goal call out to them? Are the seeker and the sought bound by an unseen contract from a time before memory?

From the first time my restless heart had heard her name, I knew that this wasn't about me alone. In the fiefdom of the Syals, a bold and peerless beauty waited for a man who would not wish to be her lord and master but would be courageous enough to love her as an equal. I was that man. Not to answer her call was to deny both our destinies, hers and mine. I slowly climbed down from my vantage point on the pale hillock and walked towards the riverbank to seek out Luddan, the boatman.

It was the third watch of day when I managed to locate Luddan and his boat. The sky lay splattered and shred over the horizon, torn and wounded, staining the waters a searing pink. A good many people were queued up in front of the pier, their fares clutched in front of them or balled up anxiously in their fists. It was the last boat of the day and many faces spoke of a desperation to get across. The river was in swell, the next crossing might not be for a few days.

There was no point in joining the queue. I had no money to pay the fare. I tapped on a few shoulders lightly and got them to clear the way up to the boat. I intended to appeal to Luddan's sense of romance. Not everyone has the good fortune of ferrying their mistress's future groom to her doorstep. In time he would be richly rewarded for the ride he would be giving me gratis this evening.

From the outside, the boat looked very handsome and spruced up, a little out of the ordinary. That impression was echoed on the outer deck which had a few rows of neat wooden benches.

Seeking Luddan, I reached an ornately carved doorway. I knocked tentatively.

'Come in!' boomed a male voice.

To say that the sight inside was a shock would be an understatement. On a large white divan, edged with silver trimmings and bolstered by many pillows, sat an extremely rotund, thick-necked, balding man, his massive paunch partially hidden by the sack of coins in front of him. Draped on his arms, on either side, were two identical women, mere girls really, dressed in bright red salwars riding up carelessly to reveal their calves, teamed with too-tight dark blue kurtis and heavily embroidered red-blue chunnis of muslin draped over their bosoms.

So this was Luddan.

It was something of a challenge to get my mind around his girth, as well as around the idea that this living portrait of crude commerce I saw before me was the man Heer Syal had seen fit to take under her dainty wing. I had been expecting a perfect rabbit of a man. If not that, at least a harried hare of a creature. The oily bull with multiple folds of flesh lolling on the divan made a very unlikely picture of someone who had been ill-used by a former master and had scuttled to Heer for protection. I was prepared for a woman of unorthodox tastes and a mind of her own, but even so, this seemed a bit much.

'You have come with the flowers for Heer's chamber? About time too. We have been waiting an age. Go in, we'll come and tell you how to place them,' said the girl on Luddan's left arm.

'It's not the regular flower fellow. Someone different,' said the girl on the right arm, getting up to follow suit.

I wasn't about to pass up a chance to see Heer's room. I walked quickly towards what seemed to be the door leading into her sanctum before anyone noticed that the flower seller had no flowers on him.

It was a huge chamber even for a rich chieftain's daughter. A dozen elaborately carved windows, six on either side, allowed the evening light in, bathing the room in a warm orange glow. At the centre of the room was a round bed. The bedspread upon it was white satin, the cushions and pillows were encased in deep red velvet trimmed with silken white tassels. A straggly-looking servant boy was lighting oil lamps on the inner ledges of the windows.

'Lay out the red silk cotton flowers like a carpet from the door to the bed.'

'Put the scented white jasmines afloat in the water tub in the bathing chamber.'

The left–right arm candy duo had walked in right behind me and were giving me instructions. Now that they were not decorating that lump of lard outside, I couldn't tell left from right. They were identical twins. It seemed the leery Luddan had struck a two-for-the-price-of-one deal.

'What are you shapely samovars of milk and honey doing next to that tub of lard?' I asked.

Beauty No. 1 giggled, one hand rising to her lips as she guiltily tried to suppress the girlish trill from escaping them.

Beauty No. 2 frowned at her, looking warningly in the direction of the servant boy.

'Stop gawking, will you?' said Beauty No. 1 to the boy.

'Go outside and press the master's feet,' said Beauty No. 2, waving the boy out of the chamber. She bolted the door from inside. I surmised she was the older twin, more cautious and responsible. Funny, how even a space of three minutes can saddle you for life with the burden of being the older sibling.

I nicknamed them Nikki and Wadi in my head. I wondered at the precise nature of their arrangement with Luddan. They were dressed more like housewives on holiday than ladies of the night, but that meant nothing. Some men like their wives dressed up like whores, others like their whores rigged out like wives.

'Couldn't you find a less ugly customer for your favours than that greasy meatball outside?' I asked. It was offensive to think of so much beauty and youth being spread out in the service of that portly, balding and greedy middle-aged boatman sitting outside the door.

Nikki gasped and brought her hand to her mouth.

Wadi glared at me angrily.

'He is our husband. Mind how you speak of him,' said Nikki. 'And now, if you will hurry up and lay out the flowers and go from here. He doesn't like us dilly-dallying unnecessarily.'

I stared from one to the other. Their beauty became poignant and painful to my eyes in that instant. My heart felt very heavy and sad to think they would be yoked to him for life, not for just a passing night.

'I am sorry,' I said. I didn't elaborate on what I was sorry about. But I was really and truly sorry that the delicate flower of their youth had been plucked so rudely and used to decorate a rich man's house. That this was the only man and all the love they were ever to know in life. Perhaps they were born to a greedy father. Or simply to an indigent one. But whatever the circumstances that led to the tragedy, here they were, trapped on this boat, in this sordid life, forever.

'You aren't really the flower fellow at all,' said Wadi accusingly, suddenly registering the lack of any flowers on me.

Before she could speak further, we heard a loud angry banging.

Nikki opened the door. Luddan burst in, followed by the straggly servant boy.

'What is going on here? What hanky-panky are you up to with this young fellow? Making eyes, always making eyes at other men. Shameless hussies. I have half a mind to give you both a good hiding and send you back to the filthy hovel you came from.'

'Hold your horses, old boatman,' I interrupted his rant. 'I have no interest in your wives. My bride awaits me on the other shore and it shall be your privilege to carry me there.'

'A passenger, are you? My boy, not all the gold in the world can buy you a passage in Heer's chamber. Keep your money ready and go stand in the queue outside,' said Luddan. 'And you two, go find out what happened to the flower fellow. The room has to be readied. I have received word that Heer and her friends wish to use the boat when we reach the other side.' My heart skipped a beat. So Heer would meet me on the boat itself. It seemed like a good omen.

'I have no money but I am here in search of Heer, to ask for her hand in marriage. You will be richly rewarded for your troubles once she knows of your part in her love story,' I said.

The expression on his face would have suited a man who had just witnessed the sun rising from the west in the middle of a moonlit night. Simply put, our man was gobsmacked.

'You cheeky dog! You brazen donkey! You penniless oaf,' spluttered Luddan. 'You think this boat is for carting around lying beggars and petty thieves and deluded madmen like you?'

'Easy, my man, you speak to the future bridegroom of your mistress. I promise to tell no tales if you see sense even now and give me passage on your boat.'

Luddan tore at the few remaining strands of hair on his bald pate and smote his forehead with the flat of his palm. Then he reached for his footwear and made a motion of chucking it at me.

'Out! Off my boat this instant!' he shouted.

'Tch ... tch ... don't lose your temper again please. Remember what the hakim said last time,' Nikki clucked at him nervously.

'Go away! You've caused enough trouble,' said Wadi to me through thinly pursed lips.

I got out of the boat and sat myself on the riverbank. I had seen the fear in the girls' eyes. I did not wish for them to get thrashed by Luddan on my account. He seemed like a nasty, brutish man.

Dusk was swiftly being overtaken by night. A handful of stars were peeping out in feeble defiance of a brooding sky, wearing a gloomy chador of clouds on its troubled face. The river was in spate, its waves raging angrily against the shore. A sudden melancholy overwhelmed me.

I thought of the ills that had befallen me in the last few months, since that night when the tree of life shook and Father's leaf fell to the ground. I thought of the unloving coldness of Mother's smile. I thought of my cruel brothers and their conniving wives. I thought of the barren stony ground the qazi had apportioned to me. I thought of the mullah's long shadow falling upon me on the steps of the mosque in Lalian. I thought of Luddan's grasping hands, which only knew the language of coins. I looked at the flood in my beloved Chanan rising higher and higher and felt an overwhelming despair, devoid of even the smallest vestige of hope. Takht Hazara with its sun-soaked, rain-kissed, laughter-filled fields was sixty kos away and Jhang Syal with its promise of love was across a river that could not be crossed. I was alone in a no man's land with only my bruised heart, my hopelessly tangled hair and my flute.

Behind me I could hear the jingle of coins and the shuffle of feet as the passengers in the queue began paying their fares and taking their places on the outer deck.

I brought the flute to my lips and began to play a dirge. It was my farewell song to this world of dead values and no sympathy for love. It was my requiem for a world that had let me down—a world where brother betrayed brother for land, where men of law stood false witness and obfuscated the truth on behalf of the powerful, where men of God were oblivious to the pain of God's faithful flock, where fathers sold nubile daughters to corrupt old men and had the gall to call it marriage, where angry rivers separated lovers who were betrothed by God himself in the holy hour when the earth was born.

As I played on, moonlight fell in cascading silver beams upon the turbulent water. The face of Khwaja Khizr loomed in front of my mind's eye. He of the green robes and the kindly visage had heard my heart's song. His spirit would take me across the river. He was the Prophet of Water, the guardian of living things. With his grace I would either swim or drown.

I stepped into the water knowing that it would decide my fate one way or the other. It was not that I was a loser, a quitter. It was just that I did not wish to fight any battle in which God was not on my side. Either you are for love or against love, being indifferent is not an option, I said to Him defiantly as I walked into the tossing waters.

I had walked only a few paces into the water when someone shouted, 'Stop! Please stop!'

A crowd of people were rushing down from the deck of Luddan's boat, led by his two wives. Before I knew it, they had surrounded me and carried me onto the boat. They laid me near a warm fireplace and gently removed my wet clothes. Nikki cradled my head in her soft lap while towelling my hair dry. Wadi massaged my feet with heated oil.

'Go put the water to heat in Heer's bath chamber,' Nikki ordered the servant boy.

'We shall prepare the lover for his bride. Bathe him and rub him with sweet perfumes and dress him in nice clothes,' said Wadi. 'Go, row the boat, good people. And sing your heart out. This is a wedding party and we are the bridegroom's side.'

Was it the music that had wrought this change of heart or Khwaja Khizr's intervention on my behalf or God Himself taking the side of love?

'Where is Luddan?' I asked through the dull haze that their tender ministrations were causing me to fall into. Would he not kill them if he knew their soft, firm hands were kneading my neck and shoulder muscles and teasing the knots out of my tired feet and legs?

'He is taken care of,' said Nikki with a quiet, secret smile.

'Hakimji recommended a small dose of opium every time the old elephant becomes too mast or out of control,' said Wadi, her eyes betraying just a flicker of pain before they became noncommittal again.

While the old boatman slept in opium's sure embrace, his two wives bathed me with warm water, dressed me in fresh clothes and tucked me into Heer's bed for the night, before quietly tiptoeing away. On the deck outside I could hear the dholaks being struck up and wedding songs being sung. I fell into a deep slumber.

II

WHAT THE CROW SAW

4

Claimed Before She Is Named

IT IS NOT AN easy decision for any crow to leave its flock and swear its allegiance to a single human being. We are not called a murder of crows without reason. Together we are invincible. We live in flocks of thousands. A huge well-knit family will occupy a single large tree for centuries, flying out in all directions in the morning and returning at dusk to pool information and resources. Our intelligence networks are formidable. We look out for ourselves, we look out for our family, we look out for others of our species and we look out for the humans in our village. An average crow is conversant with two hundred and fifty different types of calls before he makes his first solo flight out of the parent tree—calls to alert other crows against enemies like the red-tailed hawks and raccoons, calls to signal the finding of food or of a road kill, and distress calls in emergencies.

Ravens and crows share bonds with humankind that go back to the start of civilisation. We have always been there for men and their families. Picking and tidying up for them, managing their waste, issuing weather reports. We caw to warn them of unexpected visitors, we congregate on their rooftops and shout in unison if a storm is in the offing, we warn them of impending theft or loss by coming in from the south-west and of business gains when we fly

in from the north-east. It doesn't end there. If necessary, we fly in
their faces to warn them off unsavoury paths or treacherous dealings,
and deliberately steal shiny objects from their dwellings so that they
may better secure their homes. Heck, we even allow them to feed
us stale bread to redeem their bad karma. We know their language
and some of them know ours.

Not all of us choose to be auguries or oracles, but every nestling
learns the language of portents and omens. It is part of the business
of being a crow. The little ones are always volunteering to be
harbingers of happy tidings, attracted to the feasting that follows
births, betrothals and weddings. The young and importunate
clamour for the battles and blood baths that humans are so prone
to, always game for occasions that call for a raucous outcry from
the treetops. The middle-aged attend to the daily nuisances of
theft, property disputes, minor misunderstandings and accidents.
The venerable senior crow goes out on only the most important
occasions. It is a very rare instance when the whole flock makes an
appearance together.

The naming ceremony of Heer was such an event. There I was—
bright-eyed, with shining black feathers, an enthusiastic member of
the junior cacophony. Every crow within a hundred-mile radius of
Mir Chuchak's house knew that a grand feast was in the offing on the
seventh day from the day Malki delivered a baby girl of unsurpassed
beauty. Sultan was already seven years old by then. God, generous
in all other things to the Syal chieftain, had been slow to answer his
wife's supplications for another child. Much fanfare was anticipated.
It was rumoured that ten goats had been arranged for slaughter and
one-third of the meat was to be given away to the poor. The village
barber was to shave the infant's hair and weigh it against gold to be
donated to charity. A small black kohl mark would be smeared on the
child's forehead, to ward off the evil eye, before she was presented
before relatives and friends who would shower her with blessings
and gifts. Finally, and most significantly, she was to be given the

name she would carry in this life, that which would describe her and that which she would answer to. That most personal of words that humans confer on their progeny to distinguish them uniquely from every other human being.

The crows weren't the only ones who had covered many miles to be present at the naming ceremony. There were chieftains of various clans, keen to mark their presence and to register their interest in the birth of Mir Chuchak's daughter. For the Syal chieftain was an important man and the girls of the family were famous for their beauty. She was top grade future daughter-in-law material.

As part of the junior cacophony, I was one of a set of five lusty-throated young birds merrily squawking our appreciation each time someone approached Heer's parents with a gift. The Syal chieftain's wife Malki was dressed in bright red clothes, in all probability her wedding ensemble, with heavy silver ornaments adorning her wrists and ankles. Her eyes were glowing with pride. The baby was in her lap, swathed in old clothes, as was the custom. Sultan and Mir Chuchak sat on either side of her, making a small but perfect family. It was time for the infant's father to declare her name to the gathering.

Suddenly, there was a rustle as the gathered crowd parted to allow an odd pair to make its way to the centre where the family was seated.

There were two men, one bowed and limping, the other thick-set and heavy jawed, with a pashmina shawl draped over his silk kurta-pyjama. In his hand the man with the pashmina carried a golden cage with a pair of very fine pigeons. They walked up to where Mir Chuchak's family was seated on a low couch. The lame man, I surmised, must be Kaido Langra, the newborn girl's uncle. The identity of the other man was a mystery.

The pigeons were a pair of exquisite beauties. They were shah-siray—black-headed with pure white bodies—obviously a very precious gift. They wore silver anklets on their feet, which would make delicate music as they moved from rooftop to rooftop.

'Brother, Sister-in-Law, see what a special visitor we have for our darling daughter's naming ceremony. Shahji has come all the way from Rangpur to bless the baby. Such generosity, such kindness, we are truly indebted Khera sa'ab,' said Kaido Langra, addressing first the parents and then his companion, looking all the while both obsequious and important.

So, the unknown man was Shahji Khera from Rangpur. He was a fair distance from home. What had brought him here? Some ulterior motive, surely, for mere courtesy did not demand his presence at the ceremony.

'For your daughter,' said the Khera patriarch, stretching out his expensive gift towards Mir Chuchak and Malki.

'Oh, but you shouldn't have,' said Mir Chuchak. He was not insensible to the value of the gift being proffered.

'From today your daughter is our daughter, her happiness is our happiness,' said the bearer of the gift.

Mir Chuchak's face blanched.

'It is too early ...' he began.

'We are honoured, deeply honoured by your kindness, Khera sa'ab,' Kaido interrupted. 'Brother, you could not ask for a better alliance than the Kheras of Rangpur,' he said, quickly drawing out a red cloth pouch from the pocket of his long shirt. He took out a few crystals of sugar and put one in his own mouth and another into the mouth of the Khera chief and embraced him.

'Here, sister, sweeten your mouth on this doubly happy occasion,' he said with a oily smile, stretching out the sugar crystals on his palm towards Malki. She looked from her brother-in-law to her husband, unsure of what to do. Mir Chuchak stood up briskly, took his daughter from his wife's lap, strode forward and held her for all to see.

Kaido nudged Malki, looking meaningfully at the sugar he was holding before her. She took a small crystal and stood holding it between her fingers. Seeing the Khera chief's eyes on her hand and fearing that she might be offending an honoured guest, she quickly popped it into her mouth and smiled weakly at him.

Meanwhile, unaware of the little drama that had just been played out, the gathering gasped at the beauty of the baby, the rosy smoothness of her skin, the perfect almond shape of her eyes, the wispy golden-brown tufts of hair on her round head.

Mir Chuchak cleared his throat to speak. 'With the blessings of Baba Farid, a precious diamond has been sent to us. May the protection of the five pirs be upon her, this daughter of the Syals, who shall henceforth be known as Heer, the unblemished, the brilliant, the dazzling, the diamond of our clan,' he said to the gathering.

The crowd cheered at the choice of name. An old aunt rushed in to take the evil eye off the child's person. She scurried and bustled busily around the baby for a few self-important moments and then, feeling the restiveness of the crowd, yielded the stage. A signal was given for the feasting to begin. The dhols were struck and a freestyle, free-for-all dance began in the central courtyard. Elsewhere vats of thick creamy lassi began to be churned, cauldrons of oil were heated for frying puris, meat was put on skewers to roast, and broken rice was combined with gur and ghee to prepare kheer.

It was dusk by the time the merrymaking and feasting finally ended. Many crow brigades had already flown away. It would be days before the sounds of exultation and the paeans in praise of Syal hospitality would die out in our birdy skies. We crows are good at crowing and the ravens are no mean ravers either.

Much as I enjoyed the feast, I must admit I could have done better justice to it. The truth is, being witness to the morning's drama had distracted me. My eyes kept following the main actors throughout the day. There was the Khera chief, calm, grave and taciturn as he sat through the proceedings, indistinguishable from the other nobles in the gathering. There was Mir Chuchak, tall, handsome and affable as he moved through the company, welcoming and asking after his guests. Yet, I saw him pause many times during the day, swift shadows fleeting across his face when his eyes fell upon the baby in his wife's arms. After a while I saw him signal Malki to take Heer inside. The baby was restless amidst so much noise. Malki too seemed relieved to retreat to the cool calm of her chamber.

My eyes followed Kaido Langra obsessively. I had never seen greedier eyes, more grasping hands, such a leering-sneering face, in all my young life. His slanting walk, his filthy gaze, his ominous cackle, his bony fingers … all held me in their thrall. He was evil, pure and unadulterated, not a single untainted cell in his bent body. Yet, all this was apparent only to my crow's eyes. The human beings surrounding him seemed oblivious to the deformities of his character. They laughed at his jokes, clucked sympathetically at his lameness, listened respectfully to his pontification, nodding all the while.

After the last guests left, I saw Mir Chuchak hurriedly make his way to his wife's chambers. Kaido, who was supervising the winding up of the outdoor kitchen, saw him leave from the corner of his eye. He said a few quick words of instruction to the cooks and began to follow his older brother, doggedly willing his lame leg to cover the distance as quickly as possible.

I worked my way through the high branches and chose a perch on the ledge of a high ventilator that brought light and air to the room. I already had a pretty good view of the inside of his wife's room when Mir Chuchak strode in.

'What does my brother mean by getting the Khera chieftain to our daughter's naming ceremony and encouraging him to make a preposterous claim like that?' he demanded as soon as he was through the door, displeasure written large on his face.

'Kaido always has your best interest at heart. If he has brought this alliance for our daughter, it cannot be bad,' said Malki, all the while rocking the sleeping baby in her lap. She had the soft, unguarded look of a mother who has just finished suckling her baby at her breast.

'Woman, have you no sense! She is barely born, what advantage can there be to get her betrothed even before she is weaned? Why should any outsider come and lay a claim on my daughter before I have had the chance to declare even her name? It is against all decency. Kaido should have known better,' fumed Mir Chuchak.

I understood his concern. The giving of a name is not to be taken lightly. It is not a random combination of the letters of the alphabet and sounds that a parent bestows on a child. It must start with an auspicious letter. It takes into account, consciously or unconsciously, the time, sequence, season and circumstances of the child's birth. It embodies the hopes and wishes the family has for the baby. It contains the love, prayer and protection of family elders. It was not good that the shadow of the Khera name had fallen on the newborn before she had even had a chance to wear her own name. It would lie stealthily beneath her destiny as it took shape, quite like a thief who has been hiding indoors all along and can make away with the valuables whenever he chooses.

There was a knock on the door. Mir Chuchak frowned and continued to pace the floor of his wife's chamber. Realising that her husband was inclined to ignore the knock and knowing that it was probably her brother-in-law at the door, Malki settled the baby on her bed, sandwiching her between two soft bolsters for comfort, and got up to open the door.

Kaido Langra walked in, hopping on his crutches, a congratulatory smile on his face.

'So that is a big weight off our shoulders, isn't it, Brother. You will not even have to spend a single day worrying about finding a good home for her. A caste that matches ours in stature, vast holdings of orchards and farms, flourishing businesses, and not too many sons to divide them amongst—you cannot go wrong forging an alliance with the Kheras of Rangpur. Oh, what a master stratagem I deployed to get him here. My finest lalsiray, the handsome rose pigeons I had obtained from Amritsar last year, carried the letter of invitation. What man of taste can resist an invitation borne by a perfectly bred pigeon? It got him here on his fastest pair of horses to see who it is that breeds and keeps birds as fine as his. We spent the morning discussing breeding. I planted a few thoughts in his head as we spoke. Not the best of lookers, these Kheras. Could do with the infusion of some Syal blood. I tell you, sister, I worked hard on setting up your girl's future,' Kaido said, turning to Malki.

'Kaido, you might have thought to consult us, her parents, before you rushed off to secure her an alliance,' Mir Chuchak replied coldly.

'I did not know if my ploy would work. I did not want to tell you in case nothing came of it and you were disappointed,' said Kaido, apparently oblivious to his brother's displeasure.

'You do not seem to understand that I'm in no hurry to secure my daughter's future. She is beautiful, she is well-born, and we lack for nothing. Most importantly, she is only just born. Let her future unfold at its own pace. She is not a weight on my shoulders, she is a piece of my heart.' Mir Chuchak's tone was curt.

'And is she not a piece of her uncle's heart?' Kaido protested. 'Am I not her parent too? Are your children not the only family I am destined to have? I have walked loyally in your shadow since the moment of my birth. I have made your joys my happiness, your wishes my command, your success my goal. Will I want anything less than the best for my niece? If you doubt my love and loyalty, break my other leg too, I beg of you, like you broke the first. That would wound me less than your aspersions!'

I saw Mir Chuchak stiffen. A dark shadow of emotion flitted across his face and twisted it into an expression of pain. Was it guilt or helplessness or something altogether more mixed-up, I could not say.

'Hush! Do not speak like that, Kaido,' said Malki. 'What sense is there in harking back to that unfortunate accident? You know your brother was only a small child himself back then, and it was not his fault that you fell from the roof and damaged your leg while you were both racing each other. Why cause him pain with an accusation like that?'

'I am not accusing him, Malki. He started it by accusing me of not loving my niece.'

'That is not what he meant. It is just that our daughter is so young, she has come to us so recently after so many years of waiting that we do not wish to think already of in-laws and parting and other such weighty matters,' said Malki.

'Can't you see that is foolish, sentimental talk? A daughter is someone else's wealth, yours only for safekeeping. However much you may fool yourself and hold her to your heart and call her your precious diamond, she is not yours, and she never will be. Her destiny is written on her husband's palm. Foolish are the parents who harbour too much attachment towards their daughters,' said Kaido.

'This is precisely the kind of nonsense I abhor. My Heer will write her own destiny, she does not need it written on another's hand for her,' said Mir Chuchak.

'Shhh ... do not tempt fate like this! Every girl needs a husband's hand,' entreated Malki softly.

'And count your blessings, Brother, that the best in the land has been proffered for your daughter,' said Kaido.

'We shall see about that,' said Mir Chuchak grimly.

'I have given my word,' said Kaido. 'If she is married elsewhere, it shall be over my dead body.'

Malki gasped.

Kaido Langra walked out in a huff.

There was silence between the husband and wife. Mir Chuchak walked up to where the baby was lying and spoke to her.

'My daughter, I promise that you shall grow up unfettered and free, no less than any son to me.'

He turned towards his wife and held her gaze with his, willing her to join him in keeping this promise to their newborn daughter. Malki lowered her eyes and did not say a word.

I saw a dark, long, slanting evening shadow fall upon the child. It was Kaido Langra standing at a window, looking at the baby with a malevolent smile. She whimpered in her sleep, sensing the presence of something evil and unkind. I don't know what in that situation called to me—Heer's beauty, or her father's helpless nobility, or the cruelty of her uncle's gaze, but I was indentured for life.

And since that day of Heer's naming ceremony, I have lived on a high branch on the neem tree in Mir Chuchak's garden, watching out for her, for them.

5

A Doll and a Demon

THE SUNLIT COURTYARD OF the main house on Mir Chuchak's estate echoed throughout the day with Heer's name. As did the many rooms looking into the courtyard, their heavy wooden doors inlaid with squares of brass that glinted as the sun fell on them in slanting rays. The narrow stone staircase leading up to the large rooftop with its delicately latticed white parapet wall, the outhouses, the servants' quarters, the chicken-coop, the vegetable garden, the formal front garden with its lotus pond and trimmed hedges of henna bushes, the monsoon swings on the giant neem tree on which I lived, the untended wilderness of the sprawling backyard … all of these reverberated with her name.

Let me give you a view of her childhood, the scenes as they unfolded vividly before my crow eyes, the years flowing as time flows in our avian skies from moment to moment, unnumbered, without the weight of days, weeks, months or years on its back.

'Heer! Heer! Come back this instant!' Malki calls out.

But Heer shoots past her at hurricane speed, right behind Sultan, straining to catch her brother, both of them wearing only their striped cotton knickers. The music from Heer's silver anklets is soon a receding echo in Malki's despairing ears.

'Heer, little girls can't run around shirtless through the whole compound,' her mother reasons with her at night, lying down beside her, stroking her hair gently, lulling her to sleep.

'But Father said whatever Sultan can do, I can too. Let Father come back and I'll tell him how you and my grandmother are always worrying me,' Heer replies. 'I wish Father wouldn't have to travel out so often. You both are so difficult to manage when he is not here.'

I saw Malki staring long at her daughter with a worried look on her face.

In her determination to keep up with Sultan, Heer did not take into account that she was seven years younger than him. If Sultan went swimming in the river, she did too, matching him stroke for stroke. If he went riding into the nearby forests, she went along. If he was given sword-fighting lessons, she demanded them as well. She had no sense of fear. No recognition of the limitations of her own age, size, or gender. Her fierce spirit shone past it all, oblivious to any differences.

'Heer! Stop it or I'll thrash the living daylights out of you,' Sultan screams as his little sister walks into the game he is playing with his friends in the courtyard. She runs out with a fistful of marbles clutched in each tiny fist.

'That's what you get for excluding me from the game,' she shouts in reply, before running further away, her muddy feet leaving a happy, dancing zigzag trail on the courtyard floor.

Her hazel eyes shine brightly as the boys chase after her and wrestle her down to the ground. Sultan, well acquainted with her ticklish spots, knows the trick to getting his marbles back. Helpless squeals of laughter spill out of her belly into the henna-scented evening air, and the marbles tumble out of her pudgy baby hands, bouncing vigorously on the weathered red sandstone floor before rolling off in multiple directions, the boys hurrying to catch them.

'Extraordinary beauty is nothing in a girl if it does not come with malleability and some docility of nature,' her mother-in-law cautions Malki, as the younger woman stands above her in the courtyard with the furrowed red sandstone floor, massaging warm oil into her greying hair. 'Take her in hand before it is too late.'

The old lady, used to deference by one and all, makes no secret of her disapproval of Heer. The girl is the bane of her old age, defiant and entirely unbiddable.

'Sultan, come, my darling boy,' the grandmother calls out, a bowl of sweet churi—boiled rice, gur and ghee crumbled and mixed together thoroughly—in her hands, the aroma of the warm, freshly prepared sweet wafting into the air.

Out of nowhere Heer appears, whisks the bowl from her outstretched hand and runs up the stairs to the roof.

'Heer, you know very well that Bibi makes churi only for me,' shouts Sultan, taking two angry steps at a time in a bid to catch her and wrest back his bowl.

'So ask her why she doesn't make it for me,' demands Heer. 'She knows I also love churi.'

'She says it's because I'm good and you're naughty,' he replies.

'And you believe that? It's because you're a boy and for that reason she thinks the sun shines out of your bum,' says Heer, now seated precariously on the parapet wall, polishing off the churi with her fingers, knowing well that Sultan won't fight her for the fear of making her topple off the ledge.

'Heer, don't finish it all,' pleads Sultan.

'Here's your half, fair and square,' she says grandly, handing him the bowl when she's done eating. She hops down from the wall nimbly, tossing her plait back for good effect. 'I'm not a cheat like you and Bibi.'

'This girl will be the death of me,' the grandmother mutters dourly as she watches the siblings hop down the staircase together, licking their fingers, sweet and sticky with the treat.

Malki stops her wilful daughter. 'Heer, this is no way to behave,' she says in a firm voice. 'Can't you see how much you upset Bibi?'

'Can't you see how much Bibi upsets me? How unfair she is to me?' Heer says tearfully. 'She hates me.'

'Don't be silly, Heer,' chides Malki. 'She gives you so many nice things which she doesn't give Sultan. Don't sulk now. Tomorrow I'll make you a pretty doll from the old cotton pillow and that beautiful red brocade piece Bibi took out for you from her wedding trunk.'

True to her word, Malki stitches a rag doll for Heer and dresses her up in fine red and gold brocade. A miniature brass serving set, gold with pink and green inlay work, is given to her to play with. It is a Kashmiri samovar set with its own tray and six shapely long-stemmed cups that Mir Chuchak had once brought back for Malki on one of his many trips out of Jhang. Malki has a fondness for collecting beautiful objects from different places. They are displayed in an ornately carved wooden cupboard with a glass front, a small lock upon it to ward off inquisitive children and nimble-fingered servants.

For a few days, Heer and her friends hold many grand feasts in honour of the new doll. But Malki's happiness at Heer's interest in girlish play is short-lived. Very soon the brass samovar set lies abandoned, its long-stemmed cups rolling on the floor like a bunch of drunks that have forgotten how to stand straight. The imaginary feasts are over and the doll sleeps undisturbed in a forgotten corner of the house.

It is Mir Chuchak who inadvertently rescues the doll from a life
of dusty neglect. It begins when he tells Heer the story of Razia
while putting her to bed one night. Heer is a sponge for stories, she
sits by his side for long hours, soaking in tale after tale, her eyes
glowing and fixed on his face. Every word that falls from his lips is
gathered and hoarded in her heart, to be taken out and savoured
on the days he is out of town and not there to ply her with stories.

The next morning, Heer wakes up in great excitement and looks
for her abandoned doll. Amidst many shrieks of delight, Sultan's
castaway wooden horse is appropriated as a mount for the doll.
A bow and arrow set is strapped on her shoulder and a toy sword
tucked into her waistband. After some persistent pleading from
Heer, Malki fashions a turban and soldierly breeches for the newly
named doll. She is Razia, the Warrior Queen.

The reign of Queen Razia, on Heer's heart and Jhang Syal's
rooftops, courtyards and back-lanes, begins in earnest.

'Troops march!'

'Troops run!'

'Troops attack!'

A band of little girls goes from rooftops to courtyards to the
narrow lanes behind houses playing fierce war games. Their
whooping cries at pretend slayings and imagined victories can be
heard all day long. I normally follow them around at a discreet
distance, watching over them from some parapet or ledge or treetop.
Hidden, but never too far away.

'Don't call me Razia Sultana. I am no Sultana. Who am I, girls?'
Heer shouts peremptorily, holding aloft the ragdoll Razia on her
shoulder.

'You are Razia Sultan. You are our ruler, not the ruler's wife,' the
girls chorus back, knowing the answer that is expected.

'Who should we marry Razia off to today?' Hassi, her best friend,
asks Heer.

'Let me see. I think we'll make her run away with her slave Yaqut. She is the Sultan. She doesn't have to marry anyone if she doesn't want to,' Heer replies.

'Haaw!' squawk the other girls, shocked at the prospect of an eloping queen.

'Shut up, you ninnies. Don't you know she loved Yaqut? Love is better than marriage. In love you don't have to wash utensils and do the laundry.'

On another day, she allows Hassi to construct an imposing male figure out of sticks and twine and lets her lead a charge against Razia the ragdoll's army. After a bloody skirmish has been enacted to Heer's satisfaction, Hassi's stick doll asks for Razia's hand in marriage. Heer grandly accepts on behalf of her doll. 'Governor Altunia, you have done grave wrong by rebelling against me but I know that love and jealousy made you behave like that. I forgive you and accept your proposal. Together we shall rule.'

On cue, more troops, headed by Sonia the goldsmith's daughter, come rushing onto the scene and Razia and her newly acquired husband are felled.

The day's play ends with the solemn burial of the two dolls.

I could not but be amused to see how much satisfaction Heer got from the death of her hero and heroine. So sorrowful was the look she wore on her face while burying her make-believe Razia and Altunia that many of her more impressionable friends wept real tears of lament. In the hierarchy of values being formed in their little heads, dying for love, side by side with a dashing lover, ranked the highest.

Poor Malki, with her fond hopes of teaching her daughter to play with pots and pans by making her a doll. She had no idea what she had unleashed. Though in all fairness, it wasn't the doll her mother had made for her as much as the stories her father told her that were to blame.

What prompted Mir Chuchak to bring a headstrong, ill-fated queen, lying dead for over three centuries, alive once again in the imagination of his daughter, we will never know. Razia Sultan, who her father Shams-ud-din Iltutmish named his successor to the throne of Dilli, never knew peace in the four years she spent on the throne. In the eyes of the nobles of Dilli, all her wisdom and capability could not compensate for the fact that she was a woman. Even in death she knows no repose. Her grave is a matter of contention with three different claimants to her final remains. She is believed to be lying in a grave next to that of her feckless brother, Rukn ud din Firuz, in a courtyard in Bulbul-i-khana, Shahjahanabad, near the Turkman Gate entrance. In Siwan, near Kaithal, in Haryana there is a tomb for Razia and her childhood friend turned rebel governor turned husband, Altunia. And in faraway Tonk in Rajasthan, yet another pair of graves commemorate Sultanul Hind Razia and Shahide Muhabbat Quvvatul-Mulk Jamaluddin Yaqut, her Abyssinian slave, martyred in his love for her.

Razia the ragdoll, like Razia the Queen, had only a brief three- to four-year reign. By the time she was nine or ten, Heer had completely outgrown the doll, but it is my belief that Razia the ragdoll had no small part to play in the shaping of the personal myth of Heer Syal.

Heer was too much her own person for me to suggest that she was subconsciously following Razia's trajectory, yet I cannot but help draw parallels between their lives. The proclivity towards swords and horses, the trenchant belief that a woman could be whoever she wanted to be, the penchant for taking up cudgels on behalf of the downtrodden, the blithe defiance of convention in choosing a lover from a lower rung of the ladder of social hierarchy, the inconvenient existence of a prior suitor from childhood ... so many features in common.

In addition, Heer's story had a manipulative and malevolent uncle. Kaido Langra was a popular man in Jhang Syal, an able deputy to his older brother, who travelled frequently to various parts of his fiefdom, leaving Kaido incharge at home. Kaido was seen as something of an ascetic as well as an asset, a man of sacrifice as well as a useful man to know. He brokered deals of all kinds—between migrant herdsmen and farmers, between farmers and tradesmen, between thieves and law keepers, between quarrelling warlords and between parents of prospective brides and grooms. The fact that he was Mir Chuchak's brother gave him prestige, while his single status gave him the sheen of being free of worldly attachments. A busy and garrulous man, his chief business was minding other people's business.

Between Heer and Kaido there seemed to exist an inexplicable antagonism.

Even as an infant, she had a bristling awareness of him, and would wail loudly and thrash her legs about if left alone with her uncle. I remember dozens of incidents of Kaido making overtures of friendship and little Heer rejecting them imperiously.

'See what I have in my pocket for you?' asks Kaido, reaching his hand into the folds of his long shirt to take out a fistful of pine nuts.

Her eyes brighten for an instant. She takes a step forward and then hesitates and stops.

'Come on. I know you love these.' He moves forward, limping towards her on his crutches, to tousle her hair fondly.

She tosses her head out of his reach in a quick move and retreats two steps back.

'I'm not hungry just now,' she shrugs. 'Give them to Sultan.'

He scowls at her receding back as she scampers out of his sight. Yellow flecks of annoyance glitter in the white of his eyes.

Malki takes great pride in her little daughter's beauty. She loves dressing Heer up on special occasions, lining her eyes with antimony black, braiding her hair with silk ribbons, giving her glass bangles and pretty trinkets to wear.

Heer comes out of Malki's room dressed up for a wedding in the neighbourhood.

She goes to the courtyard where the men of the house are waiting for the women. Kaido spots her and beckons.

'What a beautiful bride you will make when you grow up' he says and pinches her cheeks teasingly.

'Don't do that,' she says, stamping hard on his good foot. 'I've told you before that I don't like it.'

A yowl of pain escapes Kaido's lips.

'Heer, that isn't nice,' her father reprimands her.

'Neither is pulling someone's cheeks when they don't want you to,' retorts Heer. Her eyes glitter with rage.

Mir Chuchak shrugs at his brother.

Kaido's face smudges purple in the early evening light. His eyes narrow and rest on his niece for the briefest of moments and then he smiles back at Chuchak. It is a strained smile, through lips stretched thin in annoyance.

Kaido's pigeons are a great source of enjoyment for the children who come to play with Sultan and Heer. He carries up a sack of grain to the rooftop and lets the children scatter the grain to feed the birds. The children run about shooing and scaring the feeding pigeons for fun and the entire rooftop becomes a riot of flapping, squawking, screeching birds. He lets the laughing children run amok among the pigeons till their excitement subsides. Then he coos and beckons the pigeons back one by one. He has special calling sounds for different pairs and many stories about their pedigree and their distinguishing marks.

Heer stands glaring at them balefully from a distance, refusing to join in.

'Come, Heer, sit on my lap. I'll tell you the story of how this one got a three-ring fan tail,' he says to her, nodding towards a pigeon perched on his wrist. It is a fine specimen with an elaborate set of white rings on its grey tail.

'Come on, Heer,' urge her friends. 'You love stories.'

'Not his stories,' says Heer. 'They make me feel sad for the pigeons.'

Malki has frequent conversations with Kaido about Heer. She worries that her husband's fondness for their daughter is spoiling the girl.

'My brother named her too hastily,' says Kaido to Malki. 'She is as hard as a diamond. Brightness and beauty are all very well, but she carries in her the hardness of her name.'

Heer marches into the room, sticks out her tongue at him and stomps out.

'Sister, even her natural beauty and her highborn stature will not be adequate guard against such an impetuous nature. There is nothing womanly about her. Think, what kind of wife or daughter-in-law will she make?' says Kaido. 'I pity the Kheras.'

Malki frowns.

'Your brother …' she sighs helplessly.

Kaido shakes his head bitterly. There is something in Heer's nature that has always set him on edge.

Heer's first major confrontation with Kaido takes place when Malki starts urging her to wait till the men of the house have eaten before taking her meals. It is the practice in their house, as in all the houses in the land, for the women to eat only after the menfolk. As a child, Heer has so far been exempt from the rule, but now that she is approaching puberty, Kaido has taken to dropping pointed hints and gentle barbs in Malki's direction.

'Nonsense,' says Heer when Malki broaches the topic. 'It is a ridiculous rule and I will not obey it.'

'Shh, child,' says Malki. 'God gave you a woman's body. Don't fight it.'

'My body doesn't have a different clock on it from Sultan's, so don't bring God into this,' says Heer.

'Heer, learn to obey, please,' says Malki.

'No, first you tell me why being a woman means eating last, making do with leftovers and never taking an extra serving of the good things?' asks Heer belligerently.

Their arguments continue over many days. Heer refuses to relent. Kaido decides to step in.

'Things are the way they are for a reason. Men go out of the house on important work. Your father and I oversee the lands and the collection of taxes. We see that the farmers and the cowherds are doing their work properly and that the soldiers are disciplined. We have to be looked after properly so that society does not suffer. Women eat later voluntarily. No one forces them. They just know that they stay at home all day and have only little-little, simple, unimportant tasks to do.'

Heer listens to him gravely and stalks away. It isn't till two days later that she is ready with her counter-attack.

As Mir Chuchak prepares to retire for the night, she sidles up to him.

'Father, I need your help with something very important. I need to teach Kaido a lesson,' she says.

'What has he done to annoy you now?' Mir Chuchak replies. He is familiar with the strained relationship his favourite child and his brother share. 'Tell me, what is bothering you?'

'Mother says now that I'm growing up I cannot have my food with you all anymore. I must wait for my turn and eat with the women later,' says Heer.

Mir Chuchak studies her face for a long while, trying to gauge the extent of her hurt and anger. He knows she abhors discrimination of any sort, it cuts into her deeply. From the very beginning, she has questioned everything. Why their servants are poor and they are rich, why goats and chicken are slaughtered for meat, why the calves are deprived of their mother's milk ... He has never fobbed her off with stories, has always dealt her the truth about how the real world works, its inevitable cruelties.

'It is true, Heer,' he says at last. 'Women always eat later.'

'But why? It is wrong!'

'I have never given much thought to the matter. It's always been like that.'

'Kaido says it is because men need to do important work whereas what women do is inconsequential. I want to show him what a silly liar he is. I want you to declare that no woman is going to do any work in this house for the next few days. Let everyone go hungry. Let Kaido arrange the drinking water and firewood. Let him milk the cows, feed the hens and goats. Let him do all the "little-little, simple, unimportant tasks" for two days. And let's see if it makes him want to volunteer to eat last.'

'Heer, you must not get angry with your uncle and mother,' says Mir Chuchak. 'I am equally to blame. I have never stopped to question the practice myself.'

She nods gravely and continues to stare at her father. It is obvious that she expects something more from him. The silence in the room is heavy with her expectations.

'From tomorrow all of us will eat at the same time,' says Mir Chuchak at last. 'That is to be the new rule in our house. Satisfied, my inquisitor and judge?'

But age-old traditions cannot be changed overnight. It takes many heated arguments and tantrums over the next few days, but Heer eventually gets her way.

She was tenacious, that girl. Once she began a fight, she fought it to the end. Kaido Langra stopped eating at the main house in protest. While his mother lived, food was sent to him in his own hut, which was a small distance away from the family house, within the same compound. After her death, he moved further from the main family home into a small house adjacent to his pigeon huts.

My perch on the neem tree was a fair distance from Kaido's hut and I was glad to see less of him. Later, many rumours of Kaido's corrupt ways found their way to my ears from the pigeon-quarters. I wondered if they could possibly be true. It would explain Heer's instinctive wariness of her uncle, her insistence on keeping far from him.

He had a slanting shadow, he did, Kaido the Cripple.

6

Causes and Clashes

BY THE TIME HEER turned sixteen, the lines on Malki's forehead had deepened and begun to resemble the map of Punjab, the rivers of worry over her daughter's intransigence alternating with the smooth plains of pride at Sultan's solid promise of being a caring and obedient son. Heer's toy swords had been exchanged for real ones, the wooden horses for prime mounts, and the make-believe battles for real crusades. It was quite a sight to behold, a band of Syal beauties, Heer and her closest cousins and friends, riding through the forests and countryside of Jhang, fearless and armed, unmindful of the restraints that normally applied to young women their age.

Every other day, a new story winged its way to Malki's ears, of the strange battles being fought by Heer and her gang of girls.

She had heard her daughter had a sensitivity to pain that was almost psychic. Heer could feel another's pain in her body. If someone was hungry, Heer could feel an echo of their rumbling stomach in her own, if someone was overworked and tired, she could feel a resonance of it in her limbs, if a goat was being slaughtered she could feel its fear ripple through her being, if a calf was lost in the forest, she could feel both the palpitations of its bleating heart and its mother's urgent grief as it called out for the lost child.

One day, a wisp of an elderly woman was reportedly wandering lost and half-crazed with hunger in the forests outside the settlement of Jhang Syal. It wasn't immediately clear to Heer if it was just another one of those rumours that rose up in the air like the smoke from the evening's cooking fires and soon vanished without a trace. However, once the sun disappeared into the jungle pool with a splash of crimson, and the hyenas came out baying at the moon (a silver moon the colour of the frightened old woman's hair) Heer sensed something was wrong.

She jumped out of bed, ran out to the stables, saddled her horse and rode into the moonlight, following the scent of the fear in her nostrils. She found the old woman almost dead with exhaustion, hunger and fright, and brought her back to Jhang in the middle of the night.

The woman was from a village on the other side of the forest and had been left to die by her son and his family, since they were unable to bear the proximity of her aging body. Her body, it seemed, emitted a foul odour and she sighed and moaned in the middle of the night from the ache in her limbs, disturbing everyone's sleep. Besides, her knotted fingers were no longer capable of any useful work and there was nothing to justify her continued existence. 'Better a swift feast for the wild cat than a never-ending burden on her family', her daughter-in-law had said darkly.

The next morning saw Heer and her girls galloping to Gujara to reinstate the old woman in her home. Heer seemed to know instinctively that drama has its own power. Keeping the old woman discreetly tucked out of sight behind a large tree, a small distance away, she and her friends rode up to the headman's house. Wearing turbans over their long, neatly plaited braids and carrying swords across their breasts, the girls stood in a semicircle around the biggest home in the village.

'Is there a man in your village whose excreta smelt of roses and his urine like attar when he was a baby?' she inquired of the headman when he came out.

A small crowd had gathered around them by then. They considered her strange words in a growing and voluble puzzlement. What could she mean? What kind of a question was that? Who was this beautiful girl who spoke so boldly as she sat astride her horse? Word of the unusual visitors spread through the village quicker than an itch on a monkey's bottom and before long a hundred-odd people were gathered around them. Some murmured the name of Mir Chuchak's daughter.

At last, silencing his fellow villagers, the headman spoke.

'Welcome, brave daughter of the Syals, to our humble village. We are happy to see you here, but some mistake brings you into our boundary, for indeed there is no such man to be found here,' he said.

'Then perhaps you have a man in this village who didn't cry as a baby. Every time he was wet, hungry or hurt and he opened his mouth to howl, Raag Bihag poured out?' countered Heer.

The crowd murmured like a monsoon shower on a tin roof. It was confirmed. These were the Syal beauties. From Jhang, all the way across the forest. That, right there, was the famed Heer. Every bit as flaming and beautiful as the tales went. But what madness had brought her here, talking of babies that cried in Raag Malhar? Not Malhar. She said Bihag. The girl was certainly touched in her head. Mir Chuchak had trouble on his hands for sure. What riches and beauty can compensate for such imperious madness in one's progeny? That too, a girl. Wait. Wasn't she betrothed already?

The headman walked up to her and said, 'Daughter, dismount. Stay awhile and have some buttermilk. You have come a long way. If there was such a man as you talk of in our village, I would present him before you, but indeed there is none.'

'Perhaps then there is a man who could plough the fields and harvest the grain from the very day he was born?' she demanded.

'You know and everybody knows that such a thing is not possible,' said the exasperated headman.

'Then how is it possible for a man to throw out the mother who cleaned his smelly bottom countless times when he was a baby, stayed awake through many nights because of his howling and taught him everything he knows today, simply because it is his turn to look after her?' she asked him heatedly.

The gathered crowd broke out into a rash of questions and judgements. Who did she mean? Was there such a person in their village? Indeed it was wrong if such an incident had happened. Shame on the man. Shame on his family. Shame upon the village. Shame upon everyone who mistreated old parents. Times are bad. The new generation is spoilt by too much ease. No respect for elders. Such an erosion of values. What a terrible dereliction of duty. Could it be the old mother of Durla, the one with a festering wound on her left foot? No, he couldn't have. Or could he? Maybe it was Malay Khan. Many harsh words were exchanged between his wife and his mother every day. Bad-tempered shrew, that wife of his. But why blame the wife, a man must know how to stand his ground.

The headmen held up his hand for silence.

'If indeed your charge is true, it is a grievous one. The man shall be found and flogged publicly.'

'No, no, please don't do that!'

The little old woman came scampering out from where she had stood concealed and hurried up to the headman, panting and wincing from the exertion.

An angry roar went through the crowd as the identity of the erring family stood revealed.

The son was propelled forward on the force of the crowd's wrath to face the headman. Heer gave an account of the condition she had found his mother in, in the forest.

The son stood rooted to the spot, his head hanging lower and lower in shame. The old mother implored the crowd for forgiveness for her son.

'What guarantee do you have that he will not mistreat you again?' challenged Heer.

'None,' replied the mother. 'If my upbringing has failed me once, it might fail me again. But I am not far from my grave now. I don't know how many weeks or months of life are left for me, and I don't want to go to my grave with his humiliation on my conscience. It is not for his sake that I beg you for a peaceful end to this, but my own.'

The crowd was quiet.

At last the headman walked up to the old woman and begged her forgiveness.

'We have all failed you, Mother, the entire village. It is a shameful day for all of Gurjara when you are brought back to us by an outsider. Thank you for bringing her back, daughter. I will guarantee that she is not mistreated again. She is the responsibility of every villager in this habitation. We will see to it that she is looked after properly in her son's home.'

And so it carried on. Floating rumours of wrongdoing in some house, personal pleas and furtive entreaties for help from one of the victims, a representation from a neighbouring village, and Heer and her friends would be outside the wrongdoer's door.

'You must do something to control Heer, restrain her from exercising so much power,' Malki pleaded with Mir Chuchak. 'What business is it of hers whose mother has been abandoned or daughter-in-law abused or wife beaten? Such things are best dealt with inside the family. Since when has it become right for anyone else to interfere in how a man keeps his women, children and cattle? It is only because she is your daughter that she gets away with her ridiculous meddlesome ways.'

'What powers have I given her that I can take away? How can I tell her not to see another's grief? And if having seen it, she manages to persuade the tormentors to change their behaviour, what harm is there in that?' countered Mir Chuchak.

'It is the freedom you have given her that is going to her head. Why should girls be given swords and horses? The other chieftains follow your lead in this, thinking that what is good for Mir

Chuchak's daughter is fine for theirs. No one stops to think about the consequences,' said Malki.

'That the Syal girls can defend themselves and their honour should be a matter of pride and comfort to us. How often has this land been ravaged and looted? Greeks, Arabs, Turks, Mongols— wave after wave of invaders have come seeking our land, our gold and our women. If our daughters are trained and armed to protect themselves, are we not better off for that?' asked Mir Chuchak.

I saw Malki shake her head and walk away. Poor Malki. I felt for her. She would brood upon this exchange for days, in sorrow and frustration.

Malki, who had been friendly and approachable once, had over the years become distant and isolated from the women of the settlement. Being Heer's mother had made Malki a stranger in her own life. It had forced her into cultivating a distance from her peers for she had too much pride to admit publicly that she had no say in the upbringing of her only daughter—that the liberties allowed to Heer by her doting father were not for Malki to criticise or curtail.

She had built a wall of disdain around herself that no sister, sister-in-law or childhood friend could hope to scale. Her husband was a high chieftain of the clan, her son was valiant and strong as a son ought to be, and her daughter was the most beautiful girl in the province, betrothed to be married into one of the wealthiest families in the region. Malki was living the perfect life on the face of it. But it came at a cost. This myth around her had to be maintained. Malki could not risk exposing it by becoming too close to anyone.

Only one person knew Malki's truth. It was Kaido. Kaido was Malki's confidante when her husband's lofty and liberal ideas confused her. Kaido was the one who understood her anxieties about Heer. Only Kaido knew how often Malki wished for a less beautiful, more biddable daughter. Someone who understood this most basic of tenets: girls are born to follow, not lead.

'She is living a life no woman can hope to get away with. Why does your brother refuse to see what is in plain sight?' Malki sighed to Kaido.

However, the incident of the boat worried even Mir Chuchak.

It was a strange sequence of events that led to the clash between Noora of Sambhal and Heer of Syal, on the banks of the Chenab. Heer had been sleeping poorly for the past few nights. A recurring nightmare was making her wake up in panic in the middle of the night. I had overheard her describing it to Hassi in vivid detail. There were tiny bird-sized girls locked up in her uncle's pigeon coop. They had feathers like birds but the faces of frightened little girls. *Help us, save us*, they howled out to Heer even as a big, ugly hand plucked out their feathers and broke them into two before tossing them down onto a floor already splattered with blood and broken wings. Suddenly Heer would see a little girl break out of the coop and run. Heer would run after her but before she could reach her, a gigantic hairy rat would pounce upon the feathered child and pin her to the floor, its stained teeth trying to prise her lips apart. Heer would wake up from the dream each night, nauseous, gagging and choking, as if her mouth was being violated again and again.

After one such sleepless night, just before daybreak, she heard cries of 'Help! Somebody help! Help please!'

She woke up disoriented by her dream and followed the voice, confusing these cries for the screams she had heard earlier in her sleep. They seemed to be coming from the riverfront. She mounted her horse and rode out towards the river. When Heer reached the riverfront, she was dumbstruck at the sight of a floating palace on the water. In front of her was the most beautiful boat imaginable. Not quite sure if she was still inside a dream, Heer rode closer to the boat.

The cries for help were ringing out even louder.

Inside the boat, Luddan the boatman was thrashing his twin wives. His employer Noora, the Sambhal chief, had threatened to kill him after finding out that Luddan had rented out Noora's private boat to others for a consideration. Afraid for his life, Luddan had made away with the boat in the middle of the night. Now fearful of Noora's wrath, he was beating and berating his young wives. If it wasn't for the need to keep them in fine clothes and soft mattresses, he would not be in this predicament.

Even as Heer dismounted and tethered her horse in order to explore further, a fleshy, blubbering man rushed out of the boat and threw himself at her feet.

'Help me, noble lady! Save me from my unjust master's wrath and I will serve you for life,' grovelled Luddan, rubbing his head into the coarse river sand in front of her feet.

'Boatman, first stand up like a grown man instead of flailing about on the ground like a helpless infant. Then show us your boat and tell us your story if you please,' commanded Heer, marching towards the pier. Luddan scrambled up and bustled obsequiously behind her.

It was a mistake asking to see the boat before hearing his story. The sight of the boat thrilled and enraptured Heer. Her mind, weakened already by nightmares and sleeplessness, was confused further by the boat.

As she stood listening to Luddan's tale of mistreatment and torture by his master, I think whispers from a future yet to happen began to gather around her and cloud her vision. In normal circumstances she would have been able to see that Luddan's tale was weak, like milk mixed with water by a deceitful seller seeking to make an easy profit. However, there was the fascinating beauty of the boat playing out before her eyes—its fine cedar wood exteriors, undoubtedly carved by master craftsmen. She walked, as if in a trance to the main chamber inside, and stood in the centre, gazing out at the scenes of the Chenab in the first light of the morning, framed variously in the dozen window frames of the chamber. She felt a strange restlessness assail her being. As if, were she to let go of this boat, the most important moment of her life would fail to unfold.

She felt as if she belonged to this boat or that this boat belonged to her.

'Boatman, fear not. From today you are under my protection. Stay here, moored to this shore, and if anyone should bother you even a bit, direct them to me,' said Heer.

As it happened, it did bother Noora, the Sambhal chief, more than a little that his erring boatman had sought the protection of the Syals. He was out hunting when the news reached him and he immediately headed towards the riverbank where Luddan and the boat had reportedly been spotted.

Heer was on the boat with her friends, setting off for a pleasure trip when she heard that Noora was headed towards the riverbank with his hunting party. She had the boat turned back to shore immediately.

When Noora arrived with his party, he saw that the Syal flag fluttered from high atop the boat in challenge. A band of armed girls, led by Heer, stood guarding the approach to the gangway.

'I have come to collect my boat and punish my erring boatman,' said Noora. 'Please move out of my way.'

'Luddan is under my protection now. You will have to duel with me before I let you take the boat,' said Heer, drawing her sword and slicing the air in front of her in an invitation to battle.

'This is preposterous behaviour. I do not battle with women,' said Noora. 'It is beneath my dignity. Call for your father or brother to represent you, if it is a battle you seek.'

'It is beneath my dignity to let anyone else fight on my behalf. Duel with me or concede that you have lost and leave,' said Heer.

'My hands are bound by chivalry. I can only request you once again to be reasonable and return my boat. Since the boatman has your favour, I promise to let the scoundrel off with a warning,' said Noora. 'Though he deserves a good hiding for his knavery.'

This was the ideal opportunity for Heer to have politely returned the boat to Noora. But the boat had woven a spell around her. She was loath to let it go. She stood quiet and unyielding, her eyes glinting with defiance, her chin tilted upwards, her grip on her sword strong. Finally, Noora bowed graciously and retreated.

Heer's reputation, I'm afraid, suffered considerably on account of this incident. It was ammunition in the hands of those who held her to be unreasonable and spoilt beyond measure, ample proof of her wilfulness and arrogance.

Mir Chuchak summoned his daughter to his presence.

'Heer, you were wrong to covet and take by force what is not yours. The boat must be sent back to Noora of Sambhal,' he reproached.

'Father, forgive me. I do not know what has come over me, but I cannot part with that boat. When I stepped on that boat, it was as if a flute began playing in my head and in the air I smelt the perfume of monsoon clouds bursting upon parched earth. I felt a weakness in my knees and in my ribcage the fluttering wings of a tiny butterfly eager to fly out into the open sky. Something in that boat calls to me beyond reason. I cannot let it go,' said Heer.

'Very well,' said Mir Chuchak. 'I will send a messenger to Noora apologising for your behaviour and begging to buy the boat from him as my daughter has taken an inordinate fancy to it. However, in future you would do well to remember a warrior is only as respected as the justice of his cause. The difference between a hero and a bandit lies not in how well each wields the sword, but in the cause to which their weapon is drawn.'

III

THE KEPT MAN

7

The Call of Protoplasm

SHE STORMED ONTO THE boat like a hailstorm in April, early and unexpected and in a furious rage, flattening everything in its wake. Luddan reeled and lurched like a large tree hit by sudden lightning, while his wives eddied around in circles like two small leaves caught in a giant whirlwind. Her words, swift and heedless, pelted down on my sleeping form.

'Get up! Who are you? How dare you?' she said. Her voice lashed my face like angry raindrops.

Heer had been bathing in the river with her friends when some tattletale had taken word to her that a stranger was sleeping in her precious bed. She had dressed hurriedly and reached the boat. Her anklets rang out a call to battle as she strode up the steps.

I opened my eyes reluctantly, sheltering them with the back of my hand. Heer stood there, dressed in a green majhla and a yellow kurta, resplendent in the colours of springtime in the fields. Her hair, still dripping wet, was hastily coiled against the nape of her neck and the soft muslin of her kurta clung to her moist skin. The first thing I noticed about her were her perfect breasts, round, firm and ample. I was aroused even before I was fully awake.

'Easy sweetheart, easy does it,' I said, my voice still heavy with sleep.

'Are you talking to me?' she blazed.

Truth be told, I wasn't. I was addressing a small bit of muscle wedged between my legs which was rapidly leaping to attention at the sight of her, but that is not something you can say to a woman you've just met. Even if you suspect the woman to be the other half of your soul.

True love, quite simply, is as irrefutable as an erection. It defiantly sets its own direction, unmindful of the embarrassment it causes, and the disapproval and trouble it brings in its wake.

I scrambled to a sitting position, hastily drawing my blanket over my legs and stomach, right up to my chin. My eyes refused to leave her face, even as my hands frantically searched the bed for my flute. Without it, I felt unarmed and helpless.

'Damn, you're beautiful,' I said.

She looked from my face to the flute in my hands and back to my face with a questioning, almost challenging gaze. It seemed to me that she was calling my spirit out to prove its mettle against hers.

This was my do-or-die moment. Drawing my flute to my lips, I began to play for all I was worth. Either my music would reach her or it wouldn't. There were no words for what I wanted to convey. I wanted to tell her who I was and who I believed she was to me.It is a rare man, I wanted to tell her, who leaves his father's village, his ancestral property, the entitlements that come with his forefathers' name and class, beggars himself completely, and then sets out in search of his bride with only the gift of his music. My flute played for her the song of the fakir and the free woman, of a man unchained from the burden of earning, owning, appropriating endlessly, and of a woman who declined to be a commodity, owned and possessed in exchange for security and status. Of a new, different, better world than ours, free of the rapacity of humans, their need to grab ever more and attach it to their names.

Even as I played, the nature of my connection to her became clear to me. Images of other lifetimes, other meetings and other separations flashed through my consciousness. I knew her from the time we were one protoplasm. Imprinted on each cell of my body was the memory of the distant moment when we were sundered and sent forth into the world, reeling and spinning through the ages, yearning to be united with the lost bit of ourselves.

I saw Heer's eyes darkening with an understanding of that which lay between us—a river of deep, vast, unexplored feelings asking to be plunged into without delay. I had already crossed the river, left behind the familiar childhood shore, and let my passion lead me to her door. It was her turn now to respond how she would.

When I had finished playing, she gestured to her girlfriends and to Luddan and his wives to vacate the room. Bolting the door behind her, she sat down at the edge of the bed and appraised me intently, her hands clasped tightly together on her lap.

'Who are you?' she whispered. Her eyes took in my frayed blanket and simple clothes, my long hair, the delicacy of my features, the fineness of my fingers and mouth as they held the flute. 'You look high born, your speech is smooth, yet you wear the garb of a homeless wanderer.'

'I am Ranjha from Takht Hazara, across the river. The favourite son of Mauju Chaudhry. My father was a rich landlord.'

'Why are you here, so far from your home and family, and in this penniless state?'

'My father died. My brothers cheated me of my share of the good land and gave me infertile, barren tracts to cultivate. My sisters-in-law were wicked and unkind. So I left,' I said. My eyes wandered to her feet. Her ankles were delicately crossed, her feet perfectly arched, her toes twinkled with silver rings.

'Why did you not stay and fight?'

'Fight for what?' I asked her. Her question irritated me somewhat. 'For a life of mediocrity like theirs? To be chained forever to what I was born into? To call only a spoonful of the sky my own instead of the limitless firmament? I did not fight, quite simply, because I did not want any of it.'

'What was it that you wanted then?' Heer asked, her eyes searching mine.

'To cross the river. To travel. To know the world. To explore the wilderness. Most of all, to see you,' I replied.

She flushed. I held her gaze with mine. A strong and sincere current of good feeling flowed between us.

'And now that you have travelled and have crossed the river and seen me?' she asked at last, breaking the silence.

'I could spend the rest of my life looking at you. You are so incredibly beautiful.'

'You are very bold and impertinent. I should be taking offence at your words,' she said. She straightened her spine as she spoke, lifted her neck, her chin in regal profile, a finger under it.

'What stops you then? Rail at me, walk out, send your minions in to flog me and throw me off your boat,' I challenged. 'Take offence if you will. I don't think it will change the truth even a whit. Make you any less beautiful or me any less smitten by you.'

For a moment, Heer looked uncertain. 'There is something in your voice that stops me. I feel as if it knows me better than I know myself. As if it knows ways into my heart to which I myself am not privy. That it will know how to buoy me up when I'm drowning, heal me when I'm wounded, put me together when I'm broken,' she replied slowly.

My heartbeat quickened on hearing her words. Without being consciously aware of what I was doing, I lifted her hand from her lap and placed it on my thumping heart.

'This voice and its owner are your slaves. Whatever you bid us do will be done instantly,' I said.

'I have no use for slaves. My father's house is full of servants who jump at my bidding, of people who scurry around catering to my every whim. I have dozens of obliging girlfriends who follow me blindly and obey my commands. Yet, none of this gives me real happiness. People say Heer of Syal is wilful and knows her mind. She does as she pleases. The truth is, I am confused and fearful. All my life I have only known what I don't want and most of my actions are provoked by what displeases me. I have no notion of what I do want, or what might please me. It is not a slave I need but a master. Yes, a master, a murshid. I need someone who will show me what lives inside of me and teach me not to be scared of it. Will you take me as your pupil?'

I stared at her speechlessly. She was melting before my eyes, her pride and haughtiness dissolving. Her defences were being quietly dismantled and her essential soul being laid bare to my scrutiny without any coyness or prevarication. Her capacity for honesty stunned me.

There was no place for lies in this dialogue. My truth was an insistent little muscle between my legs, wishing to make itself clear.

'I'm sorry but that is not possible. I did not come all this way to be a teacher and it is not a pupil I seek,' I said. I had no desire to stay within the boundaries prescribed by the teacher-disciple relationship. In fact, my mind was already a tumult of possible transgressions as I looked at her. I wanted to touch her. I wanted to hold her hands in mine. I wanted to kiss her feet, the nape of her neck and her delicate coral pink lips. I wanted to smell the river water in her still moist hair. I wanted to cup her breasts in my palms. I wanted to lean her body into mine, length for length, and hold her till our two hearts beat as one. And I wanted her to want me to do all this and more.

She sat there, quietly studying my face, perhaps hearing the things I hadn't said aloud. I exuded my longing for her from every pore in my skin. A gentle dew of sweat began to form on her upper lip and forehead. The intensity of my gaze was causing a slow burn to spread through her body, from the base of her spine to the back of her neck, and then slowly to her face. She held her flushed cheeks in the palms of her hands and exhaled deeply.

'Are you saying you want to marry me?' she asked.

I was caught off guard. I hadn't been thinking of bands, processions and feasts at all. Or of exchanging vows in front of our families and a stern-faced qazi. There was no social or institutional dimension to my desire for her in that moment. I certainly wasn't thinking of setting up house with her or starting a family of bawling little Heers and small snot-faced Ranjhas. I simply wanted to bury my head in her breasts and taste every inch of her skin with my tongue. My instrument was all primed and ready to play the concert of its life in the hallway of her body. But these were not things I could say to her.

I dumbly nodded my head in affirmation. Yes, I was here with the intention of making her my bride.

'I am spoken for by the Kheras of Rangpur. My hand was promised to them by my uncle at the time of my birth,' she said.

The confession knocked the breath out of my chest. Rangpur was a burgeoning township and the Kheras its foremost clan—landed gentry who had diversified into commerce with great success. It was their cargo boats that plied all along the Ravi from Multan to Lahore, trading in grain, coal and salt. Instantly, I was on my feet.

'In which case, I had better leave,' I said. I was consumed by a livid rage. My eyes were burning, my hands shaking with an urge to break something or kill someone. I had left Takht Hazara for nothing. I had crossed the river to no purpose. The other half of my soul had been promised to some undeserving son of a rich trader to wear as a decorative pin on his turban.

'Here,' she said, gathering my blanket and flute from her bed and handing them to me. 'Go if you will, but at some point in your life you will have to learn to stay and fight for what you want.'

She stood facing me, blocking the way to the door, her eyes flashing a challenge.

'Is that what you want?' I asked her. 'A man who will fight to possess you? Are you a parcel of land or a piece of gold that men must cross swords to own you and stamp their name on you? Do your mind and body not belong to you? Are they objects to be given away to whoever your family wishes?'

I believe that was the precise moment she fell in love with me. We both looked at each other, stunned. One moment it was in the realm of possibilities and in the next moment we were madly in love. Simple, stark, irrevocable love stared us in the face, too strong and swift to deny.

'Come, we need to talk,' she said, leading me back to sit on the bed. She sat down next to me, our bodies touching, my hand clasped in hers.

'Or we could talk a bit later,' I said, leaning towards her.

I drew her body closer to mine with my free arm. She turned her face to look at me questioningly. There was a pulse beating at the base of her throat. I bent my head to kiss it. I was so close, I could hear the erratic beating of her heart.

'May I?' I whispered against her skin.

When I raised my head, I saw equal parts of doubt and longing in her eyes. She was considering, perhaps, that the first time could be painful for women. A whole gamut of conflicting emotions played out on her face, while I waited with bated breath. I so wanted her to agree, to admit that what was between us was both beautiful and inevitable, already beyond the jurisdiction of cautious thoughts and careful calculations.

'Yes,' she said tremulously at last, drawing me towards her.

That first time, I took Heer like a plunderer blinded by the sight of a treasure more magnificent than even his most fervid imagination. The heat of my departure from Takht Hazara, the arduous journey with its many perils and lonesome nights and the uncertainty that had beset the last few weeks had my body tightly wound up. I was hungry, thirsty, filled with my own insecurities as I entered the oasis of her being. I clung to her with frantic urgency as if my life depended on it. Only later, when I was spent, did I read the pain in her eyes and feel like a cad.

Contrite, I cradled her in my arms and dropped a hundred soft kisses on her eyes and forehead.

'Play me some music,' she said, curling away from me.

I played a springtime raga for her. A song of the season of flowering. Of snow melting on mountain tops and the gushing down of rivers towards the plains. Of new leaves unfurling. Of fledgling birds leaving the nest. Of buds becoming blossoms. Of girls becoming women.

She sat up after a time and folded her legs up, her arms around them, her chin resting on her knees.

Wrapped in only my music, Heer looked ethereal. Her long hair was unwound now and cascading down her shoulders and back. Her lips were slightly bruised, her cheeks were suffused a gentle pink. Her nose pin shone bright and fierce like the North Star.

She took the flute from my hand and put it to the side gently.

I watched her eyes as they became smudged with small flecks of desire. I reached out for her slowly. This time I intended to get it right, stroke by gentle stroke, kiss by tender kiss. I wanted to drown her in the music of her own body, as I teased it out note by note, taking her from the lower octaves to the highest in a mounting crescendo.

'I feel as if I have just been born,' she said afterwards, her head against my chest. I knew what she was trying to say. I too felt as if I had just come alive, that the years I had existed before I met her were not life at all but some pale approximation of it. A damp, heavy, musky smell filled the room—the scent of drunken lovers, intoxicated on each other's bodies. I did not know where my body ended and my soul began and whether my hands were my hands or merely an extension of her silk smooth skin.

'Where do we go from here?' I asked her. The white bedspread beneath us was spangled red with the rose petals of her lost virginity. Clearly, the Kheras would need to arrange another prized bride for their cosseted heir.

'Will you marry me?' she asked.

'Will your father agree to call off your engagement?' I wanted to know in return. The Kheras were a family of great influence as well as affluence. To offend them would not be without repercussions for Mir Chuchak and his family.

'My father was never in favour of this engagement. My uncle, Kaido, manipulated him into it. My father is a good and upright man. He would never force me to do anything that causes me unhappiness.'

'Kaido?' I was not familiar with the name.

'My father's brother. There are no limits to his malevolence. He is like a spider that has enmeshed us deeper and deeper into its web with each passing day. He acts as if he is a selfless man of God, yet his greasy fingers are embroiled in everyone's affairs and he seems to feed off other people's problems. He first manufactures acrimony and misunderstandings and then loudly plays the well-wisher who brokers peace. There is something rotten to the core about him, yet strangely, no one seems to see it except me. In fact, he has successfully deceived even my own mother, who thinks of him as a confidante. Whereas I feel a sickness in my stomach if I so much as walk past his cottage. And I think he hates me every bit as much as I despise him.'

I sensed fear and loathing in her voice as she spoke of her uncle. I could tell it went deep. A part of me wanted to tell her that now that I was here, she had nothing to be scared of. I didn't. As long as there are men offering to protect them, women have everything to be scared of. She was better off fighting her own battles.

'I need to install you in our lives without alerting Kaido. I have a plan. If I can get my father to employ you and get to know you independently, we may stand a better chance,' she continued.

I couldn't see myself as an accountant or collector of taxes on her father's estate and I did not think Mir Chuchak would be in urgent need of a personal musician. 'I'm a man with very few practical skills,' I confessed.

'Do you have any experience of herding cattle?' she asked. 'My father keeps a huge herd in the Sandal Bar but always has trouble finding a good cowherd. The region is full of cattle thieves and rustlers and our buffaloes are constantly being stolen. The cowherds get bored so far away from the main settlement and play truant very often.'

Truly, ours was a match made in heaven. This was practically the only job I could do!

'I was chief herdsman of our clan. It is simple for me to manage large herds as animals understand my music and obey my command. But still, I am not sure it would be a good idea,' I said. To have been a cowherd to my own father's cows was one thing, but to be a cowherd in the employ of Mir Chuchak, quite another. It meant a permanent loss of caste. From a landowner's son I would become a rich man's servant. Or worse still, a rich girl's temporary diversion. A kept man. It was a one-way ticket to social downfall.

'It is away from the settlement. We could meet every day and the townsfolk wouldn't even know. I will ride into the forest with my friends and while the girls keep watch on the periphery, you and I can be together. They are loyal and will not gossip or spread tales. I will put my friend Hassi in charge,' she said.

To see her every day alone in the forest, amidst birdsong and lush, limitless greenery, sounded perfect in every way. What is social class anyway but a man-made prison, I thought. I was a free man now.

I decided I would behave like one.

8

Becoming a Cowherd

I MET HEER'S FATHER in the grounds of their home. It was a sprawling garden with a boundary of tall, fair cypress trees and hedges of the fragrant henna bush weaving through them. I could see oval ponds of water with pink and white lotuses floating on the surface. My own home in Takht Hazara, contained in a fairly big family compound, with a massive inner courtyard and a separate cooking area, an underground water tank and tall storage bins seemed like a rustic village house in comparison. The Syals lived like gentle townsfolk, unlike us Ranjhas who were simple men of the soil.

In one corner was a hoary old neem tree. I stood with my back to it. Mir Chuchak sat on a stone bench facing the neem tree while Heer stood by his side.

'Heer, what is the meaning of all this? This boy is no cowherd. Cowherds don't look like this.' Mir Chuchak remonstrated.

I don't think the Syal chieftain was blind even for a minute to the nature of his daughter's interest in me. Though Heer and I were standing far apart from each other, our bodies exuded a shared heat, our eyes were in intimate conversation, our smiles colluded. The subtext was decidedly amorous and Mir Chuchak was no fool.

'Father, you are right,' said Heer, rushing headlong before we could be discovered. 'He is no ordinary cowherd, but a cowherd he certainly is. He is from a landed family across the river and has looked after his family's herd for many years. We are lucky to have found him to look after our beasts. If you take him on, he gets a home and we get just the man we need.'

Mir Chuchak raised a wary eyebrow. Turning towards me he said, 'Speak, boy, who are you?'

'Huzoor, I am Ranjha from Takht Hazara, the youngest son of Mauju Chaudhary. Cheated by my brothers and mistreated by their wives after my father's leaf fell from the tree of life, I resolved to leave home and travel in search of my destiny,' I said. 'I believe my future lies not in my own village but outside it.'

Mir Chuchak's eyes scanned my boyish frame, taking in my smooth olive skin, sharp nose, fine forehead, shapely brows, and the mass of wavy hair framing my face and curling around the nape of my neck. He frowned.

'Son,' he said. 'You seem to have had a pampered childhood. It shows in the softness of your hands and the innocence on your face. Perhaps it was no great hardship to manage your father's cattle on the other side of the river with its wide and gentle banks. Our Syal herds are large and untamed and graze in the forests. The Sandal Bar is home to many wild beasts, besides the unscrupulous bandits and thieves who lurk in its sheltering darkness. It is full of dangers. I would not wish you torn and ripped to pieces and your weeping kin at my door. This kind of work is best left to hardy fools with ample muscles. Go back home. Make peace with your brothers. Jealousies and misunderstandings happen in all families. I will intercede on your behalf if you wish.'

'Huzoor,' I said with a quick glance at Heer. 'The dispute over land is a trivial matter, a mere excuse. It is truly my destiny that has led me to your door. I cannot return home before fulfilling it. It brought me here to Jhang Syal and to the bride of my dreams.

Having seen Heer, there is nothing else my heart desires except her hand in marriage.'

Heer stared at me, startled. This wasn't part of what we had planned to say.

I spoke too boldly, too soon, perhaps. But the taste of her mouth was still fresh on my tongue and the touch of her soft, dewy skin alive on my palms. The moment of exploding into a million raindrops inside the dark night of her body still drenched my consciousness. As she stood there, looking at me with incandescent eyes, I knew that it was my presence that had made them light up from within. Her face shone pink as if my breath had left a tell-tale trail of heat on her skin, burnishing it. Her bosom and hips arched and curved, straining against the fabric of her kurta, as if they no longer understood the purpose of the old restraints. All of her was in love with all of me. I was Heer and Heer was me. I did not see any sense in prevaricating. The sooner Mir Chuchak knew I was here to be his son-in-law, the better it would be for all of us.

'For a lad with only a staff and a flute to call his own, you aim too high,' said Mir Chuchak, fixing me with a stern gaze. 'Maybe you are not aware that destiny is in the bad habit of favouring the already blessed. Good fortune flows like water, always in search of its own level. My daughter's hand has already been promised to someone else.'

'But, Father,' protested Heer. 'You don't abide by that engagement, do you? It was wicked of my uncle to have promised me to the Kheras when I was only a baby on my mother's lap. You always told me I should consider myself free.'

'Heer,' said Mir Chuchak, 'That was before your mother and uncle agreed to the formal offer of marriage for Seida Khera and saw fit to accept the engagement gifts sent by his father Ajju Khera. Had I not been away, I would have rejected the suit, knowing it was displeasing to you. However, neither you nor I raised too many objections as we had no other suitor in mind. Now it is too late to

back out. The Kheras will take great offence at this slight to their
honour and the people of Jhang Syal will not tolerate it either.'

'Father, I have committed myself to Ranjha. In the instant I heard
his music, I felt my whole being melt and realign itself. I am not the
Heer I used to be. Yesterday, I would have bowed to your wishes.
Today it is no longer possible for me. My soul has taken a new vow
of allegiance. In all but name, Ranjha is husband to me. If you turn
him away, Heer will follow him.'

'Heer!' expostulated Mir Chuchak. 'What madness is this, my
daughter? You cannot marry for music.'

'Father, the music he creates is a better measure of a man than
the size of the mansion he inhabits. Hear my Ranjha play the flute
once, I beg of you,' said Heer.

Mir Chuchak looked from her to me and then back at her again.
I saw a flicker of worry cross his face. Perhaps he was admitting
to himself that there wasn't a Khera born who could match his
daughter's beauty like this boy she had brought before him.

'Huzoor,' I said, seizing the moment, 'I know I do not have land
or wealth to give your daughter, but she does not lack for those. If
for no other reason then, please listen to my music so that you may
understand why Heer is ready to leave all your riches and follow
me.' I was convinced that if I could play for him once, there would
be only one way his decision would go. In our favour. My music had
never failed me in all my life. Yet.

'Please, Father,' begged Heer. 'Give him an audience.'

'Very well,' he said. 'You had better be good.'

Leaning my back against the trunk of the ancient neem tree, I
took out my flute and caressed its grain gently.

In the temporal world, ours is known as the land of the five rivers,
but it is equally the land of the five saints, the five realised souls
who watch over its mountains, rivers, fields, meadows and animals.
The Panj Pir, or the Five Masters, as they are called, hold the pulse
of our people and our land between their fingertips. First, there is

Baba Farid Shakarganj of Pakpattan, the patron saint of the Syals. Then there is my beloved Khwaja Khizr, the ruler of the waters, the evergreen presence. There is Sayyid Jalal Bukhari, the brave, who transformed Genghis Khan's fire of wrath into a rosebush and later married his daughter. There is Hazrat Lal Shahbaz Qalander, the red-robed keeper of the Sindh. And then there is Bahuddin Zakariya of Multan, whose seven sons took the word of the Sufis to all corners of Hindustan.

I did not know if my music had in it the power to get the five saints to intercede on my behalf with Mir Chuchak. However, I was in love and determined to try. The energy of a hundred rutting bulls coursed through my limbs. A giddiness to match that of a thousand whirling dervishes on a full moon night was upon me. My love for Heer was making me determined to play on till her father relented and agreed to accept me as his son-in-law.

Mir Chuchak and Heer were now seated on the stone bench in the garden, facing the neem tree I was leaning against. Up on the tree, a crow focused a gaze full of loving kindness on me.

I picked up the flute and let my torrent of longing for Heer pour out of me. It emerged as a young, swift, heedless mountain brook tripping, falling and gushing down towards the ocean of love. As I played on, the nature of love made itself known to me. Our individual love stories are but the waves rising from and falling back into the vast, infinite sea of love from which the universe was created. The outburst of clouds as rain, the tumult of springs and the restlessness of rivers finally all belong to the ocean. We are all one water—rain, river, cloud, tears, blood and sea. All love bears the Creator's signature. Heer was the name I now knew God by. I could not put another name in its place.

In my mind's eye I saw her walking towards me wearing the red, gold-trimmed veil of a bride, her hands and feet patterned with fresh, dark green henna, her wrists and ankles heavy with ivory bangles.

Music is a pure art, unlike words or images. The meanings of words change with each listener, reduced or expanded to fit the comprehension of the listener's mind. Images get tainted by the judgment in their viewer's eyes. The notes of my flute, however, were not constrained in this way. They were free to sing of the ecstasy of coition without being reduced to smut by the vulgarity of the human mind or gaze. The raging of my blood, the beating of her pulse, the salt of my skin, the upward tilt of her breasts, the downward thrust of my hips, the shooting up of her legs skywards, our freefalling off the surface of consciousness into a spinning sky—all these remained what they were, the elements of a perfect symphony. I shut my eyes and played in the belief that the sufi saints who watched over all that was good and true in our land would hear my entreaty to them and persuade her father to bless our union.

I could be accused of being too fanciful for saying this, but there was a sudden and complete change in the atmosphere as I played on. The whole place was bathed in cascading particles of love and light. Mir Chuchak, Heer, I, the stone bench, the neem tree, the crow upon its branch, all of us were graced by an unseen presence. Though nothing had changed around us, the very air was charged with the presence of the Panj Pir.

The great souls traverse our land of the five rivers, shifting at will between form and formlessness. Wind, water, fire, earth, ether are like soapy liquid for the realised Masters, out of which they blow bubbles of dreams and reality into the air. Yesterday. Today. Tomorrow. Was. Is. Will be. Past. Present. Future. We living creatures cannot grasp the concept of time unless it is given to us in a narrow strip, flattened and stretched out like a tailor's measuring tape, one digit following the next sequentially. However, the enlightened soul can partake of the centuries with the ease of a honeybee in a garden, flitting and hopping from bloom, to bloom tasting the nectar of each. As certainly as I believed that I had a heart

beating in my body though I had never seen it, I believed the Panj
Pir were there in the garden with us, though invisible to the eye.
For a few fleeting moments, we were all awash in their blessings.

'Enough, son. Supplicate no more,' said Mir Chuchak. 'You play
such plaintive music, it could make the mountains melt, the waters
weep, the birds in the sky restless, and the saints lose their sleep.'

Heer rose from the stone bench with a flushed face.

'I felt as if the Panj Pir themselves were here with us as Ranjha
played,' she said.

'I too saw the visage of Baba Farid passing fleetingly in front of
my closed eyes,' agreed Mir Chuchak.

'Now tell me, Father, do you think I could be happy with another
once I have known a master such as him?'

'You know, my daughter, that you are precious beyond all things
to me and your happiness is my happiness. Clearly, this boy is
extraordinarily blessed and you have chosen well. He is a handsome
lad and from a good family. No one would have any objection if it
wasn't for the matter of the Kheras,' said Mir Chuchak. 'You have
my blessings, but how do I obtain for you the blessings of the world?
The Kheras will cry foul and there will be many amongst our own
people who will protest that I have betrayed the honour of the
Syals,' he said.

My heart leapt for joy on hearing him. I could see a hint of tears
welling up in Heer's eyes as she walked towards me. Placing her
hand in mine, she led me to her father and together we bowed for
his blessings.

'Father, your blessings are enough for me,' said Heer. 'I need no
other approval.'

'I wish it were that simple, my children,' he said, his face clouded
with misgivings. 'Honour is like a tiger that men of our ilk have
been riding for centuries. We think it adds to our glory, but in the
end it only turns its head back, tosses us down and devours us. If
I send word to the Kheras of the annulment of the engagement

with Seida, all hell will break loose both here and in Rangpur. By all accounts, Seida's father Ajju Khera is not only a very wealthy man but an extremely proud and aggressive one. At this stage I can ill afford an unpleasant controversy involving my family. I am already beset by challenges to my authority by two of my cousins. As you are aware, Heer, your uncles have been stirring up the peasantry around their estates.'

As Mir Chuchak finished, I felt an instant and overpowering sympathy for him.

'Heer, at this moment, the best I can do is to hire Ranjha as the chief cowherd for our herd. You will have to make do with that. There are too many pressing matters for me to attend to. In a few days from now, I accompany the Governor of Lahore on a delegation to Dilli. The Governor proposes to invite the Emperor to set up base in the Punjab to more effectively answer the threat and aggression on our north-west borders from the Afghans and the Uzbeks. Things have become more pernicious of late and deserve a concerted rebuttal. There are those among my own clan who foolishly side with the outsiders, thinking they may gain autonomy in the bargain. Akbar has already established his writ in the Deccan and Bengal and won over the fierce Rajputs. Unlike his father and grandfather, he is here to stay. My loyalty is with him. I do not like the frequent unrest in our region,' said Mir Chuchak.

By my reckoning, Mir Chuchak was a man with his brain firmly located between his two ears—a thinking man. Unfortunately, he was stuck leading a tribe of men who had theirs, to put it crudely, located between their legs. A man of peace trapped as head of a tribe with a predilection for picking quarrels. He was cast in the role of chieftain and rich landlord and was trying his best to do justice to it. I understood his dilemma. In a different age, he might have been a philosopher or a poet.

'Huzoor,' I said, stepping forward. 'As long as I have your blessings, I ask for nothing else. The job of chief cowherd is acceptable to me.

I have a love of animals that is stronger than my affinity with most humans. The work brings solace to my spirit. I would be happy to do it in perpetuity, if you see fit. I have no desire of owning land, either here or back in my own village.'

I meant what I said. Land and riches come with the responsibility to perpetuate them. They come with an understanding that their holder will do his utmost to leave the world more skewed in favour of his progeny than he found it. I wanted none of the narrow self-serving behaviour that comes tied with ownership.

Mir Chuchak continued to look thoughtful, hardly seeming to pay attention to what I had said.

'Once I return, I hope to have an enhanced commission of two thousand cavalry men from the Emperor. That will consolidate my position with my own clansmen. Bring ample honour to the Syal name. I will need to find a tactful intermediary to persuade the Kheras to take back their claim on Heer. If the withdrawal of the offer is seen to come from their side, it might leave their dignity intact and ruffle fewer feathers.'

'Thank you, Father. Thank you so much. I knew you would think of a way out of this,' said Heer.

'Heer, take him to the cave shrine of Shakarganj Baba tomorrow. Seek the blessings of the Panj Pir. And remember, I will not be here to shield you in the coming months. Be circumspect in your behaviour. Don't be defiant with your mother and uncle. Keep your temper under control,' said Mir Chuchak, looking at her gravely. 'I do believe this match is made in heaven, but between heaven's wishes and earth's acquiescence to them lies a huge unchartered terrain along which we have to make our own way cautiously, step by careful step.'

Two days later, Heer rode out with me some miles out of town, to a small cave hidden behind rocky cliffs, not far from where the importunate Jhelum tumbles headlong into the quietly waiting Chenab, the two rivers coming together in a cascade of rapids and whirlpools, becoming one in a tumult of passion. It was believed that Baba Farid had spent a few days here on his way from Pakpattan to Ajmer Sharif. We sought the blessings of the Panj Pir at the small cave shrine maintained by Heer's family, at a spot that consisted of nothing more than a small brass drinking cup, a walking stick and a frayed prayer rug carefully preserved from the time that the Presence had stayed there.

Our fates were now as inseparable as the waters merging before us.

9

The Unfolding of Bliss

BETWEEN THE RIVER NAMED after the sun, its waters dull gold, and the river flowing sparkling silver, carrying the waters of the moon, is the Rachena Doab, its name a composite of their names, the Ravi and the Chenab. The Ravi is the river of commerce, its rich alluvial banks providing fertile soil for the ambitions of humankind, for growing grains and nurturing grand cities. It is rumoured that ancient cities now lost to us were founded on its banks, as are present-day Lahore and Multan. The Chenab, meanwhile, is the river of lovers, poets, mystics and storytellers. Its waters are sublime with emotions and imagination. Its tales of passion never die, its music soars out into the sky.

But the river of doers and the river of dreamers each only support a narrow fertile belt along their sides. In the middle rises the untamed wilderness of the Sandal Bar, home to reeds and thorn bushes, wolves and hyenas, wild cats and deer, bandits and nomads. It is in the Sandal Bar that I pitched my tent.

I had declined Mir Chuchak's offer of a salary and shelter in the Syal outhouses. Though it was inevitable that the world would view me as a servant of the Syals, I wished that the understanding between Heer's father and me should be crystal-clear. I was the son-in-law, waiting to be acknowledged publicly, beholden to him for nothing.

Heer would bring me food in the forest in exchange for my labour. For the rest of the time I was a free man, a free agent.

The Syal herds were magnificent. I had always been an admirer of bovine beauty but my new charges had me completely in their thrall. It was obvious that cattle traders from far and wide had heard of the wealth of the Syals and brought to their doors the finest specimens of the land to sell. There were the massive blue-black Niliravi water buffaloes with their curling horns and swishing white tails, proudly wearing their Panj Kaliyan. These five (yes, five again) white markings on their forehead, face, muzzle, lower legs and tail distinguish their breed. Rivalling them in beauty were the jet-black Kundhi buffaloes, bred on the banks of the Indus and all along the coast of the Arabian Sea, their horns shaped like fishhooks sitting proudly on their broad foreheads, their necks thick and lumbering. Providing a contrast to these were the docile albino Azi-Khelis from Swat with their generous udders, slender tails and sickle-shaped horns, lying in a languishing slant across their delicate heads. Among the cows there were the matchless red and dun coloured Sahiwals, with their long tails ending in a black switch, the males with handsome humps, the females with hanging dewlaps and dappled white udders, their ears drooping gently.

These four-legged beauties were by no means easy to safeguard. The land of the many fives—five waters, five fertile plains, five wildernesses, five pirs and five markings on buffaloes, among other things—has been the scene of countless battles. Every passing century has seen conquerors and plunderers from distant lands battering on this doorway, this bastion guarding the riches of Hind. The grand battles with the early Aryans, Alexander of Macedonia, Mahmud of Ghazni and Mohammed of Ghori will find their way to the pages of written history. The audacity of the winners will be glorified, the weakness of the losers ridiculed, the clashing of arms and men, and horses and elephants, versified and sung about.

However, there are silent struggles too that beset this land; its unspoken, undeclared wars which are waged continuously and which shape it in ways more lasting than the landmark battles of history. There is the war that the bar, the desert wilderness, wages with the doab, the fertile plain, trying to hold back the army of agriculturalists coming in armed with axes and ploughs to conquer nature and reduce it to discrete squares of cultivated land. There is the war of the nomadic people versus the settled landowners. To the settled cultivator the nomad is a wastrel, of uncouth and inferior breeding, and in all likelihood hot-headed, violent, and a thief to boot. It is true nomads are sometimes thieves, for cattle thieving is a venerated art amongst them. A boy is considered a man only after he has committed his first successful heist and an indifferent rustler is unlikely to make much headway with the girls. The adroit cattle thief is something of a folk hero, an object of affection and admiration among the wandering tribes.

Cattle-rustling has a long history as a tool of resistance in this region. In eras past, the early settlers filched the cattle of new entrants to make them weaker, knowing that a nomad's cattle constituted his chief wealth. Now the tables are turned. The nomads are using cattle-lifting to unsettle the settlers, to make them less complacent as they sleep in their tidy huts at night and dream of turning the vast untamed wilderness into a neat mosaic of villages with square fields, round wells and conical huts.

As the son of one landlord and the prospective son-in-law of another, I should have considered the nomads my natural enemies. My job of looking after Mir Chuchak's herd was certainly made harder and more fraught with risk for their presence. Yet my empathy sneaked across the borders of my class, and I felt a greater fondness for the nomadic tribes than I did for my own kin. The proud Balochs with their hardy camels, the fiery Waghas and the doughty Kharrals who roamed the wilderness with their camels, horses, cattle, sheep and goats, dodging all attempts to count them, to hold them pinned to fenced parcels of land and convert them into yielders of revenue for the powers that be in Lahore and Dilli.

It seemed ironical to me that men who lived forever imprisoned within the four walls of their houses should look down upon men who roamed truly free, travelling from Balochistan to Benaras, Kabul to Kolikata, knowing the entire rugged terrain as the floor of their home and the vast skies as its roof. And that which the settler thought of disparagingly as wastelands were what provided fuel for his hearth, meat for his table, wool for his blanket, fodder for his cattle, manure for his fields, the horses he rode into battle, and the camels that brought to his door the fineries that he coveted from across the world.

As someone who had pitched his tent in a quiet woody grove inside the bar, I was part settler, part nomad. I was also part cowherd part landed gentry, part boy part man, part singleton part committed lover. To view this as some sort of mixed-up, confused state of being would be a mistake. In truth, I was perfectly balanced, poised at the pinnacle, enjoying a splendid all-round view of life.

The mornings began with birdsong. Peafowl loitered outside my tent nattering with each other. Sometimes a quail, a pheasant or a chukar partridge would drop in and end up as my breakfast. At other times, a fistful of roasted gram with gur or salted puffed rice served as my first meal. Soon after, at break of day, young errand boys from the surrounding villages would turn up carrying pails almost as large as themselves to milk the animals and then deliver their supplies to the Syal homes in town. I would encourage them each to drink some milk themselves—a few warm squirts directly from the udders, before they headed back with their brimming buckets of milk, foaming with froth. The cattle had started delivering copious quantities of milk to the soothing music that flowed out of my flute, their nerves calmed, their udders stimulated by the lilting notes.

After this, I would round up the cattle and steer them towards the river. A swim, a bath, washing and drying out my clothes on a rock, and I was ready to head back to the forest and wait for Heer. The cattle would graze freely after this till evening fell and I returned at dusk to gather them and guide them back with the sound of my flute.

Usually, while waiting for Heer, I would inexplicably doze off. Not because there was any vestige of sleep in my body, fresh as it was from its invigorating swim in the river, but simply for the pleasure of waking up to the sight of her. To open my eyes and see her kneeling above me, prodding me gently on the shoulder, her nose pin glinting in the sun, her eyes smoky with kohl and desire, her lips parted in a smile. The lurching of my heart, the excitement in the pit of my stomach, the slight trembling of my hands as they reached out to touch her, the smell of her hair and skin as I drew her to me, are all locked into my memories. Her mouth tasted sweet as her lips parted beneath mine. To keep away from her or keep her away from me was impossible as our bodies wound around each other of their own volition, refusing to be kept apart.

Afterwards, she would unwrap the food she had brought, lay it out and feast upon the sight of me eating hungrily, making short work of a large and lovingly packed meal. It always ended with the ritual of the churi. Heer knew I loved churi, mixed together thoroughly with her hands, and took it upon herself to feed me. She shared it with me, laughing all the while at the sweet messy stickiness of the proceedings. There wasn't a better dessert in the world than the churi that Heer made for me, the taste of her fingertips texturing it richly.

We talked, we walked hand in hand, we rode out together to explore the wilderness, made love again if the mood took us, or simply went out to watch the Syal girls practise their manoeuvres under the misleadingly delicate and diminutive Hassi. The girls formed a protective periphery around us while they went about their training under Hassi's greyish green eyes with a hint of steel in them. There must be very few sights in the world to match the loveliness of the Syal girls engaged in combat practice, their swords clanking as they fenced and parried with each other.

In the beginning, I could not appreciate the fact of armed women. At heart, I was a lover of peace. I abhorred violence. Women wielding the sword did not make an improved world, to my mind. Why stoop to the idiocy that had already ruined the race of men? Weren't women supposed to be our better halves and theirs the superior calling to nurture life and not wound it?

Heer, however, was adamant in her views. She said a sword was a mere inanimate object possessing no mind or morality of its own. It was like a bucket, or a hoe, or an axe or a knife. Who deployed it, where and to what purpose made it what it was. She said she and her friends picked up the sword not to harm others but to save others from harm.

'Save whom?'

'Themselves, to start with,' she said.

'What harm could come to them in their own homes?' I asked.

'Plenty,' she said curtly, her eyes narrowed. 'And have you stopped to question why we should stay confined in the home when there is a whole world out there for us to tread upon?'

'I actually hadn't.' I smiled affably at her. I preferred the mellow Heer to the militant one. This one made me squirm a bit. She made me question things I had taken for granted all my life.

'You think this is a matter of little importance, don't you?' she asked me accusingly. 'That we're just a bunch of pretty little rich girls playing soldier-soldier instead of house-house?'

'No, no!' I protested. Even though a glimmer of that thought had crossed my mind at some juncture, I wasn't foolish enough to admit it to her. Without their fathers' indulgence, there would be no horses or swords after all.

'Well, let me tell you something,' she continued fiercely. 'This whole deal, you and I, our meeting freely, our love, is only possible because I know I am safe when I come here. Because I can look after myself. And because I know my friends will look out for me and not let anyone through.'

I tried to look suitably chastened. But she wasn't done.

'Ranjha, have you ever stopped to think why a girl's place in the world is so small, why a woman's work is constantly belittled or why she is considered inferior to men, even though she is the one who gives birth to them and raises them? I'll tell you why. Because if she leaves her father or husband's house, she might be physically harmed, she might be dragged into a field or an alley and raped, she might be sold to a brothel, she might be carried off by bandits or by enemy soldiers and kept as a sex slave. So she learns, like generations of women have done before her, to trade her freedom for security, her dignity for physical safety. She chooses to live with a hundred little insults to her spirit every day instead of the threat of that one big assault on her body. In the end, it all boils down to not being helpless.'

'And carrying a sword makes you feel less helpless?'

'Not just *feel* less helpless. It *makes* me less helpless. And this isn't really about me at all,' she said, glowering at me. 'I know that as Mir Chuchak's daughter I'm safe and in a position of privilege. You have no idea what it feels like to live in an ordinary woman's skin. From the moment a girl is born, she is tutored by her mother on what she may and may not do. The list of what she is allowed to do keeps on shrinking as she grows older—cover your head, lower your neck, conceal your breasts, hide your ankles, don't go to the river alone, don't step out in the evening, don't laugh loudly, don't ask questions, don't expect answers ... Then she marries, and it only gets worse. A mother-in-law takes over to enforce the rules. Wake up first, sleep last. Cook feasts, eat leftovers. Feed sons, starve daughters. And when finally she grows older and the baton passes on to her, she starts battering the next generation with it, having seen nothing else in her life!'

'So are you saying women oppress women?' I was surprised that her tirade was directed at mothers and mothers-in-law rather than at men.

'Yes, precisely. Why blame the men alone? Why will they try to change an existing order in which they get a bonded slave to cook their food, wash their clothes, clean their homes, warm their beds, look after their aging parents and bear them children? But what reason do women have? Why do they fall all over themselves to tyrannise other women? Women can rescue each other. Women can refuse to starve, scare and suppress their daughters. They can be friends and comrades to their daughters-in-law. Women can look out for the safety of their house maids and farm labourers. Women can insist that other women be treated with respect and dignity. But for that they first need to stop feeling helpless and scared themselves. They need to stop needing a man to protect them. The price of that protection is just too high.'

Such were our romantic conversations. In the evenings, after she left, I would ponder over Heer's words, her world view. I understood Mir Chuchak's pride in her somewhat better. Heer, I could see, was not just his beloved daughter. She was the voice of his conscience. She was what he could not be—the lover of nature and wide open spaces, the protector of the weak and downtrodden, the crusader for justice. She was his sunshine girl, the one who beamed her light equally to all, irrespective of their caste or creed, their wealth and status. She dwelt still in the ideal world that he had had to quit.

Yet, I continued to brood about her insistence on women needing to learn physical combat. My own love for her told me that men and women were born not for being adversaries but for loving each other. If women carried swords, could it really change the world for them or for other women? Their physical weakness was a biological fact, wasn't it? And weren't they, as mothers, natural caregivers? Why fight the inevitable? Would not men counter their swords with bigger swords? Where would an armed battle between the sexes lead the human race to? Weren't men and women designed to cohabit and reproduce together?

'Who is to say we won't cohabit and reproduce better if we are equals?' Her voice would speak up in my head. 'Why assume relationships based on fear and bullying are better than relationships based on independence and respect?'

I loved her fervour. I loved her pride. I loved the earnestness with which she argued for what she believed in. It sometimes seemed absurd to me that a perfect, peerless diamond of a woman like Heer was with a drifter like me. I wondered at my audacity in setting out from Takht Hazara with a notion of claiming her as my own and then doing just that, without pausing for thought.

Had I paused, I may have faltered.

IV

THE PIGEON DIARIES

10

The Hidden Pigeon

OUR RELATIONSHIP WITH HUMANS is complicated. They bring out the best in us. They bring out the worst in us. We have shared caves and cliffs with humankind since the time before history. They have bent down to feed us with their own hands and they have sat down to feast on us at their high tables. We have adorned the temples of Sumerian goddesses and the wrists and foreheads of Egyptian deities. We had a starring role in Noah's story of the Great Flood and got top billing at the baptism of Christ. A white feathered ancestor sat on Mohammed the Prophet's shoulder and whispered something of import into his ears, as a consequence of which breeding grounds are still reserved for us in the holy city of Mecca, and in Medina they call us the Prophet's little friends. Outside Hindu temples the faithful scatter grains for us, for they believe that we fly the venerable souls of their dead to heaven. Even the Torah says we are kosher birds.

It's not all about olive branches though, or being messengers of hope and peace, being stage props and accessories to goddesses, high priests and the Holy Spirit. If anyone were to write a complete book about us, they couldn't do better than to title it 'War and Peace'. Hark back to 53 BC. Who carried Hannibal the Great's missives across the mighty Alps from the Battle of Modena? It was us. Who were Julius Caesar's instruction bearers during the conquest of

Gaul? Us again. Pigeons. Doves. Rock turtles. The entire family. And these ancient European worthies didn't exactly invent pigeon mail either. It had already been around for five centuries before them, courtesy Cyrus the Great of Persia. And he, in turn, didn't get the idea straight out of his fez cap. Two thousand years before him, the ruler of Sumer had sent out doves to announce to his people that the city had defeated its neighbours. The point being that for as long as mankind has been warring, our species has been there, taking care of the communications end of things. Military intelligence, that's us. Military ammunition too, if you consider the fact that the saltpetre needed for making gunpowder comes from pigeon excreta.

Not just religion and politics, but sports, farming, finance—we are tied into pretty much every important human endeavour you can name. Competitors at the Olympic Games didn't leave home without their homing pigeons. In case of victory, the pigeons flew back to their villages with the valedictory news. As for our racing skills, those are pretty formidable too. Ninety kilometres an hour isn't anything to sniff at. And that's just your average pigeon, not the racers and champions. Add to that the altitudes we can attain and the miles we can cover, and no one will wonder why a Greek poet wrote *An Ode to a Carrier Pigeon* in the fifth century BCE. Fishermen in the Mediterranean will vouch for how we keep the wheels of their enterprises well-oiled by providing information about the arrival of fishing shoals at the ports, and French vineyard keepers will certify that our guano is gold, for why else would they hire armed guards at their dovecotes to prevent pigeon manure from being stolen?

So how do we know all this? For after all, aren't we just a flock of prized pigeons in Kaido Langra's loft, held in captivity, breeding to his whims and fancies, confined to a single hut and one courtyard in Mir Chuchak's great house? Unlike humans, we carry our history inside of us and are never separate from it. What one pigeon knows every pigeon knows, for our consciousness is a collective one. Our stories travel from generation to generation not in words and songs as humankind's do, but as an inner knowledge of our own narrative. We are special. Very special. We can see colours unlike other birds and we can even view rays that elude human eyes. We can charter our course using the earth's pull. And we can recognise ourselves in the mirror. Self-awareness is a trait not common to many species. Least of all humans, who see and yet do not see, who have divested mirrors of their original purpose and made of them polished surfaces for reflecting their own vanity.

Of course, all of this may be misconstrued as excessive pride in our species. But there are types and types of pride. There is the arrogant, blind and self-aggrandising pride of humans, which is eradicating other species from the earth's surface without a backward glance. And then there is the resilient pride of the pigeons which will ensure that we are not among the annihilated species. A pride of pigeons is an invincible entity for we are programmed to breed faster every time our population is decimated. Attack gets our procreative juices flowing faster and better, so each attempt to kill us actually ends up enhancing our numerical strength.

What can actually kill us is the kind of love that we are subjected to in Kaido Langra's loft. The pigeon fancier's love for his pigeons is a more deadly thing than all the irate anger and annoyance of farmers and home dwellers added up. There is nothing more abhorrent to pigeons than captivity and forced mating with strangers from other areas in order to sire progeny that conform to human ideas of beauty. We pigeons know a bit more about conjugal love than humans. Once we have cast our troth, it is for life. We do not cheat or hanker for a little bit of something on the side. We don't keep mistresses or glibly utter 'talaaq' thrice and renege from our commitment. We don't devise religions that allow us to marry multiple times. We do not think of monogamy as monotony. We do not squander away the future of our young for a few moments of varied pleasure. We are fully invested in, and committed to, the ideal of raising our progeny in a predictable and safe environment.

To expect a monster like Kaido to understand all this would be too much to expect. He has no conception of what a species owes its children. We watch. We see. We witness. We scream, we squawk, we fly round and round in the loft and beat our wings to bring help to his victims, but to no avail.

He uses us to lure little children in. He gives them grain in their hands to feed us. He seats them on his lap and lets them marvel at a prize pigeon that alights on his wrist at his bidding. He tickles the children, makes them giggle out loud. All the while, his teeth are real and his smile is fake. His eyes glint as they zero in on a fresh victim. The one they can mesmerise into complicity, the one too timid to protest, the one too fearful to tell anyone. Bored of watching pigeons after a while, the children rush out to play in the open. All except the one.

Kaido's voice is molasses, his arms are snakes as he holds her back, restrains her from leaving.

'Wait,' he says. 'I have a special pigeon to show you.'

We screech. We squawk. We flap our wings in warning. We try to scare the child into running away after her friends. On some days we succeed. But on others, he wins. He holds her eyes with his and lassos her into the ambit of his depravity.

The game begins. He takes the child's hand and makes a show of looking for the pigeon. Naughty pigeon. Not here. Not in the cupboard. Not behind the windowsill. Is it in the pigeon loft? Not there. Nowhere in sight. Where could it have hidden? He is sad without his best pigeon. His heart is hurting. There! The child must put her head on his chest and listen. He covers his eyes with his knuckles and pretends to cry. Won't the child help him find it? The child is his special friend. She can't go anywhere till the hidden pigeon is found. The child begins to cry too. Soft tears roll down her pre-pubescent cheeks.

He wipes her cheeks. He strokes her hair. He pulls her against his deformed body. His voice is soft, his member is hardening.

'Oh, here it is!' He shouts with a laugh. 'Look where it is hiding! Wicked pigeon. Can you feel it?'

He calls them daughter, the little girls with whom he plays his dark and dirty games. The girls whose tiny hands he places on his crotch to pet the pigeon that has begun to stir in his pyjamas.

'Wake up the pigeon. It has fallen asleep,' he coos as he unties the drawstring of his pyjamas. His voice is honey, his hands are scorpions.

The talons dig deep into the child's trembling body. He is a patient teacher. Little hands learn to make his pigeon fly. Little lips learn to kiss it when it's hurt. Little skirts ride up to hide it when it's scared of the dark. We flap our wings angrily, we screech, we drum up loud hysteria in the pigeon loft. But it all only helps the fiend by drowning out the sounds of his writhing and moaning. He mutters all the while in a mounting frenzy.

Dhichod-dhichod-dhichod-dhichod-dhichod.

The abuses fly out of his mouth even as the semen squirts out in bursts from the swollen head of his one-eyed pigeon, and a child lies besmirched, torn, swallowed. A childhood lies transfixed with terror on the mud floor of Kaido's hut, staring up at him with hollow eyes.

That hidden pigeon is dirty, dirty, dirty, filthy, filthy, filthy, he tells them gravely afterwards. Whoever knows the secret of the pigeon becomes dirty-filthy too. If the little girl tells anyone she touched the hidden pigeon, its disease will come to her. Its sticky white discharge will start flowing from where she touched it. Then where will she go, the little girl who touched the pigeon? What will she tell her mother when she asks and her father when he shouts? If she tells them about the pigeon's dirty-filthy secret, they too will get the pigeon's dirty-filthy disease. Who will visit their house then, who will talk to her family after that? No one, the little girls are made to understand. They will be outcasts once others know of their sickness.

The little girls tiptoe out of his hut with the secret of the hidden pigeon coiled like a snake inside their chests. It is a secret that squeezes the air out of their lungs and makes them grow into women too scared to breathe fully, unable to claim even their fair share of air from the world. It is this snake of a secret that wraps itself around their throats and makes them choke every time they think of giving it utterance, confessing it to a parent, a sibling or a friend. A secret that slithers in and out, in and out, in and out of them as they part their legs obediently in the darkness of the marital bed and clench tight their fists and stiffen their jaws when their men come near them. It is the secret that will make them weep at the birth of their daughters and strive to make them invisible lest the one-eyed pigeon spy them and push them into a dark place from which there is no coming out undamaged.

Ironically, Kaido Langra's lameness opens more doors to him, grants him more access than would be allowed to another man of his age and standing.

His private life stinks, his public persona shines bright. His thoughts are filthy, his words are pious. His will grows weak, his sermons strong. The evening broadcast from the pigeon compound is full of warning. The cats and the crows hear us. The goats and geckos too. The humans do not heed our warnings, full as they are of their own noise.

When he is not brutalising little girls, he is advising their mothers on how to raise virtuous daughters who will be a credit to their family and community. Head full of hadiths, mouth full of platitudes, he goes from home to home advocating feminine modesty as the greatest of virtues. The lowered head, the lowered gaze, the lowered voice, the lowered hemline are eulogised fervently. A girl who lifts her head, raises her voice, flashes her eyes and exhibits her ankles will be the undoing of society. No good can come of such corruption. For boys will naturally be boys and if they respond to the invitation, who else is to be blamed but the girl who knows no containment? And the mother who failed to teach her?

Yet, throughout his career as a dispenser of homilies and platitudes, Kaido has been dogged by one problem—Heer. Heer, who is his niece, almost a daughter. Heer, who does not listen, who speaks before she is spoken to, who roams about the countryside at will, who makes her own rules about what girls should or shouldn't do. Heer, who is beautiful beyond imagination and is spoken for by the foremost family in the region, through Kaido's efforts on her behalf.

At the spinning parties, the women of Jhang Syal lament and sigh. No one can hope to teach the girls of Jhang Syal what is proper womanly decorum when Mir Chuchak's daughter is so flagrant in her rebellion. Of late, a rumour has begun to do the rounds of the spinning circles that Heer is trysting in the forests with her father's cowherd, that she has given herself body and soul to a flute player from nowhere. The girl is without shame. There is no one to rein her in and stop her.

Heer had been over-confident when she had thought she could keep Ranjha hidden in the forests, a secret for as long as she wished. The rumours about Kaido's niece are sizzling and popping like freshly frying puris in a cauldron of hot oil and the whole town is gorging itself sick on the salacious gossip.

Kaido, normally alert to every little whiff of news in the community, had fallen into a deep well of depravity, oblivious to all sounds other than the flapping of the pigeon in his own pyjamas.

A woman who works in the horse stables comes in before dawn every day to sweep the place and feed the animals. She brings along her daughter, a mute, sickly six-year-old who plays quietly on her own, wandering all over the property, while her mother works. On one such early morning, Kaido Langra is making his way to the outhouse to relieve himself when he spots the child kneeling on the ground outside, tracing a pattern on the mud. He beckons her to him, ruffles her hair, strokes her cheek, and asks her for her name.

The girl shakes her head and gesticulates with her hands to convey that she has no speech. He flips her deftly on to her back and with a pretend playfulness begins to tickle her under the armpits. She stares up at him with uncomprehending eyes, little unintelligible sounds escaping her tiny lips.

She is a pervert's dream come true.

Step by cruel step, he lures her into his hermit's hut at the edge of the homestead before daybreak each day. Though we shriek, we screech, we squawk, we fly round and round in rage, the whole pride of us are no match for Kaido's shameless pigeon.

Even as our helplessness at Kaido Langra's transgressions against humanity grows, the women of Jhang flay in frustration against Heer's flouting of society's regulations. At last, the women at the spinning party, unable to stomach her family's ambivalence to Heer's behaviour, decide to raise the issue of Heer's terrible influence on their daughters with Kaido.

Once apprised of the rumours, Kaido, seething with rage, rushes to Malki's chamber.

'If the news of your daughter's doings reaches Rangpur, we will be saddled with a broken engagement. Talk sense into her head, tie her up or lock her in if she does not listen. She cannot carry on in this way with a mere cowherd. If Chuchak's daughter cavorts openly with the house help, who is to prevent the other girls from taking their fathers' farmhands and the sons of the town's cobblers and barbers as their lovers? Is this what the Syals are to be reduced to? A race of half-castes?' he screams.

'I will speak to Heer, but you know how headstrong she is. She only listens to her father,' Malki says. 'And you know he is going to be away for some months. In his absence, who is to stop her from doing whatever she pleases? You know she doesn't care about the engagement. She will be more than glad if it is broken.'

'There has to be a limit to everything. In all other things I have deferred to him as an elder brother, but Malki, he has indulged and spoilt Heer insufferably. I cannot watch quietly while the work of our forefathers in building this settlement and consolidating the stature of the Syals is reduced to a shambles in this one generation by Chuchak's blind love for Heer. You have to make her see reason. We must send the cowherd away as soon as possible.'

Will Ranjha go? Or will he stay? Will Malki prevail or Heer prevaricate? Will the next round belong to the lovers or the connivers? We position two pairs of breeders, one in Malki's courtyard, the other on her windowsill, to eavesdrop and report. They lay their eggs and sit on watch. The pigeon loft is abuzz with excitement, the evening broadcast eagerly awaited at the end of each day.

11

Mother and Daughter

OUR REPORTERS ARE INTREPID, the drama riveting ... we wait, we watch, we bear witness to what will go down in lore as the great dialogue between Malki and Heer.

Malki summoned Heer for an upbraiding but did not know where to begin. The last time she had scolded her, Heer had been a little girl. Now she was a young woman, a supremely confident one at that, seated before her, waiting for her to speak. As always, Heer was dressed simply, too simply for Malki's taste. By way of adornment she wore only a diamond pin in her nose and the green silken braid with gold beads, which had once been Malki's, in her long plait. Yet, she looked attractive, her body perfectly shapely and her features sharp. When she had been younger Malki had insisted on putting a black spot on her forehead to ward off the evil eye.

'Tell me, Mother,' said Heer. 'What is it that you want of me?'

'I will speak plainly. There are stories about you floating all over the settlement. You have to stop seeing that cowherd immediately. People are talking. If word gets to Rangpur, we will be left with no face to show anyone,' said Malki.

Malki's intentions were right, her approach all wrong.

'Mother, when have you known me to worry about what people say or think I should do, that you expect me to begin now?' asked

Heer. 'You must have a very poor opinion of my face if you think a few idly wagging tongues can tarnish it.'

If you ask us, a friendly, more equal, mother to daughter chat would have been a better way to broach the subject, but it was already too late for that.

'And I would like to know who has been tattling to you?' bristled Heer, her spine arching in warrior mode, no longer relaxed, annoyed that despite the fact that her girls were all sworn to secrecy, the stories of her meetings with Ranjha had begun to circulate.

Heer, safe in the cocoon of her father's love and her friends' loyalty, had not even considered the many others—the kitchen-hands who saw her lovingly pack lunch for Ranjha every day, the farm labourers who saw her riding out into the forest, the errand boys who carried the milk pails back and forth every day. Between them they had all the pieces of the story to put together and embroider further with their imagination.

'That is none of your business,' replied Malki.

'I hope you had the good sense to say that to the person who came carrying these tales to you. Who I meet is nobody's business except my own,' said Heer.

'Not even mine?' asked Malki. 'What kind of mother is expected to keep quiet when her daughter is promised to one man and is carrying on openly with another?'

'The kind of mother who should not have been complicit in the writing off of her daughter's future at birth. What kind of mother allows that without protest? Two pigeon fanciers get together and decide they can treat human beings like they treat their captive birds, as some sort of breeding experiment, and you acquiesce to that,' said Heer bitterly. The story of her betrothal was no secret. The whole settlement had been witness to it.

'Heer,' said Malki sharply. 'Be respectful towards your uncle. He has always had your best interests in mind.'

'Aha, so that is who is poisoning my dear mother against me. I should have known,' Heer said as she leapt up. 'Mother, why can't you see that that phony, preachy uncle of mine has nobody's interests in mind except his own? He just likes to ensure his own importance wherever he goes. What good has he ever done for anyone? You feel beholden to him for brokering an engagement for me? Would my father and you have lacked for choices had he not done so? No. He simply stole your daughter from under your noses and promised her away to strangers. And wrote himself into a place of power while he was at it.'

'Heer, be reasonable. The Kheras are our equals in caste and our betters in wealth and status. It is an enviable match, and though Kaido was a bit hasty in fixing it up, there is nothing wrong in what he did. There was no reason for your father and me to reject the proposal.'

'Don't bring my father into this. You know perfectly well that he had always held that if and when a formal marriage proposal ever came from the Kheras, he would turn it down,' said Heer hotly. 'It is that wretched Kaido and you who accepted the engagement offer that came while Father was called away to battle against the Emperor's brother Shahzada Mirza Hakim, the ruler of Kabul. Despite knowing well that my father would not wish that childhood pact honoured, you went ahead and accepted the gifts and sweets the Kheras sent the year I turned a woman and sent them back gifts of your own.'

Malki stared at her toes, her glance resting on a missing stone in her silver toe ring. She frowned.

Heer does not know what Malki and the pigeons do. We had squawked, we had screeched, we had reproved and reprimanded. But only the squirrels and the sparrows had paid any heed to us.

The gifts the Kheras had sent to finalise the engagement were in response to Kaido's carefully timed gift of a pair of pigeons sent to the Khera chieftain with a note saying, 'Beauty begets beauty.

These are the descendants of the beautiful pair you had gifted us at the time of Heer's birth. The child whose naming ceremony you had graced is now a woman. We seek your blessings once again as she comes of age.'

A party carrying the formal proposal for the marriage of Heer to Seida Khera, the younger son of Ajju Khera, had come swiftly after. That Seida was second in line to inherit the vast Khera wealth did not matter, Kaido had told Malki. The Kheras had orchards and businesses substantial enough to distribute amongst ten sons and still have some to spare for the building of mosques and madrasas to spread the family's good name.

Marrying off a daughter into a family of a slightly higher stature and getting a daughter-in-law from one of slightly lower standing was Kaido's recipe for happy marriages. A girl should always be in awe of the family she marries into. It aids submissiveness in the woman, always the bedrock of the best marriages. Malki could not find a flaw in his reasoning. She had come to trust Kaido's instinctive wisdom over time. After her mother-in-law had passed away a few years ago, Malki had felt a great vacuum inside her heart. Though she had learnt the Syal way of doing things to perfection by then, she still missed the older woman's confidence in dealing with matters of extended family and the larger community. Kaido, who due to his crippled leg, had spent more time with his mother in his growing years, had inherited much of her uncanny perceptiveness in these matters. Malki was glad for it. She tried to speak to Heer now as her mother-in-law would have.

'Heer, my sweet child, understand that marriage is no doll's play. Once done, it cannot be undone,' she began.

'Precisely, Mother,' said Heer. 'It is best that you know without any further ado that I am married to my Ranjha, body, mind and soul. There is no undoing it now. You are better off putting my uncle's cunning to work in warding off the Kheras than in trying to browbeat me into submission.'

Malki had had enough. 'You foolish child, giving your body to a man in a moment of passion is not marriage. Cavorting on the riverbank to the tune of fine ragas is not life. You need a house, wealth and status to survive in the jungle of life. You have had your fun with the cowherd's lithe body and his serenades on the riverbank. Now cut your losses and get on with your life. Be grateful that you are a rich chieftain's daughter. A poor girl would have been dead for these transgressions by now, food first for the town's vultures and then for those of the jungle,' she burst out.

'I am shocked, Mother,' said Heer, staring down at Malki, her eyes wide, her hands flung out in an impassioned gesture. 'I did not think you had it in you to shock me, but I was wrong. Has marriage no sanctity in your eyes, no holiness attached to it? Is it just a rich people's version of prostitution to you, where the woman's body is exchanged for wealth and security, her parents no more than pimps negotiating the best deal for her?'

'I should have put chillies in your mouth every time you spoke insolently as a child. See what a juncture your father's leniency has brought you to. Which girl talks like that of her parents? We are pimps for wishing to see our children happily married? You are truly a blight on us. You will drag the Syal name into the mud and leave us in ruins. No one will want to marry a girl from all of Jhang when they hear of your wilfulness and your wicked tongue,' said Malki.

'Mother,' said Heer, sitting down again with a contrite expression on her face and placing her hand on Malki's arm, 'I do not wish to cause you grief. Why do you not see it as an occasion for rejoicing that your daughter has found the man who can make her happy for the rest of her life? My Ranjha is not only handsome and gifted but he also has the wisdom of a pir. The wild beasts of the jungle become mellow at his bidding, the buffaloes and cows overflow with milk to the sound of his flute and the cobra lowers its head and bows before him before slithering off his path.'

'He is a cowherd, Heer, nothing more. How can you erase that?' said Malki.

'Why should I want to erase that? I do not wish him to be any different from what he is,' said Heer.

'The daughter of a chieftain cannot be married to a low-caste cowherd,' said Malki.

'He is a cowherd by choice. He is a landlord's son, as high-born as any other groom you would find for me,' said Heer. 'The Ranjhas are well-respected on their side of the river. All his brothers have girls from good families for brides.'

'A man's caste is decided by his occupation in life. By adopting the work of a cowherd he has surrendered all claims to the landlord caste,' said Malki. 'Besides, his ties with his parental home are severed.'

'You bend reality to suit your wishes. You are blinded by the wealth of the Kheras, and therefore clutch at a falsehood to declare Ranjha unsuitable. Had he been born a low-caste cowherd and followed the occupation of a landowner, you would have argued the other way, saying that his caste at birth was what mattered. Mother, be that as it may, what is caste to us? We are Muslims and the Holy Book does not mention caste. The Prophet himself said we are all equally born of Aadam and Hwa, divided into tribes and races only so that we may know each other,' said Heer.

'And you have become so arrogant that you think you know the Holy Book better than your mother does?' said Malki.

'If my mother becomes too worldly and materialistic then is it not my duty to remind her that what she is saying is against the dictates of our religion? The Quran forbids parents from forcing a daughter's hand in marriage against her wishes. I would not want that sin upon your head,' said Heer. 'The Prophet only told us to look for piety in a partner, not wealth or class.'

'Don't presume to teach me, Heer. It is not for you to preach what the Holy Book says or does not say. Let the qazis do that work. It is for you and me to obey their directions on how to behave. And understand that what you call my worldliness is just practical good sense, a mother's concern for her daughter's future. Where will you live, what will you eat, how will you bring up your children if you marry a common cowherd?' asked Malki.

'We all live on this one earth, we all eat what the farms and forests yield and we all raise our children on love and hope. Larger mansions, richer food and pampered children are no guarantee of greater happiness in life. If my father gives us a small parcel of land to build a simple house on, and a few heads of cattle to start our own herd, we will need no more than that,' said Heer.

'A live-in son-in-law! You will have us rub our noses in the mud by bringing home a live-in son-in-law! A man who cannot support our daughter but is, in fact, dependent on us!' exclaimed Malki. 'How will we face the community?'

'For many months now Ranjha has been looking after the cattle my father was so hard-pressed to control earlier, and will continue to do so as long as my father wishes him to. He has taken nothing from us except the food I take for him each day. His good husbandry has added to our cattle wealth and to our income from milk. But you have no word of praise or gratitude on your lips and instead think that his association with our family will disgrace your name. But when it was my brother's turn to marry and bring home his bride, you were brimming with pride. You brought her home with fanfare, bedecked her with your jewels and approved wholeheartedly when Father allotted him a set of villages to collect revenue from, for the maintenance of his household. Why am I not entitled to a small parcel of land to set up home? What is the logic? Is the blood that flows in my brother's veins any different from the one that flows in mine that you treat us so differently?' said Heer.

'You speak wildly in the sway of your emotions. You wish that the rules of society should be rewritten so that you can carry on conveniently with your lover. The world was not constructed to do our bidding. We have to live by its rules. If individual passions were allowed to run the world, we would all be living in chaos.'

'Better a chaotic world in which people are happy than an orderly one in which love has no place,' said Heer. 'This world was created out of Allah's love for his creatures. Take love out of it and life becomes like a mouthful of ashes—dry, tasteless and impossible to swallow.'

'There is pure love and impure love. Do not speak of God's love for His followers in the same breath as your indecent cavorting in the forests with that cowherd. You are no better than the dogs and cats and monkeys who fornicate as the urge takes them. I wish I had strangled you at birth or died before I gave birth to such a godless creature,' said Malki.

'Mother, you overstep the boundaries of decency now. My love for Ranjha is purer than the first light of day, as sacred as the Kaaba stone and as unwavering in its direction as the qiblah. It does not trade itself for wealth or caste or status. It was written that Heer belongs to Ranjha, by the pen of God, on the First Day of Days. What God himself was witness to does not need parental approval or societal sanction or a qazi's signature to testify its truth. Disown me if you wish. Throw me out of this house with nothing. On Judgement Day I will answer my Maker as you will yours,' said Heer.

'Your pride and rebellion will bring you to a sorry pass. Girl, are you scared of nothing? Do you not fear destitution, dishonour or even death?' asked Malki.

'There are other things I am scared of, Mother. I am scared of the Day of Resurrection when I will rise not in the company of lovers and saints but of liars and charlatans who say one thing and do another. I am scared of the wrath of God when he finds I turned down true love for false comforts. I am scared of living a life contrary to what every cell in my body knows to be right for me. I am scared of carrying a dead soul in a living body for the rest of my days on earth,' said Heer.

'You make too much of a drama over love,' said Malki.

'The opposite of love is hatred. If I wilfully throw love out of my life, the emptied spaces of my heart and mind will automatically fill up with hatred and disgust. If I forsake Ranjha's love, I will be damning myself to a life of hatred. Hatred of myself for betraying him, of my parents for forcing me into a union against my wishes, of the man I marry for not being the right one for me, of the children I bear for being forced upon me ... This is what I am scared of, so I will not give in, whatever the consequences. Don't insist on throwing me into a dungeon of hatred, I implore you,' pleaded Heer. 'You will leave me with no choice but to defy you.'

'Heer, even if I agree to your marriage with the cowherd, do you think the community will allow it to happen? They will all be scared of the bad precedent it will set for the rest of the children. Boys will demand to marry the servant girls they take to bed and girls will take up with any low-ranking foot soldier or horse groom who takes their fancy. Your love may be true but it will throw open the floodgates of lust and bring disorder and havoc into our world,' said Malki.

'These are baseless fears, Mother. What is good and pure can only generate more good, by example. Whoever is witness to my marriage with Ranjha will aspire to a love that is equal to ours, where body and spirit are perfectly matched and in which each cares more for the happiness of the other than his or her own. If my father can understand this and has given us his blessings, what business does the community have to object?' said Heer.

'Did you say your father has given you his blessings?' asked Malki, her eyes narrowing.

'Yes,' said Heer. 'He realises that Ranjha is special and appreciates his extraordinary talent and his elevated thinking. He has seen with his own eyes how well-matched Ranjha and I are. He has given us his word that as soon as he returns from attending to his business in Dilli, he will tactfully raise the matter of terminating the engagement with the Kheras and thereafter send word to Ranjha's family across the river.'

'All I can say is that your father has no idea of what trouble he has set in motion,' said Malki, her face rigid with anger.

We fret, we fume, we fulminate over the falling out of Malki and Heer. We feel a chill in our bones and a darkening of the skies over Jhang Syal.

12

Kaido the Troublemaker

OUR HEARTS WERE WITH Heer and her Ranjha, our lives belonged
to Kaido. When body and soul are torn, suffering is a foregone
conclusion. There was gloom and doom in the pigeon compound
and prophecies were made of an impending disaster. We watched
helplessly as our crooked master played his crooked game.

Kaido Langra took all physical beauty as a personal affront. He
had long regarded Heer's loveliness as a taunt thrown at him by life,
her radiant face an affront and a mockery of his own disability. The
arrival of the deaf-mute girl in his life had kept him distracted for
a few months. With the others there had always been the risk of
being found out, the need for stealth, cunning and some restraint.
His latest find freed him to explore the depravity of his hidden
desires to their lowest depth. The shivering, speechless, terror-
filled girl had become something of an obsession with him. Each
night he went to sleep begging forgiveness for his sins, each dawn
he hunted her out, dragged her in and began to assault her again,
his pulsating lust invading her cruelly parted wafer thin limbs. His
pigeon, which he smote down every evening, threatening to kill it if
it didn't behave, woke up every morning an insatiable fiend refusing
to stop its fluttering till the child lay pinned under him, staring up
with unseeing eyes, her tiny toes pointing accusingly towards heaven.

Preoccupied with his own perversions, he had not been paying the close and jealous attention he normally did to his niece's life and movements. He had not been alert to the arrival and the hiring of the new cowherd. It had hardly been a matter of much import. His brother was hiring new lads for his herd every few months. The rascals were always making off after a while for one reason or another. How could Kaido have known that this cowherd was different?

When the rumours about Heer and Ranjha finally reached his ears, they hit him harder for having been unanticipated. They detonated through his being, leaving the taste of burnt ashes in his mouth and smoke curling out of his nostrils. That the bearers of the stories were full of hyperbole about the new cowherd's handsome good looks, and in raptures about his flute-playing skills only stoked the embers of the anger that had exploded in his belly. He rushed towards the forest to determine the truth for himself.

However, Heer's gang of girls, led by the indomitable Hassi, was always vigilant and would not let him pass through the forest without alerting the lovers first. That they jeered and mocked him in subtle ways while thwarting his progress enraged him further. That Heer, so proud and shameless always, should have the temerity to challenge him directly by rejecting the Kheras was not something Kaido intended to take lying down. When Malki came to him with the report that Heer was rebellious and unrelenting and that she had her father's support to boot, he tied the deaf-mute girl to a doorpost and slapped her repeatedly. Why couldn't the little harlot keep her legs together instead of tempting good men off the path shown by God? His helpless victim was within inches of losing her life, her eyes rolling up towards the ceiling, before Kaido freed her.

There was no point in killing the wrong girl even though all girls carried the same witchery inside of them that drove innocent men to paths of wickedness. It was Heer who had to be caught red-handed and brought to book. Kaido decided he would take the matter directly to the council of elders.

After a few days of carefully watching Heer's movements, and those of her friends, his plan was ready. Though Hassi and the other girls were on guard all day while Heer and Ranjha were in the forest, the place was completely deserted at night. He decided to brave the snakes and hyenas and make his way through the wilderness at night and hide somewhere in the vicinity of Ranjha's tent to await the morning.

It was not an easy night Kaido passed in the forest. Because of his condition, he had always been his mother's boy, sticking to her side, never accompanying the menfolk on hunts or expeditions that involved staying overnight in the wilderness. This was his first experience, being out at night in the jungle. And he was all by himself. There was no camp-fire to warm his ankles and keep the wild beasts away, no ribald man-to-man jokes to shorten the night with laughter, no snack lovingly packed by a mother or wife to bite into when hunger pangs struck at midnight. Only a cold and distant moon and stars that glittered malevolently close in the darkness, keeping him company. And the eyes of wild creatures keeping a wary watch on him from behind trees and bushes. Every now and then, he heard a rustling or slithering sound and froze with terror. It wasn't until dawn that he fell into a tired sleep.

The village boys came, milked the animals and went away carrying their huge pails of milk. Ranjha's flute played out its morning ragas and fell silent. Still Kaido slept on, hidden behind a clump of bushes. He was lying curled into a frightened knot under his blanket, with only his nose sticking out for breath and his wooden sandals and crutches lying by the side, when Ranjha, heading towards the river for a bath, heard the sounds of a fitful snoring and went to investigate.

A fakir has lost his way in the forest, Ranjha thought to himself when he saw Kaido lying with the blanket tight around him. He had a soft corner for homeless wanderers, having been one himself not many months ago. He walked back to his tent and returned with a fresh, warm tumbler of buffalo milk. He gently prodded the older man awake.

'Wake up, Baba,' he said. 'What brings you so far away from home and into this jungle?'

Kaido scrambled up to a sitting position hurriedly, his wooden bead necklace swinging furiously around his thick neck. He looked up in alarm to see Heer's paramour kneeling before him with a frothing container of milk. Hungry, miserable and shivering from the cold of the night, he stretched out his hand and gratefully gulped down the milk, still warm from the buffalo's udder.

'What brings you here? Are you new to these parts? Did you lose your way?' asked Ranjha. He looked at Kaido's crutches with concern. It was most unusual for a lame fakir to be travelling all alone. 'Have you got separated from your group?'

It was clear the boy had no idea who he was. It was just as well. Kaido had come with the vague notion of staying concealed in the bushes and surprising the lovers in the middle of their tryst and dragging a shamed, half-naked Heer with him to the town centre and summoning the council to witness her disgrace. In the cool light of day, it was clear that the plan was critically flawed. This tall, lissom, broad-shouldered young man with his fine, square-cut jaw, didn't look as if he would let a lame old man drag his girl for the many miles it was from here to the settlement. And that hussy Heer would certainly egg him on, actively abet him, who knows even get her girl gang to dig a grave for her uncle and bury him alive in it. Then there would be no one left to challenge her shameless liaison with the cowherd.

'What brings me here, you ask,' he said, staring out into the space ahead, fingering the wooden prayer beads around his neck and avoiding direct eye contact with Ranjha. 'Only The One Above has all the answers. Our feet dance to his tune. Mine. Yours. His. Hers. Everyone's feet. All servants. Only one Master,' he said in his best sing-song lunatic holy man voice, deciding to play the part of the wandering mendicant for whom Ranjha had obviously mistaken him. He would need to inveigle himself into the boy's tent on some pretext, collect evidence of Heer's visits there and make good his escape. And he would have to do all this before she appeared on the scene. It would be unwise to confront her directly, alone and so far from the settlement. His hatred for her was by no means a one-sided thing. He had felt the air crackle with hostility whenever they were forced to be in each other's presence for even a few minutes. Perhaps her subconscious mind had some inkling of the damage his conscious mind inflicted on her body in the privacy of his thoughts.

The cowherd was staring at him with a concerned look.

'Are you alright, Baba?' he asked.

'If I could rest a bit some place warm and rub some hot oil on my aching knees, I could be on my way soon,' Kaido said in his most piteous voice. He tried to stand up but his legs, stiff from being out all night in the open, buckled under him. At least physical disability was not something he needed to feign. Ranjha reached out a steadying arm, drew him to his feet and handed him his crutches.

'Come, let me take you to my tent. I can't promise you hot oil but perhaps a warm blanket might do the trick and there are some laddoos I could give you to eat,' said Ranjha. 'Or I could search the nests and steal an egg for you, should you prefer that. Nothing like a raw egg stirred into warm milk for ailing limbs.'

Ranjha led the way. Kaido walked a few paces behind, dragging his crippled leg and muttering a prayer for good effect. It was curious, but he could find no hatred in his heart for the cowherd. Even his able-bodied good looks did nothing to incite anger. Hatred, like love, demanded a certain intimacy, an intense engagement with the object of its loathing.

It was only when he was ensconced comfortably in the tent, on a fluffy down mattress, a fine woollen blanket covering his legs, a sweet laddoo of gur and roasted white sesame seeds crumbling softly in his mouth that the first small sparks of annoyance leapt to life inside his belly. So this out-of-home, out-of-caste cowherd was being pampered like some sort of prince by his niece! Fine sweets were being made and stocked in his make-shift residence and he was sleeping on the family's best linen!

Meanwhile, Ranjha prattled on unsuspectingly.

'Are you still hungry?' he asked, extending the container of laddoos towards Kaido for a second helping.

'No, son, I'm running down your supplies. It must be tough to come by food in this wilderness,' said Kaido. 'Such fine laddoos too, made, I am sure, by a mother or sister's hand. They carry the fragrance of love.'

'I must say you are astute, old Baba, to get the whiff of love from them. My wife gets these for me. And you needn't worry about my running out of supplies. She will be coming with freshly cooked lunch soon.'

Wife, was it? Kaido ground the last bit of laddoo with his teeth and swallowed it quickly. It was bitter in his mouth suddenly.

'You are married?' he said, spreading his arms to indicate the tent. 'Doesn't look like it from your living quarters. I could have sworn you were a bachelor, footloose and fancy free.'

'Well, married and not married at the same time, I suppose. You are a holy man, so you may understand my predicament. She and I are married in the eyes of Allah. We exchanged vows at the cave shrine of Baba Farid. However, there are some impediments before our marriage can be solemnised in the eyes of men. Tell me, Baba, what is more important, being true in the eyes of God or those of men?'

Kaido did not reply. His eyes had fallen on just what he was looking for. Heer's paranda. The green and gold beaded plait that she wore as an adornment in her hair, using it to extend her thick dark braid down to below her hips, lay carelessly tossed next to Ranjha's pillow. He felt his gut shrivel in aggravation and bile rise up into his mouth. His mother had made this braid with silken thread and beads of real gold, and given it to Malki when she was a young

bride. Malki in turn had gifted it to Heer. And here it lay on a lowly
cowherd's bed, a clear indication of Heer's shamelessness.

Kaido broke into a sputtering cough. His whole being shook and
rattled. Ranjha went out to fetch him water from the earthen pot.
In one swift move Kaido picked up the braid and hid it under the
blanket, as Ranjha returned.

While offering him a drink of water to soothe his cough, Ranjha
repeated his question, 'You didn't answer, Baba. What is more
important—being true in the eyes of God or those of men?'

These insufferable dreamers who thought they had a direct
connect with God were more than Kaido could bear. God only knows
what opium or hashish their mothers had been on while they were
expecting these lunatics.

'Men are the eyes and ears, mouth and nose, hands and feet of
Allah on earth,' intoned Kaido sonorously. 'You cannot break the
laws of man and blame them on the eyes of God. The actions are
yours and yours alone and so will the consequences be.'

'You do not approve, I see,' said Ranjha. 'However, if men are
truly God's representatives on earth, why do they fight and kill,
maim and oppress, rape and loot?'

Argumentative fool, thought Kaido. Full of flowery speech and
music and given to high-minded thoughts. Trust Heer to find a no-
gooder like that and throw herself at him. Well, he'd better get his
business here done quickly and leave before she arrived on the scene.

'What does my approval matter? Youth is full of folly. When did
it ever listen to reason and caution? Commit your follies. Don't let
me stop you. If you are lucky, you will have the rest of your life for
repentance. I renounced this sinful world long ago and am now only
a traveller through my remaining days. Neither its good nor its evil
is anything to me. If you will just give me this blanket to take with
me, I will be on my way. I have a long way to go, but my chest feels
rheumatic and my knee hurts. I will be glad of its warmth,' he said,
wheezing and spluttering all the while. He had started it for effect,

but the wheezing and coughing took on a life of its own. Ranjha leaned over and thumped him gently on the back.

'Are you okay, Baba?' he asked.

Best to have this strange fakir gone before Heer arrived, thought Ranjha. It might disconcert her to find a stranger sitting in his tent, a disapproving, moralistic old fellow at that, given to delivering sinister warnings.

'Baba, take the blanket if you must,' said Ranjha. 'Come, I'll walk with you for a part of the way. I am going towards the river. I was on my way there to bathe.'

They parted company where the path forked into two, Kaido headed towards the settlement and Ranjha toward the riverbank. Kaido's heart was leaping with glee. Heer's beaded green and gold braid found in the cowherd's tent was damning enough evidence to present before the council.

Heer arrived at the clearing to find Ranjha missing from his tent. She pottered around, tidying up the mattress, shutting the lid of the laddoo tin, remarking absently on how many he seemed to have gone through in a single night and looking around for the blanket, puzzled not to see it anywhere. Maybe he had indigestion from eating too many laddoos, she mused. And he must have wrapped the blanket around him. His greed for the good, simple things of life never failed to bring a smile to her face. A hearty appetite was a happy thing in a man. She settled down to wait.

But soon, she was restless again. She started walking about in the clearing in loping strides, impatient to see him coming up the path whistling to himself, the raga of the moment on his lips. But there was no sign of him anywhere. Perhaps he had been ambushed by a group of cattle thieves. A slow panic began to build up inside her. Maybe he was lying somewhere, injured and bleeding. Her mind raced on to the possibility of his being dead, thrown in some ditch by miscreants or travelling bandits from a distant village. Visions of a torn blanket, a broken staff, a stabbed back, wooden sandals abandoned by the wayside, all swept past her mind's eye. Imagining the death of one's beloved in graphic detail comes easy to all lovers, as the possibility of losing the object of one's affection sits just below the surface. The slightest scratch and it's out in the open, tossing up a hundred different versions of disaster for the mind to wrestle with. To possess love is to be vulnerable to loss. To have too much happiness is to tempt fate. And so Heer stood there with a hammering heart, her eyes peeled, gazing at the skies and the earth around her for signs of Ranjha.

Her gaze suddenly fell on a familiar pattern on the ground. Kaido had been here! The distinctive marks made on the earth by his crutches were all over the place, leading right into the tent.

'Ranjha!' she screamed in terror. 'Hassi! Hassi, get my horse ready! Kaido has done something to Ranjha,' she called out to her friend, as she ran out of the clearing and almost immediately crashed headlong into Ranjha coming from the other side.

'What's the matter, sweetheart? Where are you running to?' he asked, steadying her with his arms.

'Where have you been? I have gone crazy this past hour! How did Kaido get here? What did he do to you? Tell me what happened. Quick!'

Ranjha looked at her blankly.

'Kaido! My uncle. He was here,' she shouted.

'Relax. No one other than a crippled old fakir has been this way since morning,' said Ranjha. Even as he spoke, the truth dawned on him. Of course, the cripple had been Heer's uncle! How could he not have realised? He had been tricked. But to what purpose? The old goat hadn't harmed or threatened him. Ranjha quickly ran over his meeting with Kaido in his head.

Heer hit her palm against her forehead in frustration.

'How can you be so trusting of strangers? Couldn't you see the cunning in his eyes? Didn't you smell the corruption on him?'

'He asked to take the blanket back with him as he was cold. And I let him,' said Ranjha very, very slowly. What possible trickery could there be in that?

'Ranjha, he's up to some trick, I'm sure,' said Heer. 'I must run and catch him before he reaches the settlement and begins his slander in earnest. I will not leave one unbroken bone in his body for this. The lying, scheming, scandal-mongering thief!'

Out she ran and was soon galloping away on her horse at breakneck speed. Hassi and a few other girls followed. Ranjha watched the dust from the flying hooves and wondered whether it was likely to settle any time soon. His carelessness of the morning seemed to have set a storm in motion.

'Easy, sweetheart, easy,' he whispered. 'Don't do anything I wouldn't.'

Kaido had already managed to gather the five elders in the town square before Heer reached. He was holding up Heer's green, gold-beaded braid for all to see.

'This is a sad day for the Syals. Our honour lies rolling in the mud. Hearing worrisome rumours, I went to check on my brother's cowherd. And what do I find there? See with your own eyes and tell me, is there any other conclusion that can be drawn? She is defiling herself with her father's cowherd. Today the matter is within the community, tomorrow it may be too late. I have brought my anguish before the elders to seek your help and support.'

A crowd had gathered around the square.

At this precise moment, an angry Heer made her appearance. She marched up to Kaido and, before he knew it, her sword flew across his head, making his cap fly in the air. She tucked hard at his beard, making him yowl with pain.

'You sanctimonious humbug, is anything about you real? Pretending to be a sick fakir and stealing my braid and running here! If you cared so much about your brother or the family's honour, would you be standing here holding aloft my paranda in the marketplace?'

A wave of shock rippled through the gathering.

Kaido Langra would not back down easily. He had expected Heer to behave exactly so and was prepared. Foaming at the mouth in his anger, his words flew out in a hot spray of spit.

'You see, your honours, why it was crucial to bring the matter to you. My niece has become entirely wilful and out of control. She has lost the ability to discern between right and wrong. She even forgets that she is already betrothed to Seida Khera of Rangpur. Will we not become infamous as a tribe of liars and thieves if we steal from the Kheras the bride who is theirs by right? By the time my brother returns, it may be too late to retrieve the situation. I seek your approval in acting on her father's behalf and sending word to the Kheras to bring forward the date of her wedding.'

'You have no authority to do that!' shouted Heer. 'You are not my father. You are not half the man my father is. Stop taking advantage of his absence to manipulate the situation.'

But it was too late. The tide had turned in Kaido's favour. The council had witnessed her uncontrolled rage. It was clear that Mir Chuchak had spoiled his daughter completely and indulged her every whim. The result was self-evident. She needed to be contained before she brought further disrepute and trouble to the community. Even the story of how Heer had unreasonably appropriated the nobleman Noora's boat was revisited. The council decreed that in Mir Chuchak's absence, his brother Kaido had the community's support to act in the best interests of his family.

Heer tore her braid out of Kaido's hands. 'We'll see how you force me into anything. I'll fight this till my last breath,' she said with soft menace as she walked away.

Many of us lost our lives on that day. The disaster we had felt in our bones came to pass. Heer and her friends lit a fire in Kaido's hut in retaliation. Her cause was just, her actions unjust. Some of us escaped with only singed feathers, others were roasted alive. Kaido Langra buried our dead companions in his yard, and wept hot tears of anguish.

'Your deaths shall not go unavenged,' he promised our dead brothers and sisters.

V

THE BRIDE DEPARTS

13

The Trouble Begins

FOR A SHORT MAN, Kaido Langra cast a very long shadow. It wasn't as if I had let him steal a mere hair ornament from my tent that cursed morning, he seemed to have stolen the very sunshine from our lives. My impetuous darling had sealed the route to any goodwill sneaking towards us from her community by setting fire to his pigeon loft. Luckily, it had been detected and contained in time. But the stench of the burning flesh of his precious birds was in his nose, the memory of their roasted, charred bodies locked in his eyes. Kaido Langra was unlikely to be a forgiving enemy now. Besides, his cap had been tossed in the air publicly. The cat called Honour had been let out of the bag and into the arena, meowing, scratching, clawing and gnashing its teeth in fury. It would be a fight to the finish now.

'What were you thinking?' I later asked Heer.

'I wasn't thinking,' she said. 'I just wanted to hit him where I knew it would hurt most.'

'Well, you succeeded,' I said.

'I feel rotten about the pigeons,' she said dolefully. 'They suffered for no fault of theirs.'

I had already been summoned for an interview with Heer's brother, Sultan.

'I have been asked by the council of elders to dismiss you from my service,' he said to me stiffly, showing no interest in getting to know the man his sister had set her heart on marrying.

'You must know that I was never in your father's pay,' I said. 'I simply offered to look after the cattle and he agreed.'

'Yes, but you are in charge of our cattle,' he said. 'I will have to request you to stop herding them.'

'As a free man I must listen to my own conscience. The cattle are used to me now. Their bodily rhythms are tuned to the music from my flute. Without my music their udders will refuse to flow, and cause them great physical distress. A few might get disoriented or wild, leading the whole herd astray. Without my flute to summon it home each evening, the herd will lose its way in the forest, become prey to wild animals and thieves. Till your father returns, the cattle are in my trust. I cannot abandon them. I accepted the responsibility from him and will surrender it to him when he returns, should he ask me to do so,' I said. 'Why should these defenceless animals pay the price of a quarrel amongst men? I will continue to play my music as always. It is for you or your council to bid the animals to stop listening to it if you can.'

'You are being unreasonable and difficult,' he said.

'I do not think so. I am just honouring your father's wishes in his absence. And so should you. As his son, it is your responsibility to see that his interests are managed in the way he would like, even when he is not here. You should stand up to the council and let them know that it is wrong of them to let your uncle preside over Heer's wedding. How will your father feel when he returns to find his beloved daughter forcibly given away in marriage?'

'My sister's engagement to Seida Khera is a long-standing one, and you are the interloper who has caused all this trouble in the first place. You think with your good looks and your music you can seduce a rich chieftain's daughter and become wealthy overnight, but it isn't that simple. Heer has a family that will look after her and prevent her from doing something as stupid as throwing herself at a penniless pauper like you,' said Sultan. 'I will find another cowherd in the next few days and you had better leave after that and not provoke us to eject you forcibly from the settlement.'

'You must do what you think is right and I must do the same. Each of us must follow the dictates of his conscience. I only wish you had enough respect for your noble father to wait for him for a few months. And before you do anything in haste, do remember that wherever I go, Heer will go with me of her own free will,' I said.

Later Heer, Hassi and I met by the riverbank to discuss the next steps. The gentle river waves sloshed against the bank in mild admonition. The breeze bullied the reeds, forcing them to swish and sway to its vagaries, forward and backward, this way and that. Everything was as it had been yesterday and the day before. The cuckoo bird continued its 'coo-coo-once-is-not-enough-here's-another' coo-coo call, pleased with its own poetics, its rhythm unfaltering. So much had transpired, yet nothing had changed. I could not decide whether the riverbank's calm in the midst of our crisis was a cause for anxiety or solace. Was it telling us that we mattered not at all in the larger scheme of life or was it saying that these were small disturbances and we should repose our trust in forces greater than us?

'So where do we go from here?' I asked.

Heer and her mother were no longer on talking terms. Kaido was all over the place, talking to people, stirring up their deepest fears and forebodings. Watchful, suspicious eyes stalked Heer and her friends wherever they went.

'Can I request you both to please be very careful for a few days? Do not defy the council's orders openly,' said Hassi, looking at me imploringly.

'Perhaps it would be best if you and I ran away. Eloped,' said Heer, breaking her brooding silence.

'Where would I take you?' I asked her. 'I know it's the man's part to be reckless and willing to do anything for the girl of his dreams, but I love you too much to ruin our lives in this way. We could perhaps head towards Takht Hazara, but you know the circumstances in which I left home. My father, peace be to his soul, is dead. My brothers have wrested away my land and the qazi of the village is in their pay. My mother has many daughters-in-law to take care of her already and will have only harsh treatment to spare for you, no matter how beautiful or high-born you are.'

'I will seek a meeting with the qazi,' declared Heer. 'I will tell him plainly that I do not consent to a marriage with Seida Khera and it is wrong of my uncle and mother to force me. He must refuse to fall in line with Kaido's wickedness. Why, oh why, is my father always absent at the critical junctures of my life?'

The thought crossed my mind that perhaps it was no coincidence. Kaido, in all likelihood, deliberately played his hand when his elder brother was away.

'Kaido is like a hooded snake, waiting to poison your father's affairs at every opportunity he gets. I fail to understand how a man as wise as Mir Chuchak didn't distance himself from his brother long ago,' I said.

'You didn't know my grandmother. She favoured Kaido in everything and never neglected to remind my father, many times each day, how fortunate he was to have two legs. Kaido is a burden my father can never shake off without feeling he abused the privilege of being the healthy child. God knows how many teary scenes I have witnessed as a child, with my father swearing upon his mother's head that he would always take care of Kaido,' said Heer darkly 'How deviously she manipulated us all while she lived. If it wasn't for her constant comparisons between us, Sultan and I may have grown into friends. But she always played us off against each other.'

The three of us did not part on a very upbeat note that evening.

We took heed of Hassi's advice to not openly defy the council. Heer and I met stealthily, at night, in Mithi the barber woman's hut. Mithi was an old crone, feared and respected for her knowledge by women for miles around. Apart from brokering marriages, she knew something of making potions and medicines, of preventing pregnancies, inducing miscarriages and delivering babies. She was every woman's confidante, an ally who lived in the shadows and back rooms of big houses, at the place where life met death, day met night and blessings met curses. I had not known, but Heer had been under Mithi's care from the day after we first met. Now, I was under Mithi's care too, though in a different way. She fed me every day, as Heer could no longer bring me food from her father's kitchens. Sometimes, Heer took pity on me and brought a bit of churi and we pretended things hadn't changed for us.

The night is meant to be a time for lovers. Much is made of meeting the beloved in the moonlight and sleeping under the stars. It is true the night gave a certain fevered intensity to our lovemaking but, on the whole, I felt as if we had been thrown out of paradise and forced to live like mere mortals. The idyll in the forest was over. The endless stretches of time, the infinite canopy of the sky, the sunshine seeping slowly under our skins, the music of the birds and cicadas, the notes wafting off my flute, the non-stop picnics of food and laughter, the teasing and piquing of each other's interest and the easy, almost casual slaking of our mutual desire—all these were in the past. Now, there was a small, dark room in a poor woman's hut on the outskirts of habitation, a low wooden bed with a thin mattress, a ceiling I could touch with my arms raised, and a window we took care to shut and bolt tight before we reached for each other.

It is true I thrust deeper, stronger into her than ever before and her nails dug harder into my back as she climaxed than in times past. It is true that our bodies converged, shook and spilled into each other's with volcanic intensity, emitting a hissing heat and molten lava from their depths, the fear of loss working like an aphrodisiac, carrying desire quickly to a brimming point. We came in wave upon hot wave of pent-up feeling and afterwards we clung to each other with a vice-like grip, terrified something would come between us should we allow even a breath's space.

When the first rays of dawn peeped in through the cracked and splintered window of Mithi's hut, I dressed Heer with my own hands in the light of a hurricane lantern, my fingertips trying to memorise the touch of her skin and hair, my eyes raking in her nakedness, trying to remember correctly the arch of her back, the lift of her breasts, the hollow of her neck, the depression of her navel, all of me trembling with the thought that I might never see her again. Kneeling in front of her, I would press my head against her thighs, inhaling deeply of her scent. She smelt of crushed rose petals, a paste of gram flour and sandalwood, a whiff of almond oil and me.

The anger in her eyes stayed in the room long after she had left.

It was the first time Heer, beloved daughter of the Syals, had come face to face with her own limitations, and the fact that the man she loved was only a man, no magician. We had gone over the elopement argument a hundred times and each time it came to the same stalemate.

'I'm a very pretty man,' I joked with her. 'How will you keep me safe from all the bandits and camel traders who might want a piece of my backside?'

'I'll kill anyone who comes near us,' she said, drawing out her dagger.

'How many will you kill for me and how many will I slay for you? And will we take turns to sleep, one standing guard while the other rests? Will we burn the corpses or bury them, or leave a trail of them behind us on the open road, their stench filling the skies? And won't it be only a matter of time before we are outnumbered and overpowered?' I asked her. And this love that we would kill and die for, would it be any relation to the love we wanted to live our life out together for, I thought silently.

Our only hope was Heer's dialogue with the qazi. If she could convince him, we still stood a chance. He was an avuncular figure, unlike the stern, sanctimonious, beady-eyed qazi I had encountered at the mosque in Lalian, and had known Heer since she was a baby. In fact, he was the reason that Heer was so well-versed with the Holy Book and could quote chapters and verses with ease. She had been his favourite pupil.

'Daughter, what is this I hear of your running around the countryside taken up with the love of a common cowherd? The daughters of chieftains do not mess about with coolies and cowherds. I have called you here to ask you to stop this foolishness immediately,' he said to her gently as she sat down before him at the appointed time. 'I know you will listen to me, even if you refuse everyone else's counsel.'

'O revered qazi, I wish that it were so easy, but I am past all counsel and inseparable from my Ranjha now. At the shrine of Panj Pir, he and I have exchanged our solemn vows. He is now in my every breath; his name is my one constant refrain. Like a bald man cannot get his hair back by simply wishing for it, this Heer cannot become an obedient girl to your command or that of her parents, for she is already a married woman, loyal to her husband before all else,' said Heer.

'Heer, love is a myth, a short-lived illusion; it will pass in a few weeks or months. The injury you will do yourself by marrying unwisely, the sorrow you will cause your parents and elders, the dishonour you will bring to your clan will stay with you for the rest of your life. You must sever this connection at once,' said the qazi.

'How can you call love a falsehood? Isn't love written into each cell of this creation? Isn't it love that carries rivers to the ocean, the sky to descend upon the parched earth as rain, the blossoms to flower on trees, the crops to ripen in the fields? Hasn't love been with us since the creation of Aadam and Hwa? Isn't it true that Allah loved Muhammad? Wasn't Khadija's devotion for Muhammad true despite the gap in their age and status? Wasn't it on the strength of feelings that Fatima became the Prophet's favourite wife? Did not

Abraham love Ishmael? Was it not for love that the martyrs Hasan and Hussain were slain?' asked Heer hotly.

'Do not speak of the love of the Prophet and the martyrs in the same vein as your foolish romantic attachment, Heer,' admonished the qazi.

'Very well. Let us talk only of earthly lovers. Tell me, qazi, why is the love of Joseph and Zuleikha still spoken of in hushed tones by believers across the world? Why do we sing songs of Laila and her Qais and weep hot tears for them centuries after they are dead and gone? Why is the name of Sohni and her Mahiwal still revered by the people who live along the Chenab? If love is an illusion, how does it live on in the minds of generation after generation, how does it outlive the lovers themselves?'

'These are only stories, Heer. And notice how none of them end happily. Death is glamorous only in ballads and dramas. Cut loose the cord that ties you to this cowherd. Choose happiness, daughter. Choose life,' said the qazi.

'You ask Heer to be severed from Ranjha, but what is a kite without its string? I will flutter and fall to the ground, a dead, useless thing.'

'Heer, such exaggerated passion is not becoming in a well-born girl. A woman's virtue lies in sacrifice. A woman does not live for herself, she lives for the good of her family. For the sake of your mother's happiness and your father's good name, give up the cowherd and marry the man they have chosen for you,' said the qazi.

'I care for my father's name, not just in this world, but in the next one too. I would not cast a slur upon it by marrying a second time when I am not free from the bonds of my first marriage. It is against the laws of the Sharia. The laws are not unknown to you,' said Heer.

'Now you presume to teach me the Sharia,' said the qazi. 'Are there no limits to your arrogance?'

'Not to teach you, merely to remind you what you already know. And it is not arrogance that made me take Ranjha as my master but humility. I beg you now in all humility, let me be true to the call of my spirit. I do not care for mansions, servants or jewels. We are much more than the houses we live in, the clothes we wear, the carriages we ride in. These are false things, distractions that take us away from our true purpose. It is not to me you should be preaching but to my mother, who makes of these things a measure of a human being's worth. Now that is false pride and must cause grief to our Maker,' said Heer.

'Daughter, only the poor and the lower classes can get away with marrying for love. The daughters of noblemen and chieftains are symbols of the race's pride in itself, jewels in their father's turbans. They cannot be allowed to hurl themselves in the mud. The rich must marry strategically, furthering the cause of their clan and their settlement. Do you think the Kheras will quietly allow the bride who has been promised to them to run off with a herder of buffaloes and cows and not rain retribution on her family and kinsmen? Heer, I hate to be stern with you, but you must give up this madness instantly and prepare for your marriage with Seida Khera,' said the qazi. 'We have received word that the marriage procession is getting ready to leave Rangpur and will be here in ten days.'

'Forgive me, qazi, but you cannot solemnise my marriage without my consent. It is best that you send word to the Kheras to change their plans. Or Jhang Syal will be embarrassed even more,' she said.

Heer came straight from her meeting with the qazi to report the entire discussion to me. A terrible pall had fallen over her heart. It looked as if everything was aligned against us. The day had fallen off its ordinary everyday perch and plummeted headlong into an area of foreboding, a deep gloomy place with no air. The season of sorrows had begun unfurling before us a calendar of bleak days and desolate nights.

I did not know it then, but this was the last time I would be seeing her as a free woman. The next day, Sultan ordered for Heer to be locked up inside her chamber till her wedding day.

14

Under Duress

HASSI BROUGHT ME NEWS of Heer's incarceration. Heer had woken up the next morning to find that she had been locked inside her chambers. There was no way for her to leave home till the wedding party of the Kheras arrived. She screamed and yelled. Loud arguments took place between Sultan and Heer with neither relinquishing their positions. Sultan was determined that the wedding would take place two weeks hence. Backing him were Malki and Kaido.

'You will only leave this house in a palanquin now, wearing bridal clothes,' said Sultan to her. 'Mother, please begin the preparations for the feasts and make arrangements for the guests. My uncle has received word that a party of hundred shall accompany Seida from Rangpur on the coming full moon. My sister's wedding should be spectacular in every respect. We want the local bards to be singing its praises for years to come.'

'Why should Kaido preside over my wedding? I want my father to be there. Why are you letting Kaido steal that right from us?'

'Our uncle understands these things better than Father does, Heer. He was farsighted to broker an alliance with the Kheras when they were on the rise. Now they control the entire trade along the Ravi, their wealth unsurpassed by that of any other clan. Your marriage will be advantageous to all of Jhang Syal, opening doors to many such marriages and more trade and commerce too,' said Sultan. 'We cannot renege on an agreement of so many years, as you undoubtedly want Father to come back and do.'

'Foul play does not become fair with the passage of years,' said Heer heatedly. 'Kaido did wrong by promising me to the Kheras at birth. He is full of deceit and treachery and, though he praises our father loudly in public, he secretly sides with father's enemies to undermine his position. His heart is corrupt and he lusts for power and influence over others. You would do well to be wary of him instead of playing straight into his hands,' Heer pleaded with Sultan.

'All I know for certain is that no cowherd gets to call me brother-in-law,' he replied.

'And there is no Khera born who gets to call me wife, on that you have my word,' said Heer. 'I am already married to Ranjha. Whether you acknowledge him or not as a brother is your wish.'

'And who, may I know, presided over your wedding to the cowherd and where are the witnesses?' asked Sultan.

'I am afraid my marriage to Ranjha is beyond the comprehension of someone like you. You think of marriage as some sort of trade or exchange between parties, you have no idea of the sacred nature of the contract. Stay out of that which is beyond your intelligence or you will have cause for regret later,' Heer said coldly.

'Stop your shameless lies about being married already, Heer,' screamed Malki, barging into the room. Though she pretended that she was not the reason for Sultan's sudden assertiveness with regard to his sister's affairs, she took care not to be far from the scene of their dialogue. Sultan had not grown into the most strong-willed of men. 'I am fed up with your stubbornness.'

'Mother, you are obsessed with power and riches, your eyes are blinded by the tinsel of this false world and incapable of telling stubbornness from commitment. You would marry me off to anyone, regardless of whether we are matched in body and spirit, as long as his father has a large mansion and enough gold in his vaults. How can I renege on my vows when the Prophet himself has conducted our very first nikaah and the angels Gabreel, Mikaal, Israel and Israfael were our four witnesses? I have belonged to Ranjha from the beginning of time, our souls two halves of one whole. Your ears are too full of the noise of this world to hear the music of eternity playing before you. It pains you to have a daughter like Heer but you have no idea of the sorrow you cause me by desiring only obedience *from* me and not happiness *for* me.'

'Gabreel and Mikaal were her witnesses, she says! Israel and Israfael attended her wedding, the Prophet read out the vows! Sister, your mind has lost its moorings. Your love has made you delusional. My anger is fast giving way to concern for you. I can only pray that we can send you quickly with Seida to Rangpur, before word of your madness gets around. Your beauty will keep him blind to your faults for some time. I hope that the discipline of a married woman's life will cure you of your insanity before it is found out,' said Sultan.

Hassi was sitting beside me on the riverbank, twisting her hands nervously, reporting the whole story as she had received it from Heer.

'Ranjha, there is nothing for you both to do except run away,' said Hassi. 'You just plan your escape and the girls and I will figure a way of stealing Heer from her chambers and bringing her to you.'

Why does the world always assume that running away is a solution? That there exists a mythical place called 'away' in which disheartened people can find refuge? The truth is, our challenges are written in invisible ink inside our bellies and over our skin, in our very bone marrow, and in the blood that speeds through our vessels. Everywhere we run to, they run with us. If my own brothers could not tolerate my flute playing, free-spirited ways, and plotted to take away my land from me and drove me out of my village, what kindness could I expect from strangers? Why would a world which valued wealth and power suddenly rearrange the contours of its beliefs to cherish a penniless and dispossessed man like me for no reason? And if Heer, the daughter that Mir Chuchak had raised like a princess and trained as a warrior, could not exercise her freedom to live her life as she wished to in her own father's settlement, what was the likelihood that she would be able to do so as the wife of a poor, wandering minstrel?

Yet, to refuse to run away would be to be a cad in the eyes of Hassi and Heer's other friends. Caution in romantic matters in a man is not looked upon kindly. We are judged first on our willingness to act. Refuse to rise to the occasion and you are a loser. Never mind if the dice are loaded against you. A refusal to take the throw is not an option.

'Tell Heer to turn perfectly co-operative and docile for the time being,' I said to Hassi. 'It is better to have her family fooled into thinking that she is totally resigned to her fate. I would rather they are all engrossed in the wedding preparations and off guard. We'll try and make a run for it after the wedding party has reached Jhang. That will leave Sultan confused about what to do and have him fighting on both fronts at once. He won't know whether to come in pursuit of us or to stay back and preside over the cover-up operation before the Kheras.'

Hassi broke into a sudden laugh. She had a dimple in her right cheek and looked very pretty, the glumness gone from her face, her head thrown back in spontaneous laughter. I smiled at her even though I could not fathom the reason for her sudden mirth.

'I don't think it is Heer's nature to be docile,' she said. 'You should see her now. She's fuming and raging like a caged tigress, railing loudly about qazis who are godless sycophants, licking the boots of the rich and powerful, and women who short change their own sex to curry favour with the very men who keep them like suppressed slaves. But I will tell her to quieten down a bit. Purely as battle tactics to misguide the enemy, of course.'

After Hassi left, the full import of what had happened hit me and left me gasping for breath. Heer was a prisoner in her own house. Sultan would set guards at her door. I would not be seeing her tonight. Or any other night, unless I did something about it urgently. It felt like a body blow, a hard kick in my groin. My body was addicted to hers. The thought of going without her was unbearable, in a very real, very physical way. I felt a dryness in my mouth and a dull drumbeat in my heart. The hair on my arms prickled. I stood transfixed with the fear of losing Heer.

I hurriedly started to walk towards the town square to have a letter sent to Takht Hazara. It seemed like the only possible solution at that point. I would apprise my brothers of my need to come back home and press them to give my fair share of land back to me. I would invoke the name of our dead father (peace be upon his soul) and pray for the compassion of my mother for her youngest born and the forgiveness of my sisters-in-law for breaking their hearts and leaving abruptly. If I was lucky, their reply would reach me before Heer's wedding day and we would make a run for Takht Hazara. It would be difficult for Heer to adjust in such a large household full of subtle currents and under-currents flowing from my mother and sisters-in-law, but it had to be better than a lifetime of bondage to Seida Khera. Then, once Heer's father was back we could think of a more desirable solution, maybe settle down independently, either in Takht Hazara or here.

Over the next few days, I kept getting news of the goings-on in the Chuchak household from Mithi and Hassi. The wedding was to be on a grand scale and the preparations were fast becoming the only talk in the town. A score of cooks had already been hired and had set up their clay ovens, cooking pots and massive cauldrons for preparing the sweets and savouries which would be given as takeaways to each and every guest. For the main wedding feast an additional twenty chefs were expected from various places, each a specialist of some kind. Biryanis and pulaos, kebabs and roasted meats, kheer and halwa, walnuts from Afghanistan and pine nuts from Peshawar were all to be served at the main feast. It was understood that the whole town was invited, no exceptions. Not even the cowherd who loved the bride.

Goldsmiths, silversmiths, tailors, cobblers and henna artists were busily at work. Heer and all the pretty, young Syal girls were being measured for new clothes, new slippers and new jewellery. Several parents were hopeful that their daughters would catch the eye of the eligible young men from the Khera side. Mithi had deployed an army of young girls to collect fresh flowers from the forests and fields, and weave them into strings to be worn in the braids and coiffures of the women. I could not help but feel glum as I saw the young girls laughing and chattering away excitedly while they sat around her hut stringing flowers. There was a whirlwind of activity with Heer at the centre of it and I was only a bystander watching it from a distance.

Every day away from Heer was a day of distress and doubt for me. What if she had changed her mind and her acquiescing to the wedding preparations was no longer an act to fool her family? What if she had got swept into the spirit of bonhomie and celebration that surrounded her all through the day? Her mother had organised a huge dowry for her—trunks full of cooking ware, embroidered quilts and sheets, silver plates, bowls and tumblers, phulkari shawls and dupattas and hundreds of other things. All through the day, aunts and cousins walked into the house to admire the dowry that Malki had put on public display. What if Heer had changed her mind about me?

'Hassi, how is she?' I would ask again and again.

'I don't know,' Hassi would reply. 'She seems to be in some sort of trance. Her eyes have become hollow and distant. Her voice has lost its candour and affection. Every time I see her, all she asks me is "Hassi, how is he?"'

So, Heer was missing me as I was missing her. This thought would bring me solace for a while. We were merely being tested and soon everything would be okay. I would take her home across the river to Takht Hazara and as long as we were together, everything else could be worked out one problem at a time.

But as dusk fell and I sat down to play my flute to call the cattle home, the evening's shadows came out from behind the bushes and the trees and surrounded me. They towered and loomed over me. They shook their heads ominously. Soon it would be Saavan, the month of rain. In some monsoons, lovers come together in reckless abandon—the lightning illuminates their conjoined form, the thunder claps, the earth dons a green skirt and flowers burst out of its surface as all of nature celebrates their love-making. At other times, the season of rains brings only death and destruction; dark clouds streak the sky's face with an outpouring of tears, the rivers rage and run into floods, runaway lovers float like dead weeds on the river's surface and the moon turns a pale grey, lifeless and cold, at the sight of their entwined bodies. I sat like a rock upon another rock on the riverbank, and watched silently as the evening shadows conferred with each other in growing whispers about the fate that would be mine and Heer's in the coming monsoon.

Why had my father died before providing for his youngest and favourite son? Where was Mir Chuchak now when we needed him? What good was a true, shining, braveheart warrior woman in a world that measured a woman's worth only in units of self-abnegation and submission? What use was a man's talent if it made a homeless wanderer of him, incapable of calling the love of his life his own? So many questions circled the darkening skies and floated up slowly into the firmament. As I counted the stars later at night to help myself sleep, I wondered if any among them were answers, or were they all, every single one of them, just questions arising out of the hearts of hurting, drifting, wounded souls like myself, hanging over there, lost from one eternity to the next.

As Heer's wedding date closed in, I felt a mad rage engulf me. I, who had always stayed on the outskirts of the settlement, content to spend my time in the forests and by the riverbank with my cattle and my music, had taken to walking the streets of Jhang Syal in a dishevelled state. I wanted to be noticed. I wanted my pain to be acknowledged. I wanted to be a thorn in Sultan's flesh. I wanted word of her Ranjha's distress to reach Heer. I wanted a sign from her that she was in a comparable state of suffering and that the preparations for her nuptials were as abhorrent to her as they were to me.

In the morning, when the village boys came bearing their pails to carry back the milk into the surrounding villages, they approached me warily, their eyes wide like saucers, their footsteps fearful, their thin bodies shivering slightly in the early morning chill. Tales of the cowherd who was going mad for the love of a woman had reached their little ears in hushed whispers. And they, who knew nothing yet of either love or women, were mortally scared. They wanted to spend as little time as possible in the company of a madman, terrified that I might start tearing at my clothes and hair, or hurling imprecations or stones at them as madmen were reputed to do. They had not been taught to think of madness as a very, very quiet coming apart and drifting away of a mind weighed down by grief.

At the root of my anxiety was the non-appearance of a missive from Takht Hazara. I kept trying to think of a back-up plan should I not hear from my family. But no alternate course of action seemed available. Lovers, oppressed by society, were known to enter suicide pacts. Was that the best I would be able to offer Heer? An invitation to come share some poison with me? The very thought was repugnant to me. If all love resulted in was a snuffing out of two lives in the prime of their beauty and youth, then we needed to question love.

The questions with no answers kept multiplying in the air around me every passing day till I felt I could not breathe this air so dense with questions any longer. On those occasions I took my despair and threw it at Mithi's gnarled, misshapen feet. Her feet looked a hundred, two-hundred-years old as if they had trodden all of life's thorny paths, unshod and calloused, and there wasn't a grief left that they didn't know by name.

'Why?' I asked her again and again. 'Why is this happening to us? Why shouldn't love be the simplest, most natural thing between two people?'

She stared at me for a long time before saying, 'Being human means to reconcile two conflicting truths.'

'Which are?'

'One, that there is a benign God who made this world and watches over us all. And two, that this life is intrinsically structured to be unfair and cruel–it is in the nature of all things that exist. Plants are devoured by animals, animals are devoured by bigger animals and men, women and children are exploited by men and weak men by stronger men. And yet, life is beautiful and blessed. Between these two unalienable facts you have to learn to walk on the precipice between life and death, balancing the weight of each moment as best as you can.'

'What does this have to do with Heer and me?' I asked impatiently.

'This life is divine and there is evil in this world and all of our lives are a drama enacted to showcase these two opposing truths,' she said.

'Have you no practical advice to offer?' I asked petulantly. 'My mind cannot handle this sort of philosophising at this time.'

'Your dinner is ready. Eat it. Is that practical enough for you?' she said. 'Anything that you can do for Heer and yourself, you'll be able to do better on a full stomach.'

She was right. Even waiting was better accomplished on a full stomach than while trying to hold back hunger pangs. And all I was doing was waiting for word from my family that my home would always be my home. That its doors would always remain open for me, never mind how long I had been away.

It finally came on the afternoon before the day Seida Khera's wedding party was to arrive at the town's gate.

I listened with an impassive face as it was read out to me.

Brother, it said, we have heard of your descent in this world since you left home. It has been a source of deep pain and embarrassment to us to find out that you have become a cowherd to the Syal chief across the river, thinking nothing of the indignity and dishonour your loss of status brings to the family name. We have heard stories of how Heer, the Syal girl, has practised her wiles on you and has taken you as her keep and partner in debauchery. Your decision to leave Takht Hazara was your own. It left us grieving and hurt. For many days your mother and sisters-in-law mourned your absence and prayed for your safe return. However, what is done cannot be undone. The bellflower once lifted from the stalk cannot be put back. Glass once broken cannot be made whole again. Ashes once thrown into the river cannot be recalled. Past times cannot be summoned back. Our relationship with you is over. Do not think of coming back. Only the memories of Takht Hazara are yours to own. You have forsaken the right to its sweet waters and sacred air by your misdeeds. Know that the land of our ancestors will flow with blood before it allows you to set your feet upon it.

As I walked past the town towards my tent in the forest, I thought of the various ways in which one could take their own life–jumping from a high perch, hanging from a tree, slitting one's wrists with a sharp object, putting stones in one's pockets and walking into the river, immolating oneself. There was a cruel poetry to each of them.

None was as cruelly poetic though, as the letter my mother had got my brothers to send to me.

15

The Unwilling Bride

THE MORNING BROUGHT THE Khera wedding party to the guesthouse
at the centre of town. The balconies and terraces of Jhang Syal had
suddenly sprouted rows upon rows of colourfully dressed women
and girls peering down to catch a glimpse of the groom's entourage.
Their anklets and bangles tinkled musically as they leaned over to get
the best possible view of the bridegroom and his family. The air was
lilting and bursting with excitement. It was like spring in Kashmir
or Holi in Brajbhumi as the minstrels described it. I wondered
if bards and musicians, when visiting those parts of the country,
sang of weddings in Punjab in the same vein, as a spectacular and
spontaneous outburst of beauty and colour.

The Kheras had spared no expense in rigging out the wedding
party. There were dancing girls from Awadh and jesters from
Patliputra, minstrels from Dekkan and Malwa; torchbearers, snake
charmers, performing acrobats and drummers. The women of
the Khera family did not travel but there were a few eunuchs,
transvestites and drag queens to ensure that the Kheras could hold
their own when it came to ribaldry and crude jokes. No wedding in
our part of the world is considered complete without a trading of
insults and mutual roasting by the two sides. A wedding was as close
as it got to battle in peacetime and though the outcome was fixed

from the start, the bridegroom's party carried away the bride with the same triumph and jubilation that would normally be displayed for the spoils of battle.

I shook off my melancholy of the previous night and dressed for war. Guerrilla war, that is. The time to act stricken was over. This was the time to strike. Else, Heer would be gone forever and I would be left holding my listless flute in my hand, incapable of making any more music. I bathed, shaved, wore a clean salwar and kurta and draped a dark green shawl over my shoulders. Then I placed a turban on my head.

When I reached the guest house where the Kheras were staying, I was distracted from my purpose for more than a few minutes by the sight of the horses stationed outside. They were beauties. Piebalds, pintos, duns, greys and chestnuts groomed to shine like the sun and caparisoned in the finest raiment. There were Marwari horses with their ears delicately turned inwards, perfectly proportioned Kathiawari stallions with their trademark ambling gait and feisty Arabian mares, their reins firmly held by their young grooms. These Kheras were top-class show-offs and snobs when it came to their mounts. If their intent had been to make a statement about their wealth and status, these horses were serving the purpose very well.

Why was I there? Most certainly not for admiring the Khera fleet of horses. I was trying to figure out which part of the Khera contingent I could infiltrate with the least amount of difficulty. I had no intention of letting Heer leave Jhang Syal without me. If she was headed for Rangpur, I was going with her every step of the way.

I surveyed the guest house from all four sides. The horses and their grooms were at the front of the building. As were a few of the dancers and performers awaiting further orders on when the wedding procession would move, while entertaining the children of Jhang who had gathered around them. They hadn't seen a show of this magnificence before in all of their young lives.

I walked to the side of the building and peeped in through an
open window, taking care to wrap my shawl over my face and head.
In one corner, the older men of the Khera family sat on carpets and
low divans, smoking hukkahs that had been arranged for them, while
Kaido stood before them with folded hands, bowing every so often.
In another part of the room, Sultan stood chatting and laughing with
a group of young men from the Khera side. I cast my eyes across
the hall, trying to get a glimpse of the bridegroom.

Ah, that must be him, looking vaguely self-important!

I was struck by his ordinariness. Owlish kohl-lined eyes, thin lips
topped with a pencil-line moustache, pasty cheeks, tubby figure.
How could anyone in their right minds think of pairing him with
Heer? A swan and an owl would make a more equal couple.

If there was anything other than his father's wealth to
recommend Seida Khera, I couldn't see it. He was sitting in front of
a massive plate of sweets, his bridegroom's turban with its curtain
of white and orange flowers on his lap. A eunuch was whispering
in his ear while another was tickling him in his abdomen. The
man was simpering and giggling! I was glad I couldn't hear them.
I knew well the type of conversation that took place at these times.
I ground my heel into the mud and walked away, controlling the
urge to hurl a stone at the man for his gall in aspiring to be my
Heer's bridegroom.

I made quick business of covering the other two sides of the guest
house. This would be a good time to try and see if I could meet
Heer alone for a few minutes. I gathered that of the hundred people
comprising the wedding party, about sixty were close family and
friends of the groom. Servants, barbers, horse grooms, torchbearers,
entertainers and drummers made up the rest of the numbers. I would
have to ask Hassi to arrange a drum for me. I had decided I would
be with the drummers leading the procession to my sweetheart's
wedding. But first to go and see Heer. We needed to reassure each
other, to know we were together in this. It was a risk, but it was

worth taking. I didn't need much time with her. Even to look into her eyes and nod once would be enough.

The arrangements in the Syal household were every bit as grand and ostentatious as befitted a rich chieftain's only daughter. Food enough to feed the whole town and a few neighbouring villages was being cooked in makeshift tents. The outer façade of the main house, as well as the ancillary buildings, were bedecked with long alternating strings of marigold flowers and mango leaves. The floor of the inner courtyard was decorated with geometric designs made of rose petals and champa flowers.

From inside the rooms, wedding songs floated out, sung in reckless abandon by the older women in the family. What a riot these songs were, I thought with a twinge of longing for Takht Hazara. When my sisters and brothers had got married, I had been young enough to sneak into the inner circle of women singing and beating the dholkis and listen to the gems of gratis advice passed down from one generation of women to the next. From hoodwinking mothers-in-law to cuckolding husbands to keeping libidinous brothers-in-law in check, no topic was considered too risqué for the ears of the bride-to-be.

I waited for Hassi to come and meet me under the neem tree in the outer gardens where I had first performed for Mir Chuchak. A crow flitted from branch to branch on the tree above me as I stood waiting, as if to deliberately draw my attention. When I looked up, he fixed his beady gaze on me. It was as if he was telling me that he was my witness. That he had been there on the day when Mir Chuchak had given us his word. He knew I was Heer's rightful groom. I should not doubt my place in the scheme of things, no matter how vociferous and irrefutable Seida Khera's claim appeared today.

I saw Hassi approach from a distance. There was someone with her. She was leading a tall girl in dirty, drab clothes with a worn out dupatta covering her face towards me. It could only be

Heer, but there was nothing in the gait or the body language of the approaching figure to suggest that it was. She looked entirely dispirited and almost lifeless.

'Here she is,' said Hassi to me as they reached us. 'You had better be quick. They'll be looking to give the bride the ceremonial bath soon. I said Heer had some personal business to discuss with me and they should give us a few minutes alone. Don't take too long.'

She walked away discreetly.

So that was it. The turmeric ceremony had just been completed. The bride wears old clothes and is smeared with turmeric, sandalwood and other cleansing pastes by her female relatives and friends. Then they bathe her in rosewater and milk and dress her in bridal clothes.

Heer stood like a battered scarecrow before me, her arms limp and dangling by her side.

I tentatively lifted the veil covering her head.

'What happened to you, sweetheart?' I whispered in shock as my eyes fell on her face. It was expressionless and drawn. I put my hand to her forehead. She seemed to be running a fever. Her eyes, too large in her sallow face, were devoid of any expression.

I held her by the shoulders and shook her hard. What had happened to the brave girl I had fallen in love with? This woman who stood before me, crushed completely by her grief, seemed like an imposter.

'Heer, wake up, gather yourself,' I whispered fiercely, holding down my voice even though everything in me wanted to shout in outrage.

'I thought I would never see you again,' she said slowly. Her eyes moved over me from head to toe, noting every detail of my attire carefully: my shaven face and freshly laundered clothes. The dark green shawl on my shoulders, the proud turban on my head. And my love for her blazing in my eyes.

'Why would you ever think something so stupid?' I asked.

But I could see why. I had been easygoing before I lost her. Unwilling to run away. Reluctant to fight for her. Always looking for a peaceful way out. The hardest thing I had ever done in life was to leave Takht Hazara and cross the river and that was before I met her. Quite simply, she had no faith that I would come for her. Locked up inside her room, defenceless and unarmed for the first time in her life, her beloved father far away, her uncle treating her like a pawn in his power games, her mother and brother joining forces against her, she must have lost all hope. My Ranjha, she must have thought, will do no more than play heartrending tunes on his flute once I am gone.

I saw hope and light coming back into her eyes under my quiet, steadfast gaze.

'What are we going to do?' she asked, a tentative smile breaking through the sadness she seemed to be shrouded in. It was only a half-smile, barely reaching her eyes, but it was a lot just then. When she had walked in here with Hassi a few minutes ago, she had looked like someone who had cast her lifetime's allotment of smiles into a dark abyss and they had floated away forever out of her reach.

'I don't know, Heer,' I replied. 'But whatever we do, we're going to do it together. I am not going to allow them to separate us. I will find a way to join the Khera party, possibly as a drummer, and shall be with you as you go to Rangpur. There is nothing to hold me any longer in Jhang Syal. If the opportunity presents itself, we'll run away well before we reach Rangpur. We'll have to look for an opportune moment and make good our escape.'

She reached out her hand and gently let it slide down my cheek and rest on the nape of my neck.

'I felt as if I had fallen into a dark hole and that no one would be able to pull me out of it. To see you is to live again,' she said.

Out of the corner of my eye I could see Hassi approaching us again. I pulled Heer into my arms and kissed her fervently. She clung to me.

'I will be carrying a dagger hidden under my wedding finery. You should know Seida Khera will be dead before he touches your Heer,' she said to me fiercely, showing flashes of the woman I knew and loved, as Hassi hurried her away.

I nodded at her bleakly. This love was no easy game. It picked out enemies and foes for you when all you had ever wanted out of life was a few good friends. It asked for tributes of blood and a willingness to kill or die for it. Would I have hitched my wagon to another star had I known from before that love would prove to be such a bloodthirsty taskmaster? Too late to think of that now. I told Hassi of my plans and requested her to arrange a drum.

I stood under the tree, waiting, and tried to look for the crow I had seen earlier, but it seemed to have flown away. Hassi came back in some time with a drum. She was a resourceful girl. I gave her a tight hug. For all of Jhang Syal. It had been a second home to me. Once again, I would be on the road, looking for a place to belong to. But first, there was an elopement to accomplish. I wound my way back to the guesthouse.

'Hey, pretty boy! Nice ass you got out there,' a eunuch called out to me just as I reached. There was a clutch of them sitting and talking outside the building.

'Up your mother's,' I said pleasantly to him as I walked on.

'Who are you? Hai-hai, such smooth cheeks! I could die for you,' called a transvestite from behind me.

'The bride's lover,' I said, turning back to answer her with a broad wink. 'And you I presume must be the groom's sweetheart.'

They guffawed loudly at that.

'Oye, you look like an interesting chap. Come here and talk to us,' said the first eunuch, the one with an eye for pert posteriors.

I ambled towards them casually, trying to look as if I didn't care one way or the other for their friendship.

'You have a smoke on you?' I asked. There is nothing quite like a shared vice to make strangers feel amicable and kindly disposed towards you.

They cleared a place for me in their circle. Someone took out a pouch of tobacco and began to roll it.

I gave them my story. An abridged version of it. No lies passed between us. I was a landlord's son from Takht Hazara. I had left home after a fight with my older brothers who had cheated me of my share of the ancestral land. I worked for Mir Chuchak as a cowherd but did not wish to stay at Jhang Syal any longer as my employer was away on a long journey and his son had asked me to leave. I was of a mind to travel again and seek my fortune in the world. I was something of a musician and wanted to join the Khera wedding procession as a drummer and travel some way with it towards Rangpur.

'Oh that's easily done,' said an old transvestite who seemed to be the leader of the group. She got up, pulling me by the hand. We walked towards the entrance of the guesthouse.

'Wait here,' she said to me and walked in. I saw her walk up to Seida and whisper something in his ears. Seida looked up and squinted at me. And then he nodded.

The transvestite came out and gave me a broad wink.

'It's done,' she said.

She took me to the group of drummers standing behind the building and told them I would be joining them and that they were to take care of me.

I hadn't expected it to be quite so simple.

The drummers were wary of me and not at all as friendly as the previous group. I figured they might have reservations about my ruining their pitch by playing tunelessly so I struck up the drum and played out a few snatches of the regular wedding band themes. It didn't seem to thaw the chill.

'Latest model,' I heard a couple of them snigger amongst themselves.

It didn't feel good, I admit. But I wasn't there for social acceptance and camaraderie. I was there for my Heer. A few digs by a bunch of boys jealously guarding their turf wasn't going to sway me. I dug my heels in and waited for the wedding procession to move. It was taking interminably long, now that there was nothing to do except wait for it to proceed.

The feting and feasting inside the guest house went on for another couple of hours. It was afternoon before things began to pick up pace. Finally, the veil of flowers was tied on Seida Khera's turban amidst song and dance, and he was led out to mount the elaborately festooned horse waiting to carry the bridegroom. The horse was fed gram and gur by members of the family. A small five-year-old boy carrying a toy sword was placed on the horse in front of Seida and we were off to the Syal house for the wedding.

Beating the drums, as the bridegroom's cousins and friends danced their way to the bride's house, I lost all sense of myself. I simply became the music. I was the movement of my hands, I was the footwork of the dancers, I was the heat and friction in the air, I was the tipsy uncle twirling money over the dancers' heads and giving them to the eunuchs for good luck, I was the crazily excited little boy sitting on the bridegroom's horse waving his toy sword in the air, I was the erratic pounding and nervous plummeting of Seida Khera's heart.

As we neared the bride's residence, the bridegroom's side set off a spectacular display of fireworks. There were pinwheels zooming out into the sky and exploding in concentric circles, there were dancing discs zipping and crisscrossing on the path ahead, there were rockets that rained down in rainbow coloured stars and pomegranates that shot up with a sizzling sound and showered down in fountains of gold and silver light. Again, I simply watched. I was in the sound of the crackers, I was in the sparks flying in the air, I was in the smoke filling the early evening sky and in the glazed eyes of the children watching the display. I was in the clapping, the shouting and the hooting.

The trance I was in only shattered when I saw the bridegroom being escorted to the courtyard after the wedding feast. It was time for the nikaah ceremony. Heer would already be seated with her mother, her brother and her attorney. The qazi would be ready with the marriage papers. It would all be over for us in the next hour or so. My sweetheart would belong to another man in the eyes of the world.

I got up slowly and followed Seida and his father.

About a hundred metres short of the wedding pavilion, I saw Seida stop and turn to his father.

'Father, I can't do this,' he whispered urgently.

The older Khera turned to his son, pulled out the ornamental dagger strapped to his chest, and handed it to him. He flung out his arms dramatically and bared his chest.

'Here, kill me now and then do as you wish,' he whispered in a harsh, rasping voice before breaking into a fit of coughing.

'I'm sorry, Father,' said Seida, thumping him vigorously on the back to stop the coughing. 'Please take this back.'

The father put the dagger back in its place and the duo walked on.

Only the qazi, it seemed, was a willing participant in this strange wedding ceremony.

VI

HEER'S LAMENTATION

16

En Route to Rangpur

BABUL, I LEFT THE doors of your house weeping. Weeping I was dragged into the palanquin that was to carry me away. Carry me away to the house of strangers. Strangers who owned me now, body, mind and soul. Body, mind and soul were protesting, raging, weeping, my Father, as I was thrust out of your home. Out of your home I was evicted like a tenant without any rights to stay. Without any rights to stay in her parents' home Heer was pushed into the palanquin and sent away. Sent away from your house, my Father, the enemies lifted me away. The enemies lifted me away, my Father, on their shoulders, like the spoils of war, like a trophy or lifeless game. Like a trophy or lifeless game I now decorate the mansion of my in-laws. The mansion of my in-laws is big, my Father, but in it I weep all day. I weep all day for my Ranjha, my cowherd, my lover who Mother and Kaido betrayed and cheated of his Heer. Cheated of his Heer, he wanders in the wilderness shouting my name, O Father. O Father, my Father, find my Ranjha and send him here, O send him here, to take me away....

I grew up thinking I was some kind of princess. I believed I was special. I believed I had beauty, intelligence and the advantages of birth on my side. That I was brave and fearless. That I represented a new kind of woman and the future belonged to me. That I was unfettered, free-spirited and unstoppable. And yet, all I turned out to be in the end was a poor little rich girl living inside a beautiful bubble made for her by her doting father. My father left for a journey, the bubble burst and my home became a prison overnight, its reigning princess a bird in a gilded cage.

The fake plaster of equality and liberty covering the walls of my home came crashing down and the real bricks and mortar that held them up stood revealed. Sometimes I think everything in man's world is constructed out of the blood, sweat and tears of women. One half of our world grows louder, prouder, wealthier as the other half shrinks, swallows itself and falls into despairing silence. The solid walls of our homes and institutions are lined, brick by brick, with the time and effort of women, in a simple exchange for a place to live and food to eat. They call it marriage. It is a very advantageous system, for while servants have to be paid to do housework, wives do it for free. And once the wife has been brought in, the home-fires never stop burning, the man only has to put one bun in the oven and the hearth is always kept warm and welcoming, no matter how cruelly she is treated. The compulsions of motherhood keep her committed. No iron fences or locks or armed guards are needed to keep women from escaping. No place to take a crying infant is all that it takes.

The morning I woke up a prisoner in my own chamber, locked in by my brother Sultan, I realised the most bitter, unpalatable truth of my life. That I had always been a prisoner of my gender. My father had created for me an illusion of freedom and independence, and like any child I had thought my father was invincible, his word was decree. Yet, as soon as he left, I was just another girl locked inside a room, being compelled to marry someone she had never seen. I and my womb were being packed off to the highest bidder to produce heirs. My father was a good man, a thinking man, a well-meaning man, but that morning I realised he was not a very powerful man. He had barely left town and the age-old restrictions and society's strictures came rushing in to clamp down on me from all sides, as if the freedom he had given me to believe was mine had never existed.

Even more unpalatable than the realisation of my father's fallibility was the coming to terms with my own frailty. I was a trained warrior. I was not unarmed. I could even ask my girls to rescue me from imprisonment. But what good is physical strength when you possess no other home to go to, no land or income to keep your body and soul together? I could escape my prison chamber but I could not escape the fact of being a woman.

I did not even have the power to change my own mother's thinking. Since I was a child I had argued with her, asserted myself, pushed the boundaries of what was permissible. And yet, each time, her beliefs had rushed back at me stronger than before, their grip ever more unrelenting, their tone more high-pitched with hysteria each passing year. My mother's formidable strength lay in the fact that she was not alone in her beliefs. Her beliefs were shared by everyone around her. They were centuries deep, upheld by generation after generation of women and men, embedded deep inside the collective psyche of the land. I simply did not have a chance. My mother was the very definition of a good woman. So, to be any different from her automatically made me the bad girl.

Some part of me did realise that women like her are prisoners and slaves programmed to obey society even if it means jeopardising their own immortal souls. What can one say to someone who has never been free, never been allowed to think for themselves? How can one expect those who have sacrificed their entire lives serving a lie to stand up for the truth? Even as she exasperated me, I felt sorry for her. Her failing was that she could not love me enough, mine that I could not hate her sufficiently.

Since plunging my dagger into her was not an option and converting her to my way of thinking had proved impossible, the best I could do was to not willingly cooperate with her plans. I had a strong will. But in the days that followed my father's departure to Dilli, I found out it was worth nothing at all. I was to be married off to Seida Khera—whether I was willing or unwilling did not matter. My uncle Kaido, my mother, my brother, the qazi, the council elders, all stood aligned against me.

I suffered despair like an illness. Life turned to sawdust in my mouth. On some days I did not move from my bed, on others I did not have the strength to bathe. My eyelids became heavy and my limbs listless. I saw my friends come and go out of my room and however much I tried to talk to them, the words would not flow past my numb lips. And yet, the wedding preparations went on. Flowers were gathered, clothes were stitched, henna and sandalwood pastes were ground, dhols were tuned, and wedding songs were lustily sung.

As per the laws of our faith, the bride's consent is mandatory. I did not say 'I accept' even once, let alone three times, as required by the law to formalise the marriage. However, my attorney signed the papers on my behalf and the qazi declared the wedding complete. Those who should have held the word of Allah most dearly to their hearts turned out to be the least scared of committing perjury in His name. They would burn in the fires of hell most certainly, but of what good would that be to me? I wanted justice for myself, not punishment for the offenders. I wanted happiness in life for myself, not eternal suffering after death for them. If there was a way of achieving these, my will could not see it.

An avalanche of tears left my eyes as the Kheras lifted me into their palanquin, a torrent of pleas left my lips to my brother and mother, not to throw me out so unceremoniously from my father's home. But a weeping bride is customary. No one cared for my agony. The grief of that moment of betrayal, for it was a betrayal of everything I had been brought up to believe in, would have killed me, except for the fact that Ranjha had come that evening to see me. One look at his face and I knew I could never leave a world in which the possibility of Ranjha existed.

Even now, the hope of seeing him again is what keeps me alive. Though the nights are long in this house of the Kheras and the days are interminable, I am bound to this life by the need to keep faith with my lover. To stay alive for Ranjha as he must have fought to stay alive for me.

'Heer! Heer! Heer!' I heard him scream, the urgency of his voice tearing through the darkness of the night in the forest. 'Wait for me. I'll come for you.'

Then the sound of a big splash as his fellow drummers tossed him into the river on the way to Rangpur. Kaido Langra had got the better of us again. He had spotted Ranjha in the band of drummers and alerted my father-in-law to the infiltration of his wedding party by the troublesome cowherd who he had just thrown out of his employment for seducing village girls. Kaido had suggested that they get rid of him midway through the journey as they passed a deserted stretch of forest by the riverside. It would be better for Kaido if the cowherd was seen leaving Jhang Syal of his own choosing. His subsequent disappearance would then not be noticed by anyone.

I found this out from Seida Khera.

As he entered my tent on the night after the wedding, I was on guard, ready to attack him as soon as he came in. I leapt up swiftly from where I was seated on the customary nuptial bed, festooned with flowers, and put the serrated, sharp edge of my dagger to his fat neck.

'Touch me and you're dead,' I said. 'I'll kill you, I promise, if you lay as much as your little finger on me.'

He trembled. I saw craven fear in his eyes. He knew I was serious. His voice wobbled as he spoke and the lump in his throat bobbed up and down as he swallowed nervously before speaking to me. What a miserable creature!

'If I touch you, you'll kill me. If I don't, my father will,' he sobbed. 'It would have been simpler for everyone if I had not been born at all.'

Just then Ranjha's cry rent the night and we heard the sound of water splashing as he hit the river.

I panicked. The dagger in my hand shook ever so slightly and a little stream of blood flowed down the side of Seida's neck.

'Ouch,' he winced.

'Do you know what that sound was?' I asked menacingly. Though it was only a surface wound I had inflicted, I wouldn't have cared if he had bled to death. Something bad had happened to Ranjha.

'The beautiful drummer lad from Takht Hazara. I wanted to bring him back with us to Rangpur. My father ordered for him to be tied up and thrown into the river by the other lads. Your uncle Kaido Langra had said he should do so as soon as we reached this stretch of the journey. I argued and argued to keep him. As long as he wasn't in Jhang Syal, where he went was nobody's business. But my father is naturally cruel. He thwarts every wish of mine,' said Seida pathetically.

'*You* wanted to bring Ranjha to Rangpur! Why?' I asked.

Seida flushed. He shifted uncomfortably from one foot to the other, a mutinous look on his face.

'I ... I would have liked to know him better,' he stuttered. His lips were twitching uncontrollably in a nervous reaction and he looked suddenly tearful.

I stared at him nonplussed. And then it dawned on me very, very slowly.

'You ...?' I asked. I didn't have the words to formulate my question, but he understood it any way.

He nodded miserably.

'The hakim has been treating me since I was seventeen, but it has made no difference. I am how I am,' he said sadly.

'We'll talk about this later,' I said, getting up to go out. 'I have to go now to find Ranjha and rescue him if I can.'

'The drummer will be fine. I bribed one of the boys to tie his knots loosely so he can swim away to safety,' Seida said. 'I would have hated for him to come to harm because of me. He had such poise and grace. Such a fine fellow.'

I examined his face carefully. He seemed to be telling the truth. I looked at the cumbersome clothes I had been thrust into, heavy fabric, gaudy colours, full of embroidered stars and gold trimmings. Even if Ranjha was surfacing above the water, I would bring him down with the weight of my ensemble. Besides, I was in a new place, I would not even know which direction to run in at this time of the night. I took a few deep breaths and tried to calm my galloping heart. Then I shut my eyes and said a fervent prayer for his safety.

When I opened my eyes I saw Seida looking at me silently, probingly.

'Was he your lover by any chance? The one who they said you had tucked away in the woods for your pleasure?'

I was startled out of my reverie. This marriage was turning out to be even more fraudulent than I had imagined possible.

'Are you telling me you married me despite knowing I had a lover?' I asked. Something inside me was shaken. These Kheras seemed to be a strange family. Had marriage no sanctity whatsoever in their eyes?

'Used goods and a faggot. Both upper class, with plenty of reputation at stake. My father said it was a good pairing,' he replied. 'Neither party would be in a position to cry foul.'

'Your father …' I began heatedly.

'My father is the most ruthless man born. There are no limits to his cruelty. He abuses and tortures my mother even to this day, though he does not lack for other, younger women to fulfil his needs. When I was four years old he had my pet cat strangled in front of my eyes so I would not grow up to be a sissy. When I was seventeen I grew attached to a groom from the stables. He was the only person in the world I used to feel happy around. I would secretly run out of the house at dawn and go swimming with him in the pond behind the stables. My father found out about us somehow. Must have been one of the other grooms … I reached the pond one morning to find only his head floating in the water.'

A deep revulsion overcame me. My father-in-law sounded like a fiend. I had spent much of my life making Seida Khera out to be my enemy—the rich, older husband who was being forced on me against my wishes. And now that he was sitting in front of me, spineless and scared, a man deeply abused, I could not feel anything other than overwhelming pity for him. If this is what the Kheras did to their sons and heirs, how must they be treating their women?

'Please let me spend the night here. I promise I will not bother you. Not tonight, nor any other night. Once we reach home, the set of rooms allotted to us are amply spread out and large. I will sleep in one of the smaller rooms, er … the dressing chamber or the nursery,' he blushed.

I stared at him in alarm. If I allowed him to stay, everybody would assume our marriage had been consummated.

'Please,' he pleaded. 'My father has threatened to dress me in a skirt and put bangles on my wrists and make me dance in front of the whole gathering if I don't spend the night in your tent.'

I doubted very much if Seida's father would carry out his threat. The man seemed to have invested too much ego and effort in making his son pass off as straight to blow his own elaborately constructed cover in front of his guests. However, more abuse, private shaming and taunts were guaranteed. To send Seida away could only mean further humiliation for him. And if I was to survive till Ranjha came for me, I was better off having Seida on my side.

'Okay,' I said. 'You can sleep here for tonight. After that we'll see.'

As Seida lay curled up on the edge of the bed, sleeping a fitful sleep, I made a makeshift bed for myself on the ground. It was hard, cold, and impossible to sleep on. After a while, I got up and began to pace up and down in the small tent set up for us. There was a lot on my mind that night.

From the little I had heard about him, Seida's father was going to be my greatest challenge in the days to come. He sounded cruel, dominating, and used to having his way in all things. Subterfuge did not come naturally to me. But my brand of brazen bravery would not get me anywhere with a man who thought nothing of killing pet cats and young horse grooms in cold blood. It discomfited me greatly to think that the world would think I was sleeping with Seida Khera when I wasn't. It made me feel sullied and tainted. I was worried too, about how Ranjha would feel about it. Yet, it seemed like the only way to buy time and the space I needed to manoeuvre my life around. I did not underestimate the difficulty I was in. I had no home to call my own anymore. I had no way of contacting anyone for help. I did not know where my father was. I did not know where Ranjha was and whether he was safe, and if at all he would be able to come to Rangpur to take me away. I was fortunate to have found a possible ally in Seida Khera. It would be foolish to alienate him. Also, I had spent much of my life rescuing people ill-treated by others. Seida's sad story had already wound its way to a soft place in my heart.

At last, exhausted by my thoughts and my feverish pacing of the floor, I crept to the other side of the bed, grateful for the space that Seida had considerately left vacant for me, and fell into a deep, untroubled sleep. I had made up my mind not to be scared of anyone or anything.

When I woke up, Seida was sitting on his side of the bed, waiting for me to arise. There were birds calling to each other and the sounds of a campfire being lit. A few of the Khera men had gone hunting in the early morning and would be coming back by noon. After which we would resume our journey towards Rangpur.

'Come, I'll accompany you to the river,' he said. 'Afterwards we will have to join my father and the others for breakfast.'

I thought bleakly of the journey and the remaining ceremonies that lay ahead of me. Since the Khera women had not come in the wedding party, their part of the wedding celebrations was yet to come. There would be the bride-viewing ceremony in which the female relatives would come one by one to see my face and give me a gift. There would be games which Seida and I would be required to play for the entertainment of the younger women. There would be the filling of the lap ceremony in which Seida's mother would spread out a cloth on my lap and fill it with different fruits, symbolic of the fruits from the young bride's womb, with which she is expected to fill the house. I felt nauseous at the thought of it all.

When we returned, cleaned and freshened up from the river, my father-in-law was already sitting having his breakfast. I bowed and gestured my salaam to him.

'I hope the night was satisfactory, daughter-in-law,' he murmured, in a low voice audible only to me.

I felt the blood rushing to my face. Outrage pulsed through me, but I steadied myself. I reminded myself of the previous night's resolve, that if at all I had to be scared of anything in this world, it would be of God, not a nasty bully without a conscience.

I straightened myself and looked him in the eye.

'You need not have concerns on that account, Baba. I do not lack for experience,' I said in my sweetest voice.

It was clear from the shocked disbelief in his eyes that no woman had ever called his bluff like that before.

'Seida! Stop standing there like an oaf. Idiot! Sit down and eat your breakfast,' he said, irritably turning on Seida.

A flustered Seida looked from me to his father, not quite sure what had just happened.

'Ji, Baba,' he said nervously, biting his under lip.

Then he led me away to where we were to sit and eat. I followed him with long, measured steps, my chin up. My arrow for the day had been shot and it had not missed its mark. I had reason to grandly sweep past my obnoxious father-in-law.

17

The House of the Kheras

BABUL PYAARE … BELOVED FATHER, it was a hot, humid, stifling July when I left your shade and was sent off to stay in my in-laws' home. In my in-laws' home the storm clouds gathered laden with grief and sorrow. Laden with grief and sorrow they refused to come down in rain, they simply hung in the air, oppressive their weight, my Father, heavy with dark pain. Heavy with dark pain was my heart, O Father, as I thought of the rope swings on the neem tree in our garden. In our garden there must be young girls still swinging on those rope swings on the neem tree, their faces lifted up with laughter and hope as they watched the pelting rain. The pelting rain came down in August, lacerating my body and soul with pangs of separation, with a longing to see my Ranjha again. To see my Ranjha again, skin against skin, heartbeat against heartbeat, our limbs entwined and our souls enmeshed again was all I wished for day after day. Day after day I waited for news of him, day after day I wilted away, becoming a ghost of the girl I used to be as no news came. No news came, my Father, though August turned to September and the monsoon began to recede. The monsoon began to recede and the September moon drenched the rooftop with silver beams, harking me to remember the old days when I belonged to Ranjha and he belonged to me and the full moon was our sentry, walking beside us when we walked, standing on guard when we stopped to kiss. When we stopped to kiss, I had no idea that one day I would be left alone. Left alone hoping and praying, praying and hoping on the rooftop of the Kheras, that Heer and her Ranjha be reunited once October came. Once October came it brought with it its own torment, memories of walking hand in hand with Ranjha as the river swelled into a flood and of bathing together in its cool waters with Hassi and the girls. Hassi and the girls must still all be in their homes, still free, still happy, still alive, while Heer is a prisoner, almost a ghost, pacing the rooftop of her in-laws' home. Pacing the rooftop of the home of her in-laws, she prays alternately to The Prophet and to the man she loves, to take her away from this life, one way or the other before November comes. Before November comes, O Father, let me be with Ranjha or let me be dead....

The mansion of the Kheras was a large double-storied building in the centre of Rangpur town. The ground floor was a labyrinth of meeting rooms, halls, godowns, stables, guest rooms and servants' rooms. It was Seida's father's undisputed domain. There was a large verandah in which various tradesmen, and those hopeful of doing business with him, came to see him. Traders from faraway places like Iran, Balochistan and Mongolia, making their way towards Lahore, Dilli or Kolikata often took a pit stop at Rangpur, offloading some goods, acquiring others, changing horses and staying a night or two in one of the guest rooms, if Ajju Khera saw them as befitting of his hospitality. There was a separate kitchen downstairs and stables full of horses to meet the needs of the travelling tradesmen.

The family rooms and kitchen were on the first floor. Barring two old retainers, a man who did all the cleaning and odd jobs and his wife who helped in the kitchen, the first floor was reserved for the family. The largest rooms on the first floor were for Seida's father but he rarely used them, preferring to remain on the ground floor on most days, surrounded by a coterie of hangers-on, fawning servants, and a series of ever-changing bazaar women. The latter came in horse-drawn carriages sent especially to fetch them, veiled from head to toe, smelling of rose attar and other heavy perfumes.

I saw them from my vantage point on the roof as they alighted in
the lane outside the mansion and wondered at their fate. When the
body, which is the home of the soul, becomes a street, to which
place does the soul retreat?

Seida's mother occupied half of the upper floor, along with his
younger sister, Sehti. There had been another son, a few years older
than Seida, who had died in some sort of an accident which no one
cared to speak about. Now there were only Seida and Sehti living
with their mother. The other half belonged to Seida's older uncle,
the pigeon fancier who had been responsible for our engagement,
and his family. The two brothers were no longer on talking terms.

Sehti was a sulky girl about my own age, maybe a year or two
younger. We did not get off to a good start. The fault was mine. I
had not been a gracious bride during the parlour games Sehti and
her friends had set up when the wedding party reached home. I had
sat through the various ceremonies like a block of stone or wood,
my heart cold and unyielding. I had not smiled once at the women
who lifted my veil and exclaimed at the moon-like beauty of my
face. I had not been a willing participant in the games—the untying
of the knots on the bracelets or the fishing for coins in the trough of
water—churlishly letting Seida win without a contest. No wonder
Sehti watched me warily and preferred to keep her distance.

As Seida had said, our living quarters were ample. There was
a staircase leading to the rooftop. I spent most of my time on the
roof. The sight of the sky above was my only consolation in this
unfamiliar environment. It was the same sky that arched over my
father's home. These were the very same stars my father used to
point out to me when I was a girl. He had taught me to discern
the patterns of the different constellations and know them by
their names. It was the same sky under which my Ranjha walked
somewhere, even though I did not know where. The same stars
that watched over him when he slept. Needless to say, I was on
the rooftop also because I needed to keep a vigil for Ranjha night

and day. I had not realised that the wait for him would be so long and so soul-destroying. I had expected to see him walking down the street within a week or two of my reaching Rangpur, playing his flute for me.

Seida, too, used the staircase frequently, though in the reverse direction, to make good his escape from our chambers. He spent his days downstairs or in the marketplace, helping his father in his business dealings, and his nights wallowing about town drinking and smoking hukkah with his friends. Our rooms were like a no man's land, a deserted stretch of truce. No one found our behaviour odd for newlyweds. In the world of the Kheras, being attached to one's wife was a sign of weakness. Wives, like slippers, were utilitarian objects meant to be kept under the man's feet.

The first two months after the wedding passed relatively quietly. I thought of myself as a boarder who would be leaving soon and thus did not bother with anybody in the house. Rabel, the servant woman, would leave my food and bath water for me and apart from a curt 'thank you', I had no words to spare. I wondered at the patience Seida's mother was showing me, but only briefly. My mind was too full of myself, my own sorrows and fears for Ranjha's safety.

One day, the servant woman came to the rooftop and said Seida's mother had summoned me to her room. I considered refusing, but then followed the woman downstairs. The truth was, I was curious to know why she had summoned me after all these days. Apart from wishing each other when we happened to cross paths, we had not had much of a conversation yet. She was a very quiet woman. As was Sehti. The first floor of the house was mute in contrast to the noises that carried upstairs all day from the bustling quarters on the ground floor. Except on the rare days when the man of the house was in residence and the walls of the first floor shook with invective and abuse and the scurrying feet of the two old servants trying to keep pace with the master's demands.

She was a wisp of a woman, almost a shadow. She seemed to occupy no space at all. Standing in front of her, I felt too tall, too solid, too alive. Her face and hands had a crisscross of fine lines and from under them her skin shone translucent. She was dressed simply in a light coloured salwar and kurta of fine muslin, her head partially covered with a matching dupatta. I was surprised to note that her eyes were full of compassion as she looked at me.

'Sit down,' she gestured.

I complied awkwardly.

'You are not happy here?' she asked me in a low, husky voice. 'You were forced into this marriage?'

I said nothing. There was nothing to say.

'Seida has had a difficult childhood. Very, very difficult. My husband is a harsh man and Seida was a sensitive child. He is weak and under-confident. You are just the girl he needs. A strong woman like you could help him mend his ways and also stand up to his father,' she said.

'How do you know I'm strong?' I asked her. She had seen very little of me so far.

'The old aunts in my family used to say that you can tell within a week of a new bride's arrival which way she will be treated in her in-laws' home—like a maharani or a mehtraani. You, my dear, have maharani written all over you. Such regal disdain,' she said with a wistful smile.

A queen or a sweeper woman, there were only two ways a woman's life could unfold in her husband's home, according to her aunts' theory.

I did not understand what she was getting at. I had been so intent on not getting involved with the Kheras that I had behaved in too proud and haughty a manner. I felt ashamed of myself. Perhaps I had taken too much for granted. I was an unwilling guest, but a guest all the same. I owed my hosts basic courtesy even if I was unable to love them or regard them as my family.

'I am sorry,' I said. 'Would you like me to help with the housework? I do not wish to burden you in any way by my presence. Just tell me what you would like me to do, and I will try my best to do it.'

She laughed a short laugh.

'My dear, I have been a servant long enough in this house to have paid in advance the debts of the next seven generations of daughters-in-law to cross this threshold,' she said.

The words were bitter but her voice was calm, unruffled and full of quietude.

'Your queen-like bearing brings solace to my old and battered heart. When I see you standing at your window, proud and solitary as you stare out of it, willing life to bend to your wishes, I wish I could go back thirty years in time and begin again,' she continued.

Again, I felt bereft of words. I had decided I would keep my own secrets and not confide in anyone here, but I wished I could tell her not to think of me as her daughter-in-law. It seemed wrong for me to be listening to her innermost thoughts when I was nothing more than a passing visitor in her life.

'I will be leaving soon,' I said. 'Once I have word that my father has returned home. I cannot go back to Jhang while my uncle Kaido is at the helm of the family's affairs. He is manipulative and scheming and there is little love lost between us.'

'I made the mistake of returning home once, so let me tell you what I know,' she said, shaking her head. 'I am not speaking to you as Seida's mother, though for his sake, I do hope you will choose to stay. I speak to you as an older woman who has suffered life's vicissitudes. The house you go back to is never the same as the one you left as a bride. It is happy to see you as a guest, but should you expect to find a refuge there from your marriage, you will find that the old open places of affection and freedom you once inhabited, are now diminished. You will be relegated to a small, dark corner with very little say in anything. You will find shame written on the faces of your parents, resentment and suspicion in the gaze of your siblings, pity in the eyes of your friends. Even the servants of the house will regard you as the one without a future.'

'You speak from your own experience?' I asked. 'You left and then came back?'

She nodded.

'When I returned to this house after making a dramatic exit with a baby in my arms, it was far worse than it would have been had I never left. For now everyone, including myself, knew I had no place to go,' she continued. 'The thought of not having a roof over my head leached me of the last ounce of my courage.'

I felt sorry for her. Deeply sorry. In my mind's eye I could visualise her as a delicate young woman married to a man who battered and bruised her at will. A fragile flower crushed by a furious fist, its petals torn, its fragrance disregarded.

'Were there no older women in the house to shelter you or help you out?' I asked.

'My mother-in-law was there and my older sister-in-law. My mother-in-law was a very hard woman. She watched me like a hawk all day and swooped on every little mistake I made. I used to quiver with fear, trying my best not to incur her wrath, but the harder I tried, the angrier and more displeased she became,' she said. 'She kept every little thing under lock and key and used to measure every ingredient precisely before giving it to me. Just to put together the simplest meal I had to get past seven to eight locks, each staring at me with stony disapproval. Except for salt, everything else was stored in a separate locked cupboard—milk, sugar, flour, spices, coal, everything.'

'And your sister-in-law?' I asked.

'She made good her escape from the clutches of my mother-in-law as soon as she could. I came into the house and she retired to her bedroom with a headache that never went away. She didn't come out of her quarters for long and was always complaining of some ailment or ache. She never tried to be friends with me. She wanted to keep to herself so that she wouldn't have to tolerate my mother-in-law's tyranny again. She persuaded her husband to give her a separate kitchen. She was a smarter woman than I was. Also luckier. She had a husband who doted on her.'

'Is that what makes you so kind towards me?' I asked. 'The fact that your mother-in-law made you suffer intolerably?'

'I don't think it works like that. This life, human nature, it all eludes me. The more I try to make sense of it, the less logical it seems. I'm kind to you because that's how I'm made. My mother-in-law was cruel because that was in her nature. A mountain doesn't become a river, a river doesn't become a tree and a hawk doesn't behave like a lamb or a lamb like a tiger. We are all tied to our natures,' she mused.

'Are you saying life doesn't change us?' I challenged her.

'Oh, of course it does. Mountains get eroded and rivers get muddied and trees get chopped down or grow more branches as life goes on. A hawk might lose a wing, a tiger's roar may soften with age and the lamb might become meat. Life happens to all of us, altering us irrevocably. Yet, the essential nature of things doesn't change. A tiger doesn't become a tree or a lamb a river. The change that life brings about is so slight compared to what nature has originally created that it barely signifies,' she said.

'But experiences change a human being's nature,' I insisted. 'Sinners become saints. There are so many stories told to us of miraculous transformations.'

'That is the belief I based my whole life on. But when I look back, I do not think it worked out that way. I thought if I show myself to be an obedient and willing worker, my mother-in-law's experience would teach her that I could be trusted and she would be less angry. But she went to her grave raging. Her experience of me did nothing to change her behaviour towards me,' she said. 'Sometimes she would soften for a few days. But then, out of nowhere, she would erupt with anger and suspicion yet again. Whatever was inside her was so much stronger than my desire for her to be calm.'

I wanted to ask her about her husband but could not find the words to do so without seeming intrusive. Perhaps talking about her mother-in-law was her way of talking to me about my father-in-law.

We talked some more about inconsequential things. She told me that she was concerned about the gout that was troubling the old servant and she did not know how long he would be able to discharge his duties. She asked me whether I would like to keep my ornaments in my own trunk, in my own room, under lock and key. I told her I was happy to let them remain in her safekeeping. As I was leaving, she said to me that Sehti had been very excited about getting a new sister. She was a shy girl, she feared rejection too much to try and approach me again, but if I tried I would find in her someone who would be a devoted friend. It was a pity that two girls of the same age should live under the same roof and not spend time together laughing and chatting.

I felt terrible. It was not my intention to hurt these people. Yet, I was mortally afraid of settling down in this house, of forging relationships with them. I did not belong in this life, this family, this marriage, and I did not wish to deceive them into thinking I did. I had to keep faith with my real marriage, even if it had begun to seem like a false dream.

18

Sehti Becomes a Friend

RANJHA BELOVED, THE MONTH of December is cruel and cold and I long for the warmth of your arms. For the warmth of your arms Heer is ready to sell her soul. Heer is ready to sell her soul to any passing devil who will give me hope of being with you again. Hope of being with you again makes me consult clever charlatans and wandering soothsayers who read the lines on my palms and tell me what the stars say of my fate. What the stars say of my fate is uncertain, my beloved, no one tells me how many days more I must spend in the house of the Kheras. In the house of the Kheras January arrives bringing further chills and a biting wind that eats into my bones. A biting wind that eats into my bones and brings on a raging fever that refuses to go away. Refuses to go away and refuses to let me die for the will to live is leaving me as January saps my strength away. January saps my strength away and February taunts me with the first signs of spring. The first signs of spring wreck havoc in my heart and my mind. My mind curses Malki for giving birth to a daughter who was to know such pain in life, who was to know such separation and loss. To know such separation and loss becomes intolerable, my beloved, when March brings with it festivals and weddings. Festivals and weddings hurt me, O lover, for everything around me is in celebration while I stand solitary and apart. I stand solitary and apart on the rooftop of the Kheras, my beloved, while young girls dress up as brides and coyly let their lovers take them away. Take them away from my sight, I pray, lest I lose my sanity, lest my grief rip open my mind and soul. Rip open my mind and soul and on every cell you'll find there is Ranjha's name. Ranjha's name is written upon every pore and every unit of Heer's blood and skin. Heer's blood and skin burn and simmer under the April sun and catch fire in May. In May the sun is livid and angry as it sets her breasts aflame and she beats them in lamentation and from the rooftop loudly shouts out Ranjha's name. Ranjha's name leaves Heer's lips again and again till nothing of Heer remains. Nothing of Heer remains, my beloved, nothing of Heer remains I tell anyone who cares to pass my way in the scorching heat of June. In the scorching heat of June I tell them, you can call me Ranjha from now for in loving Ranjha I have become Ranjha, I am no longer Heer....

Six months passed in the Khera household before I finally gave up thinking that Ranjha was going to arrive any time soon. Something had gone wrong, either he was sick or injured, or something had made him forget his promise of coming for me. Terrible thoughts swarmed into my head each day. Had he hit his head against a river-boulder and lost his memory? Had his legs or arms been crushed irreparably in an accident? Had bandits attacked him and knifed him and was he lying somewhere recovering from grievous wounds? I could not believe he was dead. My heart told me he was alive but distracted or incapacitated in some way, that somewhere he was living a life of challenge and deprivation and that he too was suffering just like I was. A theory had formed itself in my head that we were both being tested by the heavens, that such a love as ours could not be given just like that and that it had to be earned. I prayed to the Panj Pir every day to show me what I needed to do to be reunited with Ranjha.

Seida Khera and I were like two travellers who did not speak each other's tongue but were journeying together for a long distance through rough, unknown terrain. We were scrupulously attentive to each other's needs, spoke only of bare practical necessities and looked out for each other's safety, guarding each other's back. Without any discussion on the subject, we had arrived at an understanding that he would take advantage of his newly married status to not let his father bully him any longer.

On the rare days that Seida's father moved into his rooms on the first floor and ate with the family, mostly around festivals and special occasions like the visit of an out-of-town relative, I took care to stay firmly by Seida's side. The elder Khera was a domineering presence in the household, making everyone scurry around, bending, scraping and bowing to his convenience, but he was wary of me. He was used to seeing submission in the eyes of women. In mine, he read a quiet defiance he did not know how to deal with. His eyes would move from Seida to me, back and forth, trying to puzzle out what was happening, but we were united in the stand we presented to him, as two people who had no complaints of each other. Short of hiding in our bedroom, Seida's father had no way of getting to the truth, and he was too overbearing a man to hide anywhere.

The language he spoke was of a kind I had never been exposed to in my parents' home. Somewhere on the edges of my consciousness there had been the awareness that men sometimes used swear words, but I had no real expectation of ever coming face to face with them and was therefore completely unprepared for the onslaught. It was a form of warfare, a method of violence I had not been trained to handle. I would become totally immobile at the sound of his loud voice hurling abuses at all and sundry. I used to wonder how the rest of the family continued to go about their work—eating, chatting and sleeping. How they could carry on with whatever they were doing as if those high-decibel, coated-in-poison, mixed-with-acid and hurled-at-full-speed imprecations were nothing out of the ordinary.

Once, Sehti and I were together on the rooftop, hanging out the washing to dry. Her father's voice reverberated up from the verandah of the ground floor. He was shouting at a servant who had annoyed him for some reason that was not clear to us. It took very little to annoy him. On a bad day, even a speck of dust on his window ledge or a few grains of salt more or less in his mutton curry could bring on a whirlwind of expletives and send plates and tumblers flying across the verandah or through the rooms.

'You donkey's prick! You brainless cunt! You monkey's shit! Motherfucker, who do you think you are? I'll tear your ass and stuff it into your mouth, you asshole,' we heard him say from two floors down.

I was hanging a pyjama on the line. My hand stopped mid-action and I froze in that position. Sehti's eyes darted up to my face. I don't know what she read in my eyes. Terror or revulsion or a mixture of both. She lowered her gaze and began to hum a tune under her breath, all the while deftly bending and stretching, picking up the laundry and hanging it out to dry piece by piece. I stood rigid, unable to react or do anything to diffuse the sudden tension between us.

At last, the storm of words blew over and there was silence downstairs. I turned to walk down to my room, seeking not to embarrass her or myself any further.

'Don't go yet,' she called out to me very softly. 'Come here and talk with me for a bit.'

I hesitated. But then I turned around and walked back to her.

'I'm sorry, I'm not used to this. I don't know how you can remain unaffected and just carry on,' I said after a moment of silence had passed between us.

'They are just words,' she said. 'They can't hurt you unless you let them. They have no power or meaning other than the one you give to them.'

More invective from her father came hurtling through the air and crashed against our eardrums. I flinched involuntarily.

'Motherfucker. Sisterfucker. Daughterfucker. Bastard. Cunt. Prick. Balls. Backside. Asshole,' she said in a musical voice looking straight into my eyes and shrugged, 'So what?'

She was a delicate-looking girl, with her mother's fine frame and translucent fair skin. A long, neatly plaited braid of dark hair snaked down to her waist. The whole of her was pretty in an understated and quiet sort of way. That that sweet mouth of hers could roll off such a foul string of abuse was a revelation. I was deeply perturbed.

'This is all very shocking for you?' she asked. 'That I should curse like this?'

'Yes,' I nodded. 'No one should speak like that, especially not a gentle, well-brought up girl like you.'

'They used to terrify me, these words. I used to be scared everyone would know me as the girl whose father only spoke in abuses. I was scared to let any friends come home to play with me lest they overhear my father rant. I was scared to go to their houses to play lest I be expected to reciprocate by calling them over. Every time I heard him shouting at my mother or the servants, I wanted to dig a hole in the backyard, lie down in it and die. Every time I walked down the street to the market, I imagined that everyone was staring at me as if the abuses were branded on my skin and written on my forehead,' she said. 'But, the harder I shut my ears, the further I tried to run from them, the more I trembled on hearing them fly, the louder and meaner his words seemed to become. It was as if I was feeding them with my fear.'

'Did your father not notice how frightened you were?' I asked.

'What if he did? Displays of any kind of weakness only enrage him further,' Sehti replied. 'He takes them as a signal to attack more viciously.'

I felt overwhelmed by sadness that she should dislike her father so intensely. Even though I had been at loggerheads with Malki most of my life, there had been a bond of exasperated affection connecting us. I had never hated her, just the way she thought about certain things. Here, I sensed no mitigating currents of love or understanding.

'What happened to cure you of your terror?' I asked.

'I was once ill with a high fever for several days. The hakim whose care I was in had almost given up on me. Only Mother refused to give up. She and Rabel sat by my bed, night after night, bringing down the fever with cold compresses, fanning me gently to cool my brow. One night, I sat up in my bed in high delirium, a string of abuse leaving my fevered lips. Every foul word or expression I had ever heard raged out of me in hysterical sobs. I laughed wildly, I cried, I pummelled Mother with my fists and then I put my head on her chest and wept inconsolably. Rabel tried to silence me, but Mother told her to let me be. When all my rage was spent, she rocked me to sleep in her arms as if I was a baby. When I woke up the next morning, the fever had begun to recede. And over the next few days I realised my fear of father's terrible tongue had also gone,' she said.

'Your mother is a very remarkable woman,' I said. 'It must have taken a lot of inner strength for her to retain her gentle goodness amidst so much cruelty and harshness. I see no bitterness or anger in her.'

'It is only now that I have begun to appreciate her. When I was younger, I hated that she never stood up for herself or for us, that her only response to so much injustice was to quieten us down or to weep silently and unseen. I always thought of her as a very weak and helpless person,' she replied. 'I wanted her to break a few things, hurl a few objects in return, at least shout back occasionally.'

'To rail when nothing will come out of it is to weaken yourself further. I had always thought of myself as a very strong woman,' I told her. 'I could fight, I could always speak up for myself, I was truly scared of no man. Yet, when it came to the first real battle of my life, I realised I was as weak and helpless as the next woman. You see, I had nowhere to go. I did not have a square inch of land or anything at all to call my own. My very existence, the food I ate, the clothes I wore, the roof I slept under would always be some man's largesse to me—my father's or my brother's or my husband's.'

'That is what Mother said to me when I asked her why she never left despite the fact that Father treated her so badly. She said there were no real choices she had in the matter. She could choose between being miserable and neglected in her father's house or hectored and oppressed in her husband's house, and whichever choice she made, it would be the wrong one. An old family servant, who had looked after her since she was a baby, advised her to return to my father's house. The servant told her that what my mother thought of as her father's home would soon become her brother's. Her husband's home would ease out after her mother-in-law died and her son grew into a man,' Sehti said. 'If she was going to be unhappy in both places, she said it was better for her to be unhappy where her children at least had a chance of happiness.'

'Why are we such abject creatures, Sehti?' I burst out. 'Completely without pride, bearing whatever is thrown at us in order to survive? First, we live on the dream that our husbands will be nice to us. And if that fails, then we carry on living on the sorry hope that our sons will be kinder than our husbands. Are we nothing in ourselves? Why do we not own property? Even the children we bear out of our wombs carry their father's names. Are women weak because they own nothing or do women own nothing because they are weak?'

'Mother says there are always more questions than answers in a woman's life. The ones who learn early not to ask too many questions are the ones who seem to be the happiest,' said Sehti. 'The ones who ask questions and insist upon answers are labelled witches and burnt alive or stoned to death, or become abandoned old crones living as outcasts outside mosques and temples with no one to call their own,' she replied.

'Come, this talk is too wretched. Your mother must be wondering what is taking us so long,' I said. I had already opened up to her much more than I had intended to.

As we walked down the stairs together, she spoke again.

'Heer,' she said. 'From today can we be sisters and friends, please? To have me as a friend may not solve your problems but it might make them easier to bear.'

She was right. To have her as a friend was the best thing that happened to me after coming to Rangpur. My grief was such that no one could cure it. The only cure lay in being with Ranjha again and there seemed to be no sign of him. To have known so much happiness so briefly and then to have it taken away without explanation was cruel beyond endurance. Where was he? Why had he disappeared? My eyes resembled hollows staring into the far horizon, imagining even distant specks of dust to be Ranjha, waiting for him to materialise out of the thinness of the air, take shape, become palpable, hold me in his arms and tell me that I had just been having a bad dream. I was losing my mind. I had begun to hallucinate, to see him in the doorway, to imagine him in my bed, to talk to him in my head and sometimes even out loud.

Through this illness that was creeping up upon me, I had Sehti by my side, holding my hand for comfort, giving me a shoulder to lean against, combing my hair gently on the days I forgot to comb it, and leading me silently to my room when I got fretful and forgot myself. I had fallen into a deep darkness and Sehti's soft smile was the only sliver of sunshine peeping past the dense clouds in my head.

Still, I did not speak of Ranjha to her. I did not want to lose the intensity of my pain. It was all I had left to remind me of him. Everything else was slowly slipping off the edges of my memory. The touch of his skin, the timbre of his voice, the warmth of his gaze were all flying further and further out of my recall, like the sight of a flock of birds vanishing into the distant blue of the sky.

It was Sehti who surprised me by telling me of Murad the Baloch.

VII

WHAT THE CROW, THE PIGEON AND THE GOAT WITNESSED

19

The Crow's Testimony

I DO NOT KNOW if you recall, but we have met before. The first time we met was at Heer's naming ceremony and the last was when you saw me trying to convey courage and sympathy to Ranjha as he stood waiting for Heer under the neem tree on the day of her false wedding with Seida Khera.

That was a day of departures. It was the day of Heer Syal's departure from her happy childhood home into the state of homelessness that every married woman knows. Some know it for a few days or weeks, after which they are able to make the new place a default home of sorts. Others know it for the rest of their lives, the sense of dislocation never leaving them. Rare is the bride who does not weep copiously at her departure from the childhood home, for she knows that it is not just the home of her parents she is leaving behind, but also, more irrevocably, the certainties of girlhood for the vagaries of womanhood.

It was a day of departure for Ranjha too. It was true this wasn't the first time for him. He had already left so much behind. He had left Takht Hazara and the comforts afforded to him by his birth, he had left all claims to leading a landowner's privileged life, he had left a mother, brothers, sisters-in-law, and the happiness of belonging in a family, however flawed that family might be, he had left his

beloved cattle herd behind. And on that day when he decided to
follow Heer to the land of the Kheras, he left behind his nonchalance,
his carefreeness too. It was a departure from being his own man,
responsible only for his own life, and becoming someone who,
despite his natural instincts to avoid being tied down to anything, was
now at least partly responsible for another person's happiness. It was
a departure from an idyllic romance in a safeguarded environment
to the challenging reality of surviving in a world with no sympathy
for lovers.

As I watched Ranjha promise Heer that he would follow her to
Rangpur, a grim realisation dawned on me. My hours on the neem
tree, which had been home for the last eighteen years, were now
numbered. As her guardian in the natural world, it was my duty to
follow her to her new abode. Her affairs were far from settled, her
life's trajectory full of uncertainty and danger, her heart and soul in
upheaval. I would need to look out for these young lovers as they
defied the strictures the world was trying to put them under.

The neem tree I had lived upon most of my life was no ordinary
tree. A hundred feet high, a hundred years old, it was a living witness
to the complete history of the Syals in Jhang, its shade benign and
life giving, its every part a source of protection and healing. I was
nervous at the thought of leaving its purified air. I was no longer
young. At twenty years of age, I could not expect to live more than
another two or three. Leaving my home might mean cutting that
life shorter. I would perhaps never see my beloved neem again. But
it was clear to me that I had to follow them, it was my dharma.

That fateful night, the stars were pale and lustreless in the cold,
white light of an unsympathetic moon, when Heer departed sobbing
in a palanquin, Ranjha departed grim-faced with a drum around his
neck, and this aging crow left Jhang Syal on a wing and a prayer.

On the first night at camp with the Khera party, I was very fearful
and restless. I had a premonition of impending danger. The Khera
patriarch had chosen a deserted stretch of forest along the river, only

a few miles outside Jhang, to set up their camp. Perhaps they were tired after all the feasting and ceremonies, but the place felt sinister to me, the rustling river reeds were full of whispers and sighs. I looked around in the surrounding canopy for a local crow flock to whom I could offer my respects and maybe elicit some intelligence and help from. However, I could not locate any. It was an inauspicious start and confirmed my suspicion that the terrain was shrouded in bad luck. I found a high branch that gave me vantage of the bridal tent with one eye, and the open fire around which the drummers had gathered for the night, from the other. The main tent where the family of the bridegroom slept was behind me, just out of my line of vision.

I had barely been asleep for a few hours when something moved towards the bride's tent. I realised the bridegroom had just walked in, in all probability to claim his conjugal rights. I bristled with tension, the small feathers on my back standing up. I expected to see a screaming, bleeding Seida Khera fleeing out of Heer's tent any minute now, for I knew Heer would not be unarmed or unprepared for his advances.

Instead, a scream rent the air from the opposite direction, from near the river.

'Heer! Heer! Heer!' I heard him scream, the urgency of his voice tearing through the dense darkness of the night in the forest. 'Wait for me. I'll come for you.'

Ranjha!

He was in trouble. Before I could fly to him, the sound of a huge splash in the river reverberated through the night.

Suddenly, a scene I had witnessed a little before I turned in to sleep came back to me. As I watched from the tree I had chosen as my night's perch, I had seen the elder Khera and Seida having some sort of discussion before retiring for the night. Seida was making what appeared like an impassioned plea to his father, to not much apparent effect. Then the Khera patriarch strode up to the drummers, signalled two of them out of the group and gave them some instructions. Seida hung in the shadows. After his father had left, I saw him approach the two drummers again and give them a few silver coins.

It all made sense now. The instructions I had seen being issued must have been to throw Ranjha into the river. In a split second, my course in life changed. I rushed to the river after Ranjha.

It was a treacherous track of water. The grey waters eddied rapidly as the river moved through a series of sharp bends. Fortunately, the moon was full and illuminated the entire length of turbulent water. I saw a speck of white hurtling downstream on the swift current. I flew ahead at an angle, taking note of the speed of the moving speck, so as to position myself over the river as Ranjha flowed under.

He was floating, his white garments billowing out, his hands and legs tied. The drummers had not taken care to wrest the drum from around his neck before they threw him in. It must have brought him up to the water's surface. There was a blindfold around his eyes. He was struggling to free his arms and legs and the river was buffeting and tossing him rudely. I swooped down to tug at the knots around his wrists. They came off in a single pull as if they had deliberately been left loose. Next, I tugged at the ankles. Those knots were loose too. He turned over on his belly and began to swim swiftly. His blindfold was still in place. I was hovering over him, looking for a way to dart in and remove the blindfold, but he used his now freed hand to forcefully tug it off and began to swim shorewards. The drum bobbed on the water, with no master to claim it. It had served its purpose twice over, first in getting him his passage into the wedding party and then in keeping him afloat when he was tossed into the river.

He swam in strong strokes towards the shore and was almost there when the next calamity struck. I saw it a few seconds before him and squawked out a panicked warning that only served to startle him further and he hit the boulder with a cracking sound and a yelp

of pain. Although it was a moonlit night, that part of the water had
fallen into a shadowy darkness created by the river reeds near the
approaching bank. I saw him slow down, obviously in deep pain, and
laboriously make the last few metres of the journey before hoisting
himself out of the water's edge and onto the shore. He dropped to
the ground and lay on his stomach, one arm flung out and the other
listless by his side. There was a deep gash on his forehead and his
breathing was ragged.

Come on, Ranjha. Come on, move a bit further on the land lest
the water carry you away again, I said to him silently in my head.

He lay there panting for breath and unable to move.

Come on, come on, you can do it, I urged him from inside my
head.

Still he lay there.

Get up, man. For Heer's sake, move, I was shouting aloud at him
now, uncaring that my speech would not make any sense to him.

He groaned and brought himself up to his knees, crawling
forward bit by bit, his right arm or shoulder obviously in excruciating
pain as he manoeuvred himself onto a dry patch of sand.

I cried out in delight. It was good to see him out of the water's
sweeping reach.

The very next minute I heard him gasp and fall down insensible on
the sand. Either the blow on the forehead or the pain in his shoulder
had knocked him out cold. I flew down to where he was lying and
circled around him inspecting him from all sides. His breathing was
steady. But I could not tell how badly injured he was. There was
nothing to do but wait until he came around, or until morning. It
was an evening in July, hot and humid. I hoped he would be none
the worse for sleeping in wet clothes.

As Ranjha lay there unconscious to the world, my thoughts
flew to Heer for the first time since I had left my watch at the night
camp and rushed after Ranjha. I wondered if she had heard his cry.
I calculated that she must have. Her tent was only a little further

from where I was perched. I wondered how she had fared. I sent a quick prayer up for her. It was clear my next few days were going to be spent looking after her lover. Though I had no idea what I was going to do to help him when he came to consciousness. Choosing a perch from where I could keep an eye on him, I fell into a fitful sleep.

Dawn broke in shards of pink and gold light rippling on the waters, but Ranjha lay there motionless and insensible to its beauty. I had something of a plan forming in my mind. I did not know if it would work, but it was all I could think of. I would fly back to Jhang Syal and fetch Hassi, or failing that, one of Heer's other friends. I estimated we were barely fifteen or so miles out of town. Though I was no longer in the prime of youth, it would not take me much more than three quarters of an hour to reach Jhang. The challenge would be to communicate with Hassi and get her to follow me. I decided to take my chances.

On reaching Hassi's house, I positioned myself on the low parapet wall of the terrace and began my vigil. If I was lucky, she would come here soon with some household task to do. The terrace is the place for drying many things—clothes, vegetables, hair. And sometimes it's just good for catching a few moments alone in a busy household. But over an hour passed and there was no sound of footsteps coming up. It was the morning just after a grand wedding and everything was running late. I would have to be patient.

It was almost noon and I was ready to give up and go to Sonia, the goldsmith's daughter's house, when I heard Hassi's voice as she moved up the staircase. She was talking to someone about the wedding last night.

'My heart bleeds for Ranjha. He has been ill-used,' said Hassi.

'Heer was pretty broken-hearted too. I wept for all of us, for all the women in the world who must sacrifice their lives for the wishes of their families, when I heard her crying,' said the second girl. It sounded like Sonia. No doubt they were coming up to discuss the wedding privately, out of the hearing of family elders. I would have to hustle Hassi out of her leisurely chatting and onto her horse as quickly as possible. Ranjha had been in bad shape when I left and it had already been about four or five hours since.

They settled down on a string cot that lay in a corner.

'Uff, I'm still wearing these heavy earrings,' said Hassi. 'I was so tired yesterday I fell off to sleep with them on.'

She began to take off the gold hoop ring secured with a gold chain running from behind her ear into her plait. Having taken the first one off, she put it down on her lap. I saw my opening.

I rushed to pick it up and flew off.

The girls shrieked and came after me. I flew down and dropped it on the ground where they could see it. They rushed downstairs to pick it up. Just as they reached the spot, I made off with the glittering gold earring again and flew a short distance. I did this three times before I conveyed my meaning successfully.

'Hassi, the crow is trying to lead us somewhere!' said Sonia.

I crowed loudly to indicate she'd got the right idea.

'You're trying to tell us something?' Hassi said, eyeing me dubiously.

I squawked excitedly in response and flew towards the stables, where I perched on her horse.

I dropped the earring and let Sonia pick it up only after Hassi was mounted. Sonia tried to get on behind her, but I shooed her off. Hassi would need to bring a passenger back.

'You stay here,' said Hassi. 'I'll follow the crow. It's trying to show me something. Maybe someone we know is in trouble.'

And so, I brought Hassi, still wearing one large gold earring, to the spot on the riverbed where Ranjha lay prone upon the sand. He was moaning in discomfort, conscious but barely so.

Hassi's eyes widened in shock as they took in his prone figure and then flew swiftly to me in astonishment. She nodded in brief acknowledgement towards me and knelt down to attend to Ranjha. It took a lot of effort and persistence on her part to manoeuvre him on to her horse and ride back with him to his tent in the clearing in the forest outside Jhang Syal. It was dusk before she returned.

Immediately, she went to the local bonesetter's house and enlisted his daughter Fattiya's help. A sling was made for Ranjha's broken arm and poultices applied to bring down the swelling. Through all of this, Ranjha only muttered Heer's name from some far off place in his consciousness, slipping in and out of wakefulness.

Morning brought a small contingent of Heer's friends to his aid. There was Sonia the goldsmith's daughter, Mirran and Bano, the woodseller's girls and Sanpatti, the shepherd's lissom daughter with her gift of a she-goat for milking every day. However, morning also brought with it a raging fever. The gash on Ranjha's forehead had turned an angry, throbbing red and did not look too good to me.

Hassi swore the girls to secrecy. Ranjha's presence was not to be made known to anyone else. She feared what Kaido or Sultan might do to him if they found him back in their radius of influence and in a vulnerable state. Ranjha needed to be restored to health before anything else. They took turns sitting with him, applying bandages of cool water on his fevered brow, fetching food and water for him and tending to his requirements. The fever raged for over a month and many were the days that I thought he would not make it. I feared the mosquitoes on the riverbed that night had left him with their tiny kisses of death. He seemed to be in the throes of the shaking and shivering sickness, with the fever at its highest every evening, his teeth chattering despite the fact that it was the hot part of the year and he was covered with many blankets.

Finally, the fever broke and it looked as if the impulse to live had won. The arm too was on the mend, according to Fattiya. Yet, he was weak of body and spirit. Maudlin. Morose. He was unable to accept that he had failed to rescue Heer on that fateful night and now she was lodged in the house of the Kheras. His days had been stolen from him by the ill-timed fever and it tortured him to think that Heer must have waited for him and not known what had become of him.

Another month passed in acute physical weakness and self-loathing. He would sit there brooding, not knowing what was to come. The girls tried hard to restore his spirits, bringing him the churi he loved to eat, but he pushed it away. It was the flavour of Heer's fingers that he craved, the churi was nothing by itself. They urged him to pick up his flute again, but the music seemed to have dried up in him. He broke his flute in frustration and tossed it away. Again and again, he asked if there was any news of Heer, but the girls had nothing to offer him.

As he regained his health, Ranjha was able to cook and look after himself. Heer's friends' visits became less frequent. Only Hassi continued to visit every day, bringing any provisions he might need, staying on to talk with him.

'Forget her now, Ranjha,' she said. 'She has been in Rangpur for over two months and there is no word from there. No complaints, no news that the bride is missing her home, no threats to send her back. She must be well, settling in.'

Hassi's pensive eyes communicated other things to him as she looked at him. In the soft touch of her hand on his arm, in the accidental brushing of her breasts against his body as she leant over to give him a blanket, she was offering him a chance to forget Heer.

Ranjha sensed the overtures she was making and they made him acutely uncomfortable. 'Hassi, you forget I belong to Heer,' he said. 'And you forget she belongs to Seida Khera,' she snapped back at him.

A grimace of pain disfigured his face.

Hassi rode away and did not visit again for many days. Perhaps she was embarrassed that he had read the invitation in her eyes and rejected it so directly. Perhaps she was angry at his listless self-pity and refusal to come to terms with what had happened. Perhaps she was overtaken with guilt for desiring her best friend's man. Whatever the true reason may have been, she stayed away.

Left alone to brood for days on end, Ranja talked aloud to himself. He did not know if Heer was happy in Rangpur and he should leave her alone, or if she was trapped and desperately waiting for him to come and take her away.

'One sign, just one sign,' he asked of the unbroken expanse of blue sky above him, day after day.

'Just one word, just the smallest hint,' he asked of the river, chucking small pebbles into it to ruffle its calm.

He drew patterns in the mud with a stick and stared hard at them for clues to his quandary, but they revealed nothing to his impassioned scrutiny.

When Hassi came next, it was with Sonia and Sanpatti, and Ranjha sat laughing and flirting with the three girls, filling the awkwardness between them by creating once again the mood of the days when Heer was in Jhang Syal and flirting was just a game they all played together as friends.

'Hassi,' he said, as they were leaving. She waited while the other two walked ahead. 'Thank you for saving my life,' he said, opening his arms and holding her tiny frame in a tight clasp. 'It is time for me to go from here. I will be leaving in a day or two.'

'Don't go,' she said. 'I'm not Heer but I am a woman with a heart that aches for you. You can bury your sadness in me. I will make a home with you and keep you from succumbing to the madness that takes lost lovers to their graves before their time.'

'You are too brave and beautiful a woman to condemn yourself to living with a man whose soul is enmeshed with another's irrevocably,' he said. 'You deserve better.'

'Where will you go?' she asked.

'I don't know,' he said. 'All places are equal to those who have no home.'

'I fear for you, alone on the road. You are only just recovering,' she said.

'I won't be entirely alone. Tell Sanpatti her goat goes with me. For milk and for companionship,' he replied. 'Go now, the others are waiting for you.'

The hurt in Hassi's heart played hide-and-seek on her face as she waved to him.

Over the next two days I watched him make arrangements for his departure, packing all that he might need for the life of a travelling mendicant, into a bag he could hoist on his shoulder, and I wondered what this new departure meant for me. I did not know of what further use I could be to him. I watched Ranjha leave Jhang Syal with a sorrowing heart. I had grown to love him in these months of watching over him. For now, however, my home in the neem tree was calling out to me. I would rest there for a few days and then fly out to Rangpur.

Even as the crow flies, it was a long journey, but my heart was restless to see Heer.

20

The Pigeons Bear Witness

THE CORPSE OF THE deaf-mute girl was found by her mother outside the cowshed some ten days after Heer's wedding. The girl had gone missing on the night of the wedding. Her mother had looked everywhere but could not find her. When she did, she wished she hadn't. Her clothes were torn and barely covered her frail body. There was blood in congealed streaks along her thighs and dark bruises on her back and stomach and teeth marks on her nipples. It was clear she had been brutally and repeatedly raped.

We screeched. We squawked. We flapped our wings in anger.

On the night he stole her from the wedding feast, Kaido Langra ripped her clothes in front of our eyes and dressed her in red and gold like a bride. His bed was strewn with flowers taken from the wedding pavilion. He was not a drinker, but that night he drank fermented brew and let it go to his head and into his groin too, till his organ was engorged and full. That night he did not hide his pigeon or play any seeking and finding games.

That night we heard him say, 'Enjoy your wedding night, my beautiful niece.'

We screeched. We squawked. We screamed. We flew round and round in a flutter of outrage. To no avail.

For nine nights we watched him celebrate his niece's wedding, each night more depraved than the one that preceded it. Each night, lust and hatred combined to torture his trapped prey in a new abomination. We saw the deaf-mute girl's soul departing from her eyes and yet he heaved and thrust and spilled his corruption inside her body, unaware that his victim had escaped him through the only door that swung open for her. We heard the wailing of her soul as it spun out of the orbit of this earth's evil, finally free of her mute body.

We hung our heads in shame. For we were guilty by association. This was the hand that fed us our daily grain. We fluttered and flapped in our own ignominy. We wept for our keeper's sordid soul. We cried for all of humankind, for the sorry mess of creatures it called its own.

We watched as Kaido Langra put her back in the clothes he had ripped off her on the night of the wedding. We watched him drag her body in the stealth of dawn and leave it outside the stable for her mother to discover. She looked like a broken doll as they heaped earth upon her in her grave.

We heard him weep in loud lament.

Girls, little girls, he said, were like flowers. Creation's most tender gift. Delicate and pure. It was the duty of their parents to be like thorns, sharp and hard and always at their side, guarding them. These are pearls given to us, he said. Don't throw your pearls in the gutter where the pigs will get to them, he begged. The girl's mother was thrown out of her job at the shed. A mother who was so careless with her own young one could not be trusted with the care of other beings. The guilt and shame of having a daughter raped to death was hers to carry. She too would die soon of heartache and the unkindness of the world towards those it wrongs.

The little girl's death turned Kaido Langra into a crusader. A saviour of delicate flowers in the garden of life. There was immorality and depravity all around them, he warned the people of Jhang Syal with grim foreboding. They had to kneel down and ask forgiveness for their sinners' ways. One precious life had been brutally snuffed out. How many more did they wish to lose before they came to their senses?

He called meetings of women in Malki's courtyard and made forceful pleas to them to cover their daughters from head to toe in chadors, not even as much as an errant strand of hair visible to an outsider's gaze. He beseeched fathers not to let their daughters out of the house without a male family member chaperoning them. Not to the nearby shop to get salt or grain for their mothers. Not to each other's houses to play or run around wasting their time in useless laughter and games. Not even to the mosque to pray or to celebrate Eid.

He sat for long hours with the qazi, persuading him to discontinue Quran lessons for the daughters of the chieftains. Such lessons were turning their heads, making them challenge the authority of their fathers, bringing disrepute to their families. He went from house to house, meeting each elder in the village council individually. Girls, he said, must be stopped from learning horse riding. That would ensure their safety as they could never be too far away from their houses.

The air of a town, its very climate can be changed by insinuation, by sowing fear and doubt in the minds of men, by fanning dormant anxieties. Fresh fears don't need to be created to trigger feelings of insecurity and panic—just a reminder of old traumas buried in the collective subconscious is enough. Human history has more memories of bloodshed and assault written on its pages than that of any other creature. The fear in Kaido's voice was real perhaps. He saw a rapist and a murderer in the mirror each morning and he had every reason to believe that the world was a terrible place.

The earth of Jhang Syal was becoming suspicious of the beauty of its own daughters. Daughters it had once proudly shown off as the most beautiful and accomplished in the land were now being hidden inside chadors and homes. We watched as their playing hours became shorter and hemlines became longer and laughter began to be reprimanded and tears began flowing unbidden from the eyes of little girls starved of friends and freedom.

It was only a few months since Mir Chuchak had left, but the town had changed beyond recognition. Its streets were less colourful and looked deserted by early evening. Women did not stand at doors gossiping with each other, their daughters hanging on to their mothers' dupattas and soaking in their casual conversations. Only dour old men hung around at street corners after dark, cogitating over the town's declining morals over their hukkahs. Its playgrounds and rooftops no longer resonated with the jumbled voices of girls and boys fighting for turf. All outdoor terrain was male terrain. In the month of Saawan no swings were put out on trees, as it made little girls giddy with happiness and unmindful of which way their skirts or hair flew. In any case, too much sunshine and fresh air was not good for girls as it might tan their skins, make them less fair and not desirable enough for their future husbands.

It intrigues us, this human notion of a 'fairer sex'. Male pigeons can't be told apart from female pigeons on the basis of colour. The concept of the 'weaker sex' is even more incomprehensible to us. Male and female pigeons equally grunt, growl, peck and flap their wings to protect their nest and their young ones against threats. And the division of labour in our species is something that humans would do well to look at. Even the hatching of eggs is done collaboratively. The female pigeon sits on the egg from mid-afternoon to the morning. In the morning, the male takes over and is on duty till mid-afternoon. Both sexes take turns feeding their baby chicks by regurgitating food into their mouths. And no self-respecting, able-bodied male pigeon would think it was his female partner's job to serve him food. And yet, human beings are considered the more advanced of the two species. At least in their own lexicon.

We sometimes debate among ourselves if the human is the weakest and darkest of God's creatures. Is that what makes humans susceptible to the glint of gold, the seduction of silver, the clutter of coins? Is his own light so dim that he needs the light of shining metals to make him feel safe? Is his sense of self-worth so slight that he heaps upon it continuously the weight of more and more gold and yet fails to measure up in his own eyes, no matter how much wealth he amasses? Does he strive to get all of nature under his control to compensate for the fact that he has no control over his own nature? He is the only one of God's creatures who wears clothes and yet there is none more naked than him—his greed, his jealousies, his hatred and insecurities always on display.

There are others amongst us who argue that money isn't the root cause of the evil inside man. It was the accidental discovery of fire that turned man from being just another one of creation's creatures into destruction's most promising child. It is the arrogance of possessing fire that makes him think of the rest of creation as merely food for him to cook and eat. Cooked food has corrupted the soul of man. Isn't it the desire for unending supplies of cooked food that makes him chain his own other half to a life of servitude and drudgery? He wounds himself and then wonders why he bleeds. He suppresses his own mother, sisters, wife and daughters and then rues the growing injustice in his society. He cuts himself off from the sources of goodness in life and then bemoans the evil in the world.

Kaido Langra was a prime example of the race of men. He was convinced that his terrible sin came from the ease with which temptation was strewn across his path. He flagellated himself in the privacy of his thoughts, but not for long. He blamed the deaf-mute girl for being such an easy victim, he held her mother responsible for compromising his soul by leaving her girl unchaperoned to be taken by anyone at will.

But more than them, he blamed his brother. For giving birth to Heer. For giving her the freedom to be who she wished to be, to go where she wanted, to do as she pleased, taunting men with her desirability, making their blood boil with her wantonness. Never again, Kaido swore, would Jhang Syal be vulnerable to a temptress like Heer. Never again would fathers, uncles and brothers be tempted to transgress God's laws.

In the beginning, not everyone in Jhang Syal believed in the new creed that Kaido had begun to preach. Yet, as the months passed, his hold over the town increased. Those who were tolerant at heart began to feel defensive, unsure of their place in the new dispensation. They were scared their own casual attitude in the changed environment might harm their families. Those who started observing the new strictures became more rigid in their adherence every passing day. To enforce the irrational, more irrationality is required. To be cruel on a continued basis calls for an inuring of oneself, further and further from the pain of another. To disrespect another, one must move a great distance away from one's own self, so as to lose sight of the truth that all are born equally deserving of respect.

In the midst of this churning of mentalities and moralities in Jhang Syal, a carrier pigeon arrived from faraway Dilli carrying a message from a father to his son, bearing glad tidings. Sultan rushed with it to his uncle and they both listened silently as the qazi read it out. The Emperor Akbar was impressed by Mir Chuchak's representation. He had been accorded the status of an amir with an additional charge of fifteen hundred horsemen. There was a substantial increase in the jaagirs allotted to him for the purpose of administration and revenue collection. The Syal banner would fly higher than ever before.

In the days that followed the arrival of this missive from Dilli, many carrier pigeons flew from Jhang Syal to neighbouring settlements. Mir Chuchak was not without his share of enemies. He had two cousins from his father's side, Mir Bhulla and Mir Tullia, who were greatly jealous of his increasing power and prestige among the Syals. While ostensibly declaring their allegiance to him, they worked behind the scenes, encouraging the farmers to renege on the payment of their taxes from time to time. There were also a couple of commanders of the forces who resented Chuchak for imposing fines on them for maintaining substandard and underfed horses and poorly trained men in their units. And finally, there was the qazi, who had become a more important man than he could have ever hoped to be while Mir Chuchak was at the helm of affairs. Kaido Langra inveigled upon the qazi to call a secret meeting of these disaffected noblemen and disgruntled commanders.

We flew out with the invitations. We flew in with the acceptances.

A group of five whole men, one cripple, and a young man who found his father's boots too large for him, met three times in the months that followed. The agenda on the table was how to contain the permissiveness in society, how to lead the common population back to a life of piety, how to maintain the independence of the tribe against outside influences.

It must be said, in Sultan's defence, that he had no direct role in the plot against his father. He was a mere pawn in Kaido's manipulations against his older brother. As was the qazi, who unknowingly served to give a veneer of holiness to Kaido's unholy enterprise of gathering his brother's chief enemies together into a confederacy. Kaido would have left them both out of his secret designs except that Sultan was needed to maintain the communication with his father and the qazi was the official scribe.

The first missive that went from Sultan to his father congratulated him on his success in Dilli and informed him that all was well in Jhang Syal. The second missive enquired about his father's plans for returning home. The third missive conveyed a humble entreaty from his uncles, Mir Bhulla and Mir Tullia, that their esteemed cousin should break his journey between Multan and Jhang Syal to partake of their hospitality en route. They wished to hold a feast in his honour in their village. The peasants of their zamindari too would be honoured if the clan chief stopped by and gave them the glad tidings personally.

Their words were pretty, their intentions ugly.

There were wheels within wheels, subplots within plots, devious plans hidden inside of apparent plans that Sultan and the qazi got no whiff of. Only we knew. Only we were privy to the late night gatherings of the conspirators in Kaido's room. We should not have been shocked. Brother has killed brother out of jealousy in the history of humans from the time Qayen killed Habeel. And they were the first pair of brothers known to mankind, the sons of Aadam and Hwa.

Only we knew that Sultan was being made an unsuspecting accomplice in the conspiracy to remove his father from the helm of affairs, indeed from life itself. Only we knew of the deal that Kaido Langra had struck with his two cousins and the two defecting commanders, of ceding administrative and military controls to them in return for the power to exercise moral control over the lives of their people. Only we knew the full extent of his ambitions to usher in a new moral order. If his plans came to fruition, there would be good days ahead for dyers of black cloth and weavers of prayer mats.

Only we knew that the laddoo Kaido would send with Sultan, to sweeten his father's mouth upon his return, would be poisoned.

21

A Man and a Goat

Ranjha did well to tuck me under his arm as he walked out of Jhang Syal forever. Conventional thinking would have you imagine that a man and a dog would make for ideal on-road companions. Or a man and a donkey. Or perhaps a man and a horse. However, dogs, though more devoted than us to their master's feelings, lack a sense of adventure. A dog is not a natural explorer and adventurer like a goat. It likes, after a bit of rushing about chasing birds and squirrels, nothing more than to return to the familiar hearth, the comfortable rug or cool floor of his master's home. A moping, homesick dog is not quite what a man on the road for an indefinite duration needs to keep his spirits high. A female donkey, I concede, would not be a bad choice of a travelling companion. Its milk is rich in nutrition and healing properties. And a donkey is better for carrying a load or offering the occasional ride. But a donkey can't rival a goat's agility, its ability to skip along on nimble feet through narrow, treacherous paths and negotiate mountainous terrain and high cliffs, or its ability to survive on a vast range of thorny shrubs and find food even in the most inhospitable terrain. And as for a horse, let's not even go there. Horses are high-maintenance creatures, definitely not what I would recommend for a poor broken-hearted cowherd with no place to call his own.

It made me giddy with happiness to be on this trip with Ranjha. There is nothing a goat likes better than to travel with a friend or two. Travelling solo is not our thing. It would make a goat bleat in fear and feel helpless to wander without a companion. But unlike our cousins the sheep, we do not have a herd mentality. We don't wish to flock together and spend our lives baa-baaing away inside enclosures. We value our individuality. We are capricious— whimsical, fanciful and fond of change. So off-roading, camping in the open, climbing trees—yes, climbing trees—and trekking and trying out our survival skills under extreme conditions appeals to us. I was more than happy to be giving my milk to Ranjha in exchange for this chance to see the world. It was such ripping good luck to not be in Sanpatti's yard with my brothers and sisters, waiting to become curry, and be out there roughing it out instead and clocking miles under my hooves.

I was also Ranjha's guide to spotting and picking edible berries to eat. In this he tentatively followed my lead, watching what I ate and trying it out for taste. I led him on to interesting discoveries. Not perhaps as interesting and lucrative as the discovery of coffee beans, which my ancestors in Ethiopia led their goatherd friend Kaldi to, but appetising enough and full of essential nutrients. The rule was clear to him. He was to follow my example. If I didn't touch it or go near it, he wasn't to either.

He spoke to me. Miles upon miles of monologue flowed off his tongue. His heart was heavy and I felt good that I could help lighten his load. That is the beauty of travel. Leave two creatures alone and they fall into step with each other, develop an empathy that overcomes barriers of species or creed. In the regimented life of a village or town, each creature is bound to his own role in the economy, his own slot in the social space, caged inside his own narrow conception of the other's place in the scheme of life. But leave them alone on the road, the sky above them and the ground beneath, united by their basic survival needs to find water, food and solace, and they can discover the whole firmament in each other's eyes, the oneness of the soul that permeates the living world.

He called me Nanhi.

'Nanhi,' he said with a sigh during our very first chat, 'whoever wields the stick owns the buffalo.' We were sitting on a knoll together, tired after walking silently for many miles. It was three or four days since we had left Jhang Syal. I did not know which way we were headed. I don't think he did either, but the sun used to rise on our backsides and set in our eyes.

I knew, of course, that he was speaking metaphorically. About power and resources. Those who had the power appropriated what they wanted and others learnt to do without. It was an eye-opener for me. I realised with a shock that what separated man from other species was also what separated man from man. Man hadn't just hijacked the planet from under the noses of the other species but carried the tendency to appropriate by force from his own kind too. Ranjha was heartbroken because his bride, Heer, had been herded into the compound of the Kheras using the stick of wealth. Moreover, his own claims to property, and the power that came with it, had been wrested away through cunning by his brothers. Though he hadn't put up much of a fight either.

He was an idealist, a bit of a dreamer and philosopher. In our many conversations he was trying to understand his own life, figuring out why something as simple and obvious as the bliss he had taken for a given after meeting Heer had eluded him. He had loved Heer, she had loved him, neither of them asked for anything more than to be with each other. Yet, she had been forcibly married off and he had been thrown into the river by her husband's family. Now, separated from her for months by the play of fate, he no longer knew how to reach her and whether she wanted him still.

'Nanhi,' he said to me a few days later. 'The truth of the matter is, I can't deal with the thought of another man in Heer's bed. It makes me physically sick to imagine that owl of a Seida going anywhere near her, let alone touching her and being naked with her. How can Heer even tolerate such an abomination? And yet, had she refused to consummate her marriage she would have been sent back home by now. What use would the Kheras have for a bride who refuses to warm their son's bed?'

I could only bleat in sympathy but it seemed to comfort him somewhat. He wrapped an arm around my neck and buried his head in my back. We sat like that for many minutes listening to each other breathe. If I could speak, I would have told him the sexual politics of a goat pen are even more brutal than that of man's world. The strongest billy just rams through all the available does. Love isn't a variable at all in our mating choices. However, I understood jealousy. There was a lot of it amongst young billy goats, constantly locking horns and head butting each other, mounting each other in sheer frustration while the old buck played the entire field of does on his own.

'Nanhi, am I a selfish cad to think nothing of what she must have to go through to survive in the house of the Kheras, thrust out of her home by her own brother and mother, abandoned by her Ranjha, who promised to rescue her and then disappeared without trace? What is a woman to do in such a situation? A woman is not a man even if she is a warrior like Heer. She still bleeds each month. She cannot simply run away and live a life on the road. Her body's curse goes with her. On those days, she needs a place to be private in. Even a temple or a mosque will not allow her in because she is unclean. Don't you think it is unreasonable, Nanhi, that the Maker should turn his back on the body he created, during those days?'

I stared at him a bit blankly. In our species, the natural cycles just came and went, a signal to begin procreating, nothing else. We didn't think of ourselves as unclean and felt no particular need to hide. In fact, it was the female goat's time of the month to wag her bottom and invite attention. But Sanpatti, I remember, used to be confined to a small, dark room in her house and not allowed to cook, or water the plants, or milk the cattle or goats. For those three or four days she was required to be invisible, for apparently, even her shadow could turn milk rancid and spoil the year's supply of pickles.

'In any case,' Ranjha continued. 'What am I thinking? The life of a travelling beggar isn't what Heer was born for. If that is all my love can offer her, she is better off as a bride of the Kheras. Or is she? Is she truly? Why do we think of nomads as beggars and thieves? Maybe I am a madman, but Nanhi, I sometimes think this whole idea of farming was a huge mistake. We think we own the land, while in fact the land becomes our master. We are constantly tilling, hoeing, weeding, watering and tending to it, in an effort to grow food. What is food anyway but tomorrow's shit? Is our shit any better than yours, or the tiger's or the camel's? We sell our souls to own land, we draw boundaries on it, we beget children to bequeath it to—children who must bear our name to inherit the land that we have put our name to. And yet, that does not bring us peace. We constantly fear the man who does not have our good fortune and may covet it.'

I sighed deeply. Man certainly had no reason to fear goats. Our lives were fully surrendered to his needs. We did not have the tools to win any argument against the race of men—axes, saws, daggers, butcher's knives.

'It doesn't end here, does it,' he continued. 'We pay taxes, keep armies, go to war for the sake of this land. Some men become kings and soldiers, others toiling peasants to meet the demands the desire for land makes on us. The peasant lives in fear of being wiped out by the king's fury, the king goes to bed scared of being murdered while he sleeps by the peasant's envy. We imagine we are planting and sowing just crops, but the truth is we also sow fear and reap mutual hatred in our greed for growing more and more food.'

He was being romantic, utopian and impractical perhaps, in wishing for earlier, less complicated times. But I could see his point. Domestication does that to you even while it gives you more assured access to food and a more secure environment. In the goat pen, we were well fed but constantly afraid. We were scared of each other, of boredom, of man, of being milked dry, of becoming meat. These few days of the open sky and the limitless earth had lifted my spirits. The surprises of the road, the unpredictable weather and changing topography brought my senses to a fine alert and made me skip as I had never known I could. We may not have had abundant amounts to eat, but we hadn't slept hungry, or at least, intolerably hungry, on any day. Perhaps all of us creatures need less food and more happiness than we imagine.

It is possible that appetite expands in response to the availability of food. Plenty creates its own hungers. Because we see too much, we want excessively. And maybe a happy heart overflows and fills the stomach too, making it less demanding. Of course, in our case, we only had one happy heart between the two of us. Ranjha's heart was full of sorrow for Heer.

'Nanhi, without the air that flows through it, what is a flute but a useless piece of bamboo riddled with holes? What is an ektara without the hand that plucks at its string? What is a conch shell without the breath that blows into it? What is a drum without the sticks that beat it? What is a boat without oars? A river without its banks? How does it serve the world to separate two parts of a whole that are rendered useless without each other? What in the whole world is worth gaining if the music inside us is lost?'

Go back to your music, Ranjha, wanted to tell him. It had been a mistake to chuck away his flute. Heer was lost to him. Music wasn't. He was confusing the issue. You don't cut off your second limb to protest against being deprived of the first one. His music would have healed him, kept him going, helped him sublimate his sorrow and rise above it. But then, he did not want to be healed. He wanted a grand, all-consuming grief, the kind that would kill him and release him from the need to go on.

'What was more precious to her than the laughter on Heer's lips, the smile in her eyes, the glow on her daughter's face, that

Malki should throw her only daughter into the arms of strangers? However much gold the Kheras load her bosom with, will it ever compensate for the lack of her lover's touch?' he continued on his own caravan of thoughts.

He ranted against Malki and Sultan. I had learnt from Sanpatti's chatter with her friends that Kaido Langra was the real villain of the piece. However, Ranjha seemed to have no rancour against him. I guess he had expected such treachery from Kaido, but he had naively viewed Heer's mother and brother as future family to be loved. Their actions baffled and hurt him.

'You know, Nanhi, I wouldn't confess this to another human being, but I can say it to you without fear of being judged. I was momentarily tempted by Hassi's offer. Heer and Seida. Ranjha and Hassi. Maybe she shuts her eyes tight in his bed and thinks of me as she climaxes. I could have done the same—held Heer in my imagination even as I gave my body to Hassi. This whole question of what to do next, where to go now would have been answered,' he said. 'You and I would not have been on the road like this.'

It would have worked, I suppose. Hassi was unattached, not betrothed as Heer was. Ranjha was high-born enough; a cowherd only for Heer's love.

'Maybe I should think of becoming a part-time lover to young women with a taste for social outcasts. How's that for a career, Nanhi? Stay a few days here, a few weeks there ... find Heer in the glint of one woman's nose pin and the swing of another's plait. I could spend a lifetime searching for the scent of her in every girl I meet, catching a whiff of her in someone's hair, another glimpse in some other's swaying gait, perhaps in the sound of anklets hitting the ground, or the spreading of lampblack beneath a pair of drowsy eyes. Instead of one Heer I could re-imagine a world full of Heers Everywhere I look, I would see her,' he mused.

I bleated out a high-pitched warning. That seemed like the fastest route to being beaten into pulp.

'Oh, I'd get out of there when they discover I am only half a man, my heart missing from the frame. Heck, if I'm lucky, their brothers and fathers may come in pursuit of me and I might even get killed for my troubles.'

I looked at him, a mute spectator as he went on.

'I really don't think Heer is so shallow or fickle as to develop a love for the wealth of the Kheras over and above her devotion to me. It is not for nothing that she calls me her murshid, though you might think it strange for a woman to think of her lover as her spiritual guide. But Nanhi, sometimes one person's touch can awaken the snake of consciousness that sits at the base of another's spine and send it revolving through the energy centres of the heart and third eye and open them up to a knowing of the divinity that dwells within. I am that person for Heer. And yet, I can't help but wonder, what if Seida's touch has also left its imprint upon her by now? What if she is already with child? There is no Mithi there to help her with that business,' he said. His face was cupped in the palms of his hands, his elbows rested on his knees, as he squatted against a thorny, leafless acacia. The expression in his eyes was bleak.

I had to concede that his fears were not unfounded. If the love of Ranjha was to wage a war against the compulsions of motherhood in Heer's heart, who could say which would win? Motherhood changes not just the contours of a woman's body but also floods her being with an overarching maternal instinct. And in man's world, children belong with the father, his name stamped upon theirs. Goats, of course, don't care too much about paternity. We have no property to bequeath.

Though I recount our conversations at one stretch, they took place over months. The rainy season yielded to a brief season of leaf fall and then the winter was upon us. More and more we left the deserted stretches of road and tended towards the warmth of villages with their offer of a hot meal or a warm fire to gossip around and an enclosed barn to sleep in. There was much allure to starlit nights, the stars hanging so low and bright that you imagined they twinkled only for you and the man sleeping by your side, his unruly locks covering his forehead, his arm flung out at an upward angle. But the charm of sleeping under a starry sky was beginning to wane. I could feel the chill in my bones and we woke up with dew on our skin, shivering slightly.

We halted at a village engaged in preparing the land for the sowing of winter gram. Ranjha offered to work in the fields in exchange for a few days of food and lodging. It seemed like a good way to keep ourselves warm and well-fed as the days shortened and the evenings became nippy. However, I wish we hadn't stopped, for it is here that he met the naked jogi with the torn earlobe. With his bare ash-smeared chest, his long hair tied in a top knot, his ears pierced and adorned with earrings, his chillum billowing out a sweet smoke around his head and his eyes drowsy and half shut all the time, the jogi made for a startling sight.

Night after night I saw Ranjha seeking out his company and directing question after question at him, which he answered in a voice that rose and sank, peaked and plateaued and went on for hours on end. I was jealous, extremely jealous. The jogi seemed to have answers for him, something I had never been able to give him, in our many conversations over the months.

And then, as suddenly as it had begun, my life as a travelling goat came to an end. He hugged me and wept as he took my leave. He was gifting me to his host in the village.

'Nanhi, you have been my best friend ever in this life. I will always be indebted to you,' he said. He was headed to Tilla Jogian, to see if the great Balnath Yogi would accept him as a follower and agree to initiate him into the secret practices of his sect.

There was nothing left for me to do but wait for Eid in this village of strangers.

VIII

BEING AN ASCETIC

22

At Tilla Jogian

AFTER OVER A MONTH and a half of walking north along the right
bank of the Jhelum, I reached my destination. The Hill of the Jogis
stands at a distance from the highlands of the Salt Range, on a
solitary spur rising 1000 metres above sea level, the highest peak in
the vicinity. On the top of the hill stands the ancient monastery, a
complex of domed temples, square courtyards and pillared halls built
out of grey sandstone. The entire hermitage is silhouetted against
an azure blue sky, and covered in the shade of wild olive, pistachio
and pine trees. There are semul trees too, their silky bare white arms
lifted to the sky, waiting to burst into flame at the touch of spring.

The sound of mantras reverberated in the air, a low distant
mumble floating to my ears. I began my slow, laboured ascent up to
the hallowed monastery, which went back at least sixteen centuries
or more. It was here that Guru Goraknath had started the order of
the Kunphatta jogis. The same Great Gorakhnath who had rescued
Puran, Prince of Sialkot, from the well he had been thrown into by
his father Salwan at the behest of his stepmother Loona, and restored
to him his severed limbs. Puran had turned down the offer to reclaim
his father's kingdom and sought instead to be initiated as a follower
of the jogi. It was to Goraknath and this hermitage that Bhartari,
the ruler of Ujjain, had come after abdicating his crown in favour

of his younger brother, Vikramaditya. Clearly, greater men than me had given up the world and come to this sanctuary seeking peace.

The last fifty years had seen the area around the hill becoming militarised. The heavy boots of soldiers and the flying hooves of horses had trampled all over these parts in recent times. Sher Shah Suri, the wily Pakhtun, had ordered the building of the mighty Rohtas Qila on a cleft in the mountain, just a few miles north of the Tilla, to prevent the return of Humayun after having routed him in the Battle of Kanauj and forced him to flee to Persia. Millions of rupees were spent by Raja Todar Mal to get this fort up against the resistance of the local Gakkars, who were fiercely loyal to the Mughals. Todar Mal paid as much as one gold asharfi per stone cut to the labourers who dared work there against the diktats of the Gakkar chief, Sarang Khan. Yet Sher Shah Suri, at whose command the Qila was built, died after seeing the fort only once. Ten years after Sher Shah's death, when Humuyan crossed the Jhelum again to reclaim the kingdom that Babar had established, the Rohtas Qila, so formidable from the outside, was already deserted inside. I had learnt from gossip along the road that Akbar's brother-in-law Raja Mansingh used it as a summer home now.

Temporal power can come and go like that in a matter of decades. Spiritual power endures. The renown of the current guru of Tilla Jogian, Balnath, rivalled that of Goraknath Baba of fifteen-sixteen centuries ago. And I was headed to his seat, seeking to be initiated into the Siddha practices of the Nath jogis.

Though they were followers of Shiva, the Nath jogis were held in affection by the pirs and walis of Islam too. They did not worship idols of gods and goddesses as other Hindus do, but instead sought to realise their own powers, perfecting their bodies through asanas and controlling their mind through mantras and meditation. It was this mastery over the self that I had come seeking. I wanted the arrogance of one who has nothing left to lose, similar to the kind I had witnessed in the naked fakir I had met during my stay in a

village a few weeks ago. There he was with scarcely a loincloth on
his person, with no idea of where his next meal would come from,
and yet he walked with the pride of a conqueror, for he had won
the greatest battle there is to be won. He had conquered his own
fears and established dominion over his own desires.

What had the love of Heer Syal given me in contrast? I was an
abject, fearful creature even in my own eyes, listless, self-pitying and
full of sorrows. My desire for her held me in its grip, making of me
a madman who lived only in his dreams. In the real world everything
had the power to hurt me—a passing remark, the tinkling of cow
bells, the singing of cicadas, the changing weather—so fragile was
my sense of self. When I saw the kunphatta sadhu walk through
the street for the first time, I knew he had something I wanted.
Invulnerability. The power to reject the world. I wanted that
power for myself. I wanted the power to reject the many worlds
which had for one reason or another excluded me—the world of
the Ranjhas of Takht Hazara, the Syals of Jhang, the Kheras of
Rangpur, the world of kings and emperors, the world of ordinary
men. I wanted nothing from any of these worlds. Not food and
shelter, not sweethearts, not approval, not kindness, not largesse. I
wanted self-mastery. The ability to walk naked through the world,
knowing it was mine to take or leave as I wished, every moment
in time detached from the moment that preceded it, my whole life
complete unto itself, in each and every instant.

I prostrated before the great Balnath Jogi, my knees on the cold
stone floor before him, my head at his feet, my hands stretched out
with the palms joined together in supplication.

'Lift up your head, boy, and look me in the eye,' he said.

His forehead was six inches wide, almost half his face. It sat atop
a too-long, aquiline nose. His eyes were rolled upwards towards the
sky, their whites speckled with a fierce bloody red. His outer ears
were adorned with a succession of gold rings. His hair flowed jet
black and straight to mid waist. He looked ageless and powerful.

I straightened up, my hands still folded respectfully before him. I felt tremulous in the waves of energy emanating out of him.

'What brings you here? Let me see. Family quarrels? Disputes over land? Jealousy? Girl trouble? All of these, one after the other? You think becoming a jogi is an easy escape route? That this place is a refuge from worldly troubles? You are fed up of being tossed around by life and think Balnath Baba is going to mollycoddle you, apply balm on your wounds, rock you in his arms till you fall into peace. Go away, young fool, this isn't a hospice for the hurt and maimed. We don't take damaged goods here. This isn't a patchwork unit. This is where the brave come to become invincible.'

A sob escaped my throat. My eyes stung with tears at the truth of his accusation. It was true I was a beaten and damaged piece of humanity looking for an escape route. Yet, to admit it would be to be turned away from here after these arduous months of walking and hoping. I had to convince him that I belonged at his feet, that I was worthy of his tutelage.

'I cannot lie to you who sees through the veneer of all things and into the heart of life itself. It is true that I left my father's house with a broken heart, cheated of my inheritance by my jealous brothers and their conniving wives. It is also true that I have loved a woman deeply and have been left bereft of my beloved who is now the wife of another man. And that is not the full sum of all I have lost. I have lost my faith too. I, who trusted the boat of my life to the blessings of the Panj Pir, sure that they would guide it to the shore safely, no longer believe in their love for me or its power to overcome all obstacles in my path. I stand before you shorn of love, faith and hope,' I said in a breath.

He stared straight ahead, his expression giving nothing away. I rushed on.

'But I am no coward. I am brave. And I wish to be invincible. Do not send me away without testing me. There is a fire inside me which will leap alive at your touch. Take this dry wood, O guru, and ignite it with your spark and see how brightly it burns.'

'Your words are pleasing like your face. Yet, the sons of landowners make poor disciples in my experience. Their insides are soft,' he said. 'And their heartbeat erratic. Their stomachs growl too easily at the thought of cooked food, their pulse races too fast at the sight of comely women.'

'Nothing you say is untrue, but there are layers and layers to each being. I do not deny those layers shrouded my personality once. But I have cast them off and left them behind me on the road of life. The fineness of a feast, the softness of a bed, the loveliness of a woman no longer mean anything to me,' I said. 'I am done chasing the pleasures of the world, I now seek only to know the ecstasy inside of me.'

I saw his eyebrows move almost imperceptibly. Just the slightest of twitches in his forehead muscles told me my answer had not gone unnoticed. I just had to push home the advantage and I would have him for my guru.

My eyes fell on the spiral conch shell lying to his right. The oldest wind instrument in the world, extant in the world from the time of the great ocean churning, the sound of ocean waves present inside it, even now, in this mountain monastery miles away from any sea. There it lay beckoning to me, the father of the flute which had rescued me at every critical juncture in my life. In what I knew was an act of extreme audacity, and likely to have me thrown out should I fail, I leaned over and picked it up and put it to my lips.

The sound of the brahma naada, the cosmic hum, filled the air, starting as a low, barely audible rumble and expanding in concentric circles, out, out, out, further out, till it contained inside of it the entire monastery. The Hill of the Jogis stood as if suspended in time, not a leaf stirring. Finally, I put the conch down and met his eyes, which were now directed straight at me. They were a glistening grey, the colour of river gravel from a high mountain stream.

'You are already a jogi,' he said. There was tenderness in his gaze. My heart leapt for the joy of it. I, who had been so disenfranchised by life for so many months, now had a master, a refuge and a purpose.

'Teach me, Nath, what lies inside of me,' I said, resting my head at his feet in obeisance again.

The rigours of the next six months are beyond description. The macrocosm and the microcosm are one. The endless universe of stars, planets and space, oceans, lakes and rivers, mountains, plateaus and plains is only a projection of the infinitude inside. The outer world and the inner body are mirrors to each other's complexity. The organs, glands, energy centres, blood vessels and nerves come together in the body to form a universe of infinite intelligence and endless possibilities. What I knew of myself was worth less than a fingernail compared to the body of knowledge available to the great jogis. The intrepid explorer sets out to climb a peak or discover a lost river. The spiritual aspirant sits in silence, waiting for the mountain to bow before him, the vanished river to come seeking him, for he knows it cannot have a life outside if it isn't already mapped inside his consciousness.

Many lifetimes can be spent learning the geography of the soul's house. There are nine gateways to the inner abode—two eyes, two ears, two nostrils, the mouth, the anus and the sex organ. The average householder spends his lifetime at these doorways to the self, looking outwards. The jogi learns to train his gaze inwards. He learns to still his body, sitting in vajra asana, till his body loses sight of itself, of pain and of the memory of pain, becoming nothing more than a channel for his breath. He then learns to watch his breath. *So*, in, *ham*, out. *Soham*. Twenty-one thousand six hundred complete breaths pass through his nostrils every single day. Twenty-one thousand six hundred separate moments to check the surging of thoughts and fall into an awareness of the infinite are available to him. Each moment won is a step closer to the kingdom within. He also learns *kumbak*, the science of holding his breath, for eternity lies in the gap between two successive breaths.

It is only after the disciple is established in the practice of stillness and a constant awareness of his breath that the guru initiates him into the knowledge of chakras and mudras and techniques for awakening the coiled serpent at the base of the spine and training it to rise slowly up to the crown chakra. Prana and apana, in-breath and out-breath, blend at the naval centre and the awakening begins, activating the lower centres first and then slowly rising up. Worlds unfold before the jogi's eyes, spiritual powers manifest at his command, music and madness rage through his being as each energy chakra expands and spins out to its fullness, activating the one above it sequentially.

At any given time, there were about eighty to one hundred of us at the hermitage, at various stages of our practice. Some sat in groups, while others preferred to be alone, practising stillness and controlling the breath, or the correct enunciation of mantras. There were group discourses and collective meditations that went on from new moon to full moon. We fed sparsely on fruits, nuts and milk and wore no clothes. To be naked is not difficult. After the first few hours it ceases to seem unusual. Shame is a conditioned response. It arises not from our actions but from the gap between actions and expectations. When the expectation of clothes gets shed, left without a place to stand, the shame too falls off. In conditions of extreme cold, we gathered wood from the surrounding forest and lit bonfires. However, at most times, privation, austerity and self-reliance were the norm. We grew our own food and took turns tending to the cleaning of the premises.

Despite the hardship, there was a free flow of music and mirth. Marijuana too. Madness was not frowned upon. Many lost their head for a few days or a few months, muttering, abusing and running wildly along the hallways or in the surrounding forest, as the purgatory fires awakened inside them through the initiation process threatened to consume them. Others sat doused in a haze of sweet cannabis, smoking away, taking a break from the process of becoming enlightened, just watching time float in a diffused yellow haze around their heads.

I came to this fountain of knowledge feeling soul-deprived and with an all-consuming thirst to rise above the circumstances of my life. I wished to be an elevated being, above passions, beyond pain. My progress earned me the approval of the senior jogis.

Some spent months at the Tilla, others years, before their ears were bored by Baba Balnath and adorned with hoops in the final transfer of Shakti from master to disciple. After that they were free to roam the world as they pleased, the sign of a Nath yogi on them earning them the fear and respect of common folk wherever they went. Some chose to be itinerant sadhus all their lives, roaming through the populace casting birth charts, dispensing healing herbs, predicting futures and performing minor miracles. Others set up their own deras in far-flung corners of the world, becoming masters in their own right. Yet others vanished into distant mountain caves and became self-realised mystics, bairaagis, with no relationship to the world. The last of these was my goal. I dreamt of travelling northwards to Kashmir and disappearing into the snow-clad mountains, my connection with the world severed for this lifetime.

It was in the month of June, nearly a year since I had been separated from Heer, that the hallucinations began. Every time I left the main hall alone, a crow would appear in my line of vision. And not any crow. I was sure it was the crow from the neem tree in Jhang Syal. It followed me into the forest, its eyes boring into mine as I did my morning ablutions. It sat on the parapet of the well when I went to draw water for my bath, it flapped its wings to draw my attention when I went to collect firewood. Yet, no one else seemed to see him. Only when I was alone did I see the crow. I was certain I was imagining him. At night, as I slept, he spoke in my dreams. *Rush to Rangpur, fool. She needs you urgently.*

It was only a few days before my final initiation. Suddenly, a storm of memories came cascading through me. Then a torrent of thoughts and a flood of tears followed. Who was I without Heer Syal? What was I doing here on this mountain so far away from her? What were we all trying to do here anyway? Trying to achieve a union of Shiv and Shakti inside of us? What if the entire hypothesis was completely flawed? Shiv's Parvati wasn't a concept in his mind, she was a living creature by his side, wasn't she? It was from his dialogue with her that the entire science of self-realisation was born. Why then would Ranjha be required to be without his Heer?

I thought of all the women in my life. My mother, who had given me the gifts of life and milk. My sisters and sisters-in-law, who had variously loved, hated, pampered, teased and bullied me, and helped me grow into the man I became. I thought of Sahiba, her tart tongue and waspish ways and our days of friendship. She had wanted to fix me up with her younger sister. From this distance, it no longer seemed like a great crime, misplaced affection at the most. I thought of Nikki and Wadi, Luddan's twin wives who had helped me cross the river. I thought of Heer's band of cousins and friends who had made our love possible with their vigilant guarding of our trysts in the forests outside Jhang Syal. I thought of Hassi, who had rescued me as I lay dying by the riverbank and of Fattiya, who had repaired my broken bone. Sonia and Sanpatti and the woodseller's two girls—Mirran and Bano—who had nursed me back to wholeness. What a cad I was to believe that I would become a superior being by excluding women from my life!

The apparition of the crow made me fall into a deep well of doubt. If Heer was in trouble and needed me, did anything else matter? Yet, I was only two days away from my initiation. It was too late to renege. I feared the anger of Balnath Baba. I feared being seen as a deserter from the ranks, an ingrate.

On the appointed day, I bathed and prostrated myself at the guru's feet. He raised me and pierced my ears, adorning them with rings. I stood rigid with pain and resolve. A few drops of blood trickled down to the floor from my pierced earlobes. He began to administer the vow of celibacy. I was to repeat after him that henceforth all women would be mothers and sisters to me.

The vision of Heer's face, ill and transfigured with grief, flashed before my mind's eyes. *She was dying.* And then plop!

My crown chakra had a liberal splotch of crow shit on it. The crow was for real, after all. It had burst into the main hall and splattered its protest over my head. That's what it thought of my taking the vow of celibacy.

'Forgive me, O Guru,' I heard myself saying, 'As Gauri is to Shankar, Heer is to Ranjha. I cannot take your vow of celibacy. Release me from it, O Nath, before it is too late. This path is not for Ranjha. Send me with your blessings on the road that leads me to Heer.'

IX

WHAT SEHTI SAID

23

Memories and Dreams

DREAMS AND MEMORIES—MUCH of my early life was spent between these two. Before my brother's bride came to live with us, I did not have much use for reality. I made good my escape from it as quickly as I could, disappearing for hours on end into imagined games or impossible futures. On most days, the present was too much for me to bear. My father's temper was a thunderstorm one day—full of lightning, drama and livid rain, which left my mother and us soaked in tears—and the next day it was a desert wind—hot, dry, and unrelenting, leaving us parched and sapped of all strength. Like an arbitrary weather god he kept changing the micro-climate of our home, tossing us from one extreme to another every few hours or days, as the mood took him, even as my mother struggled to maintain the calm and shield us from the worst. I think of my mother as an awning, trying to protect my brothers and me from the harsh sun, pelting rain or torrential winds. I saw her becoming more tattered and beaten over the years, and sometimes just collapsing upon us, unequal to the task.

It is difficult to make friends in such a situation. As if the violent words tripping off my father's tongue hung permanently in the air around me, audible to everyone I met. My own words came out in ragged, watchful whispers when I was a child, scared that if I did not screen them before letting them escape my lips, the illicit words from my father's vocabulary might rush out to replace them. And then no one would ever want to be my friend. Yet, I did not lack for friendship. I had my two older brothers and five cousins, my uncle's children who shared the house with us. We were a sufficient universe unto ourselves with our shared canopy of a sky dense with verbal abuse.

However, little by little everyone was lost, only mother and I remained. My older brother Rajju was engaged to my cousins' cousin from their mother's side. Imarti, my aunt's brother's daughter, was the sweetest, liveliest girl imaginable. She would visit her aunt's house often and during those times, she and my brother were inseparable. They were constantly sitting in the stairwell holding hands and talking, her thick long-lashed eyes looking up at him in utter devotion, his ears hanging on to her every word. My mother already loved her like a daughter, I like a sister. There were grand plans for the wedding. Seida, too, was betrothed to Heer Syal. As my uncle had no sons of his own, only five daughters, he had offered his nephew's hand for her when the Syals showed interest in an alliance with our family.

However, before Rajju and Imarti's wedding could take place, my father and my uncle had a falling out over some business matter and my father in his rage declared that our two families would not speak with each other again. I lost my five cousins on a single night, the year I turned ten. We woke up to big brass locks hanging from doors that had always swung freely between the two sides of the house. My aunt, always a taciturn woman with a delicate constitution, retreated into a wounded sulk. My uncle made a few tentative attempts to persuade my father not to mix business dealings with family matters but was beaten back into a heartbroken silence by the force of his brother's fury.

The engagement was called off and the couple forbidden from seeing each other again. It was Rabel, the family maid, who found them lying dead with their arms around each other in the storeroom where the quilts were kept. Unwilling to be separated, they had taken poison together in a suicide pact. I still remember the sound of the maid's scream filling the whole house. We were forbidden by my father to ever take my older brother's name again. The lovers died together but were buried separately in hushed-up burials and the silence between my uncle's family and ours now became a mile-high wall of mutual blame, which could never be dismantled or scaled.

My uncle took the quarrel with his brother to heart. The dispute between the families was the beginning of his decline into a listlessness which got worse with every passing year. His pigeon loft, built with an all-consuming passion for breeding beautiful pairs of birds, fell into a state of total neglect. The pigeons died or flew away to make their homes all over the town, as it pleased them. Sometimes, an occasional beauty with a turquoise throat or a perfect fantail still alights on our rooftop, a talisman from the forgotten days.

My cousins were married off over the years but we did not receive invitations to the weddings. My aunt died of one of the many aches, pains and fevers she had nursed assiduously through her life. My father forbade my mother to attend the burial. My uncle lives alone with his servants. The sound of his lonely, rasping cough through the night does not seem to disturb my father's sleep. Some men thrive on enmity, it swells their pride, makes them feel indomitable. My father is one of them.

Once upon a time, my brother Seida and I were good friends. Although he was several years older than I was, he did not treat me like a child unworthy of his attention. He liked the imaginary games I devised and entered into them with an enthusiasm matching mine. I like to think I had a talent. We didn't just play marbles or spin tops or fly kites. We fought historic battles, time-travelled into the future, and discovered new galaxies as we played with these things. In this imaginary world of mine, a marble was a foot soldier in Porus's army, a spinning top was a time machine and kites of course were emissaries to other planets. But the year he turned seventeen and began to sprout hair on his chin and speak in a deeper voice, Seida lost interest in my rooftop playground and deserted me for a new friend. He fell completely in the thrall of Meru, the groom boy. In their boyish bantering and horsing around, there was no place for me. I watched with forlorn eyes as my brother stole out from the house to be with his new friend, never seeming to get enough of his company.

My soul is smudged with Meru's blood. I have tried many times to forgive myself. I was only a child, less than twelve years old. I had lost my only remaining childhood companion and was feeling jealous and bereft. I could not possibly have imagined the extreme step my father was capable of. But nothing changes the fact that it was I who squealed to my father about Seida's morning swims with Meru. I only wanted my brother back. Though Seida never found out who carried the tale to my father, I lost my brother. He was never the same after Meru died. From a friendly boy Seida became a man with a shifting gaze overnight. If my mother or I could look into his eyes, we might find again the son and brother we lost the day Seida found Meru's head floating in the pond, separated from his torso, the waters a deep crimson. But his eyes elude us. His gaze rests on our toes or our hands or upon the furniture or on the walls as he speaks, it refuses to meet the solicitousness in our eyes, it declines to acknowledge our concern for him. Years have passed since the incident, but we live in its shadow still.

Since then, Seida has lived like a stranger in our midst, coming home to bathe and sleep, spending his waking hours following my father's orders at work or with friends in town. I had hoped his wedding would change things for us all. Heer Syal was reputed to be the most beautiful woman in the land. I thought my brother would be completely smitten with such a bride and we would see more of him at home, drawn back into the family fold by his lovely wife's charms. I had imagined she would be like Imarti, vivacious and friendly, her laughter spilling into the empty spaces in our hearts, her beauty dispelling the gloom that had settled into our lives.

In my daydreams, I saw us sitting on the rooftop, Heer and I, oiling each other's hair and weaving strings of fresh white scented flowers to wear in our plaits. I saw us nattering over the fire as we cooked the evening meal together, giving old Rabel a much needed break. I saw us dressing up and walking arm in arm, exploring the shops in the marketplace, buying coloured bangles and silver toe rings as the fancy took us. I saw her blushing and giggling as my brother manoeuvred to get her out of my clutches and into his own arms, beckoning her away beseechingly to the privacy of their bedroom. I saw my mother's eyes fill with gentle hope as she fussed and fretted over a daughter-in-law heavy with her first child.

I thought I would confide in her of my secret love for Murad and she would draw my head against her shoulder, stroke my hair gently and let me sob my heart out. And then she would tell me that love is an impractical, impossible girlish dream and how it was best I forget him and marry a good man of my parents' choice as she had done. I had thought she would teach me to be a real woman, fluid, flexible, ever-yielding.

She came. She looked at us briefly. She looked away.

It was as if we did not exist. We became invisible in our own home. She looked at no one. She spoke to no one. Indifferent to everyone and everything, even to her own flaming beauty, she stood splendid and solitary at the window of her room, gazing out into the distance. She positioned herself on the rooftop, as distant from the denizens of the house as the moon in the sky. As lovely too.

I had been brought up to believe that sorrow, like menstruation, was something women were meant to suffer in secret, hidden from the eyes of the world. The everyday suffering of women was as ineluctable as their bleeding each month, and as inappropriate to show. Good women did not reveal tear-stained faces or blood-stained clothes, besmirching the reputation of their families with untoward displays of the weaknesses of their minds and bodies. They wept, like they bled, in quiet, darkened rooms and emerged out of them only when they were clean again, clear of all tell-tale signs of bodily fluids.

I had heard that Heer was a brave woman—that she and her friends used to go dashing about the countryside on their horses, armed and dressed for battle, that she was respected and feared by the common people in the villages around Jhang, that she had once taken on the nobleman Noora and wrested his personal boat away for her own use. However, it was none of these tales that convinced me of her bravery. It was the way she wore her grief out in the open that left me awestruck. She did not pretend to be happy, or behave politely, or hide her pain away discreetly. She grieved in the manner of one who believed that she was entitled to her feelings. What made her a revolutionary in my eyes was the fact that my sister-in-law believed that it was not her job alone to defer to the world. That it was equally the world's job to earn her pleasure. I could not think of another woman like her in my experience.

I cannot say I took to her immediately. It would take an angel's temperament (or my mother's all-forgiving heart) to love someone who is so dismissive of your existence and I was no angel. I resented her sorrow. We had not caused it, why was she inflicting it on us?

Angry as I was about her rejection of us, I could not rid myself of my fascination for her. I watched her all the time, unable to fathom her intensity and yet drawn irresistibly to it. What must it be like, I wondered, to possess a heart that beat to its own compulsions? How could a woman dare to stand so alone and upright and not be scared of inciting the wrath of men and God alike? And yet, when I watched her with my father, the most fearsome man I knew, I realised that it was his eyes that turned away from hers in discomfort, her gaze remained clear and straight. Her courage was real and came from somewhere deep within.

Ironically, we became friends only because of my father. One day, as we were hanging out the washing on the rooftop, I saw her completely shaken as the sudden volley of abuse from my father's mouth flew up to the air around us. Heer looked completely out of her depth. His uncouth words seemed to affect her, to pierce even her seemingly impenetrable exterior. For the first time since she had come, I felt tenderness for her well up in my heart. She was only a girl, just a little older than I was, and she was all alone in a new family, hundreds of miles away from her parents and her childhood friends. I thought she could use a bit of sisterly guidance.

The thawing of the silence between us was for a long, long while a one-way phenomenon. I spoke, she kept quiet. But I knew that she was listening and was no longer indifferent to my company, and therefore I carried on speaking. Also, I was bursting at the seams. I had held my secret inside my heart for too long. I needed to tell someone about Murad, to rescue him from the world of my dreams and memories and make of him a real person. Till I could not speak of him to anyone, it was as if he did not exist.

Every year at the start of winter, the Balochi caravans came down from the high mountain passes and the cold deserts in the north-west to our more salubrious southern climes. As soon as news of the sighting of the first camel train reached our ears, hoards of children from Rangpur gathered and ran out to watch them arrive. Line upon line of camels would arrive over the next few weeks, carrying upon their backs whole families, household belongings like beds, bedding, cooking pots and pans, and huge trunks of goods for trading. They settled on the outskirts of Rangpur, selling their wares of wool, butter, pistachios, dried figs, almonds and pine nuts to the locals. There were more exotic wares too. Frankincense and wild dates from Arabia, muslins from Europe, carved ivory from Africa, which they obtained through trade with other caravans they had crossed along the way. These they would carry to sell to nobles and rich gentry in Dilli and Kolikata. They stayed for ten–fifteen days, grazing their camel and sheep and exchanging goods in town, selling some and buying others, while the children of Rangpur gawked at them in wonder. The tall, turbaned, hawk-nosed men with their flowing robes, the women with their bright loose-fitting embroidered long shirts and loose trousers, the children who it was rumoured were required to bathe only once a year, the strange tongue they spoke, filling and renting the air like the sound of a flock of wild birds cooing and mating—all these were a source of endless fascination to us.

It is not clear whether I started stalking Murad first or he started stalking me. There was a boy on a camel whose eyes met mine and I looked away. Only to look back again. He smiled, a toothy, lopsided smile laced with impudence. Every day after that, my eyes went in search of his, a huge excitement building up inside me as we locked glances. I waited each year for the camel caravans to arrive and ran down to see if the boy was there and whether his eyes would still seek mine out and smile at me. I spotted him in our street once and walked the length of the market with deliberate steps, never once looking back but making sure that he was following me. There was a warmth on my back and my plait swung to my gait as it had never done before. I would do it again and again, over the next few days, as I led him down a maze of streets and he followed, not once losing sight of me.

The streets I led Murad down, the corners I peeped out at him from to see if he was still following, the shops I artfully stopped at to let him catch up with me, remained lit up in my mind's eye months after the Balochi caravans left. Every place that he had walked behind me made my heart race when I walked past it again. The days after the caravan left our town rolled along dull and indistinguishable from each other, turning into weeks and months without any relevance for me. I lived inside the snatches of time I had stolen away from my life and spent zig-zagging through the streets of our neighbourhood with Murad walking behind me, reliving those bright-hued moments again and again.

Despite the fact that I flirted with him and should have anticipated what came next, I was completely shocked when he stood before me last winter, a full grown man (admittedly, the most handsome I had ever seen) proffering me the gift of a topaz blue sarig, the head scarf worn by Balochi women, and asking me to marry him. I shook my head at him mutely.

'Run away with me. My people will welcome you with open arms,' he said. 'We make much fuss of new brides, spoil them with love and attention. You will be happy amidst us.'

I stood there transfixed with terror. Suddenly the dance I had been leading him through the years had stopped mid-step and its consequences stood looking me in the face.

'You are scared?' he asked.

I nodded in affirmation. It was too big a leap into the unknown.

'I do not know you,' I whispered.

'I see this is too sudden for you. When the caravan returns to Kuhetta in spring, I will stay back for a couple of months on the pretext of some work in these plains. Then we can meet again. Perhaps, after you know me better, you will agree,' he said. He bowed formally and left.

I stood there clutching the blue headscarf, my entire being in upheaval as I watched him walk away. Was I in love with him? Was he in love with me? Was love, then, not a game one played in one's head but a real thing which demanded actual decisions and irrevocable actions? The thought of running away with him filled me with deep panic. It meant never seeing my mother or my home again. It meant leaving the familiar vocabulary of my childhood days and learning to speak in a strange tongue, leaving the comfortable food my palate loved for unknown tastes, abandoning the sedate home-bound life I had been raised to live for unending adventure on the road. Everything in my heart wanted to say no to Murad's proposal except my heart itself.

Spring had come to Rangpur this year and brought with it an importunate Murad. He and his camel had set up a solitary camp on the outskirts of town and awaited my answer.

I still did not know what my answer was. I had hoped Heer would offer me counsel, tell me what to do.

She listened woodenly to my story.

'Heer, what should I do?' I asked her.

'How can I tell you what you should do? We are such different people. You are scared of a life based on love, I fear a life without love more than I fear anything else,' she said.

'Can love be trusted? Will it not vanish as suddenly as it has arisen, fade away and die, leaving in its wake only disappointment? Will Murad turn out to be the person I dream he is, or will he be entirely different? What if I disappoint him? What if he is not how I imagine him to be? What if everything goes horribly wrong?' I asked.

'Your mother married the man her parents chose for her. Did everything go absolutely right for her? There are no guarantees in life, Sehti. Either way, one takes one's chances. It is for you to decide which regrets you are willing to live with and which you aren't,' she replied.

She was not being much help.

As Murad waited for my answer, spring was slowly giving way to summer. I pleaded for some more time.

24

A Death and a Revelation

THE NEWS OF HEER's father's death came to us like a bolt out of the blue, sudden and cataclysmic.

Sultan, her grieving brother, sent word of Mir Chuchak's death, requesting Heer's presence at her mother's side at this tragic time. Mir Chuchak, returning from Dilli, had suffered a fatal bout of food poisoning at a feast thrown in his honour by his cousin, Mir Tullia. Heer crumpled to the floor on her knees, her head bowed and wept uncontrollably on hearing the emissary's message. My mother and I tried to hold her and comfort her, but we were helpless and ineffectual against the raging tide of her grief and the devastation it brought in its wake.

'Daughter, get up. Be strong for your mother's sake. She will need your support in this terrible hour,' my mother said. 'You can take Seida with you or go alone with a groom to accompany you, as you wish.'

She stared at my mother with uncomprehending eyes.

'The messenger waits for you. I will send two horsemen for your protection. It is best if you leave at the crack of dawn tomorrow. It is only proper that Seida go with you,' my father added.

'I do not wish to go,' said Heer, through her tears. 'My father is dead and with him my connection to Jhang.'

We all started at her declaration, not sure if we had heard her right.

She turned towards the messenger and spoke to him in a trembling voice.

'Please tell my mother that she succeeded in expelling me from my home against my wishes, now she must live with the consequences of her victory. Let her embrace the emptiness that she so wilfully created in her life. Heer will never return. Please tell my brother Sultan that my tears for my father are true. I would not taint them with mourning for him in the company of those who feigned false respect for him while conniving with those who wished him dead. Tell the people of Jhang Syal they do not deserve a daughter like me, so I will spare them my presence. And tell my dear childhood friends and cousins, all the daughters of the Syals, that even if Heer loses her life in this battle for love, they must not give up. The war must go on.'

Saying this, she retreated to her room and shut herself in. The house felt leaden with the weight of her grief.

It took much gentle cajoling and soft persistence on my part to get her to open her door the next morning and drink a few sips of water and eat a little food. Nothing remained of the strong woman who had bid her brother's messenger to go back to him with her stern refusal to go home. She was listless and weak beyond recognition, her eyes full of a deep, dark despair. I had no words of consolation to offer her, at least none that seemed adequate in the circumstances. I simply held her tight as she leaned into my shoulder, her tears flowing soundlessly.

Over the next few weeks, Heer began to, quite simply, fall apart in front of our horrified eyes. She hardly ate anything, forgot to bathe, and let her hair become unkempt, declining the maid's offer to help disentangle it for her. There were dark circles under her eyes and her collarbones stuck out, while her clothes hung loose. It seemed as if she had fallen into a death wish and was willing it to come true.

Shortly after the news of Mir Chuchak's death came from Jhang, I noticed that a black crow had come and positioned itself in our house. It watched over Heer through the day, sitting guard upon her bedroom window.

She was in the throes of a raging fever. I applied bandages of tepid water on her forehead and brow to take the temperature down, while Seida watched me helplessly, unsure of what to do for his ill bride. He brought offerings of apples from Kashmir and grapes from Kandhar to tempt her into eating something. The maid gently pressed her arms and legs in a comforting, kneading rhythm. My mother sat with her beads, her lips moving soundlessly in prayer for Heer. All of us were too preoccupied to shoo the crow away.

When Heer opened her eyes, they fell upon the crow and for the first time in many days, I saw her smile weakly.

'You have come,' she said tenderly to the crow. 'My childhood friend.'

The crow became a regular visitor to our house, flying in to sit on the windowsill to watch over the supine Heer. Later, after her fever finally broke and she was able to climb up to the rooftop, the crow would keep her company on the parapet wall. They seemed to be in some sort of communion with each other. We were glad to see that there was something that seemed to calm Heer, leaving her looking less wretched than she normally did.

The maid tied a red string on the crow's foot to confirm that it was the same bird each day. It was.

'Do you think it is the spirit of her dead father that visits her?' Rabel speculated.

'Hush! Don't speak such nonsense about the spirit of the dead. May his soul be at peace,' my mother scolded her.

I had begun to believe that the crow had actually flown in from Jhang Syal expressly to watch over Heer. It was not an impossible thought. Why should there not be communion among all of God's creatures? We were made of the same clay after all, as Murad said to me when I laughed at him for having long conversations with his camel, who he called Brother.

Murad and his Brother waited outside town. If I wanted him to leave and never come back again, I was to just tell him so in as many words and he would go without as much as turning back to take one last look at me, he said. I could not get my lips to utter those words. Yet, even if I wished to run away with him, how could I leave Heer in this state?

She drifted between coherence and incoherence on most days. Her grief was a sweeping, ravaging, all-consuming force that was impossible to quieten or contain. She seemed to be suffering from some sort of delusions. Paranoia about her uncle consumed her.

'I know it in my bones, Sehti,' she said. 'Kaido, my uncle, is behind my father's death in some evil and scheming way. Otherwise, why should a healthy and strong man in the prime of his life die in the middle of a feast? If the exertions of his travels did not kill him, why would his return home do so unless someone bore him ill will?'

'Hush, Heer,' I tried to dispel her fears. 'Your thoughts have become too morbid. Your illness is making your imagination hot and fevered. Perhaps, if you agreed to go home even now, it would be good for you. It will calm you to be amongst your own people for a while.'

She began to laugh hysterically.

'A woman like me, with a mind of her own, has no one who she can call her own people. I am as much an embarrassment in my mother's home as I am in your father's house. As much a stone around my brother's neck as I am around your brother's,' she said.

'Heer,' I protested, 'don't say such things.'

'I need truth to breathe in, Sehti,' she pleaded. 'I cannot live in a world made up of polite little lies. If we are to be friends, let not courteous inanities flow between us. Are we such weak, pitiable creatures that a small dose of plain speaking will kill us? Are you not better off for admitting that this so called sister-in-law of yours is a great embarrassment to you all? What meaningful conversation is possible between us if you put so much effort into hiding from me the upheaval I am causing in your life?'

It was true.

There was much speculation buzzing around our town about Seida's new bride and her strange ways. It was inevitable, given Heer's behaviour. She stood on the rooftop for hours like an unmoving statue. On other days she paced it like a madwoman, laughing wildly for no reason or crying unceasingly without cause. She was not just mourning her father. Her father's death had shattered her silence and reserve about her lover. I heard her sobbing Ranjha's name over and over again.

'Heer,' I said. 'If he had to come for you, he would have come by now. If you do not wish to return to your own home, learn to accept this one as your own. Seida may not be the man you love, but he is not a bad man and he means well. My mother will love you like a daughter if you will only give her a chance. What is the sense of this endless grief that lets you neither live nor die in peace?'

She stared at me with unseeing eyes.

'I cannot die in peace till I know what became of him,' she said at last. 'I cannot take with me to the grave this huge pain of not knowing what happened to Ranjha. No grave would be deep enough to contain the unrest of my soul.'

The light was leaving her eyes. She was becoming a living ghost.

I overheard her begging the crow to go find her Ranjha and bring him to her.

'You who are free to fly in the skies, won't you do this for Heer? Find him, tell him Heer is dying, tell him to come back to me,' she whispered to the crow evening after evening. The crow sat listening to her gravely and then one day it simply flew away, vanished into the dusk, not to return the next morning as it usually did. I was sorry to see him go. He had become a comforting presence, a sign that creation was not indifferent to our family's strange plight.

'Mother, what should we do about Heer? She will die like this,' I said to my mother.

'I am doing the only thing I know how to do,' she replied, her hands firmly on her prayer beads. I did not have my mother's patience and faith. I decided to go and talk to Seida. To find out his thoughts on the matter. Of late, he had started staying downstairs for longer and longer periods, sometimes not coming up even to sleep.

As I reached the corner-room downstairs that Seida usually occupied, I heard my father's voice lashing out from behind the closed door in a low but contemptuous tone.

'You pig's shit, do I have to teach you how to keep a woman satisfied? Should I do a practical demonstration for you on how to untie your pyjama string and use your prick? Ten months that snooty bitch has been with us and instead of lying moaning on the floor in the throes of labour pains, she is standing upright on my terrace, muttering her lover's name aloud for the whole world to hear.'

Don't call me Heer. All that remains of Heer is her longing for Ranjha. Call me Ranjha instead. That is what she had been telling all and sundry from the rooftop today. Word of Heer's latest transgression had undoubtedly reached my father.

'Baba, I ...' I heard Seida mumble.

'Baba WHAT, you spineless faggot? You'd rather have a horse groom's cock inside your pretty pink ass than get between a woman's legs and do a real man's work? Don't I know, you motherfucker? Bunch of fairies, that's what your mother's side of the family is full of. But at least the buggers had the decency to keep their wives pregnant and busy, whatever else they did. Didn't I tell you before your marriage that what you do for your jollies is your own business but the family and its name must go on?' hissed Father.

I felt as if I had been pushed off a high mountain cliff, limbs flaying, heart sinking, lungs squeezed of all air, plunging into nowhere with a gathering momentum. I felt I would hit the ground in smithereens. As I spun through the void, incidents from my life flashed before my eyes in swift snatches of memory—my mother's youngest brother's kohl-lined eyes and delicately mincing gait and the derision with which my father always spoke of him; the decapitated head in the water and the blood in the pond that had followed my innocent disclosure of Seida's friendship with Meru, the groom; the succession of hakims and vaids who had come and gone from our house over the years trying to cure Seida's unnamed, invisible illness; the something-isn't-quite-right quality of Heer and Seida's pretend marriage that I hadn't been able to put a finger on, their deliberate complicity in keeping us all fooled. All of these were clear as daylight to me now.

I crept back upstairs on trembling knees, my brow covered in a cold sweat, my hands clammy. I could hear the hammering of my heart, feel the fluttering of fear in my stomach, the nausea in my throat and the taste of ashes in my parched mouth.

So that was Seida's secret. The reason his eyes never met Mother's and mine. I felt a terrible pity for my poor brother. Pinioned under my father's scathing scorn, he had never breathed fully or fearlessly. His life was in many ways worse than the self-inflicted death of Rajju, my older brother. And then I thought of what my father had deliberately done to Heer. Heer, who had been more precious than a diamond in her own home. Whose name had become a synonym for beauty and strength for hundreds of miles around us. She had been brought like a cow into our house, the best pedigreed cow to be kept for foaling, to breed a few Khera bulls, her happiness no concern of ours. Had my mother suspected or known that Seida's marriage was a sham and deeply unfair to Heer? I realised she must have and yet, what exactly could she have done to stop my father once he had decided to go ahead with it? The helplessness of my mother's life sobbed out from each and every brick of our house. I saw it in every awning, every crevice, every crack in the floor where her wishes had fallen over the years and tried to remain out of sight, undetected, taken for dead.

When morning dawned, I knew what I must do. I must gift to my mother the hope that her daughter's life would pass better than her own.

I stole out of the house to meet Murad.

Standing in front of him looking at his gentle eyes and lopsided smile, I was suddenly without doubt. I would take my chances. For better or worse. In marrying a man who had waited so patiently for me to make my own choice, I was definitely off to a good start. But first, there was something else to clear with him.

'Murad,' I said. 'Much as I yearn to be your wife as soon as possible, I cannot leave Heer to her plight. She has been used terribly by my family. We stole her from her rightful partner and brought her into our home where there is nothing for her. My brother cannot be a proper husband to her, or she a loving wife to him. We must locate her Ranjha and take her to him.'

'How do you expect me to find him? He could be anywhere,' Murad said. 'Or nowhere,' he added slowly.

'You are a man and free to go where you wish. Travel to the spot where he was last seen. Go to nearby market towns and spend time at street corners where men from different places gather. Go to mosques and drinking houses, if you must. Send out word through other caravans. Someone must know of him. He is said to be a man of great beauty, an accomplished musician, a well-born lad. Someone, somewhere would know which way he went after he was thrown into the river on my father's orders. Allah forbid that it should be so, but even if he were dead, there would be some news of him. He could not have simply disappeared without trace. For my sake, Murad, do your best to find him. I am sure you will get some news of him if you try,' I implored.

'I will go today itself,' said Murad.

I stood in the circle of his arms, breathing in the soft mountain pine scent of him, the uncertainty of the last few months behind me at last. It was a relief to let my heart say aloud what it had known silently for so long. He was the one for me. This was where I belonged, right there, cradled against his broad chest, his breath fanning my hair lightly.

He soon left and was gone for over a week.

The news Murad returned with from his trip was mixed. There were rumours that Ranjha had lost his mind and now wandered in the forests around Jhang Syal, sobbing like a madman for his Heer. Others averred that he had returned to Takht Hazara and his family had found another bride for him. Another rumour, the strongest by far, was that he had travelled northwards along the banks of the Jhelum and become an ascetic. He had forsaken the world after losing Heer and joined an ancient sect of naked sadhus living in the mountains of the Salt Range.

I had hoped fervently that Murad would return with Ranjha. Now, I did not know what to believe. Or what to do next. Having said yes to Murad, there was no going back on my word. In any case, I was no longer capable of holding back my feelings for him. I was awash in them from head to toe. Yet, to leave Heer in this condition was not an option.

Someone, somewhere, somehow must have heard my fervid prayers for a miracle. I woke up one morning to be told by old Rabel, that a most astoundingly good-looking young sadhu with pierced ears, long hair and ash smeared on an all but naked body had come to Rangpur the previous evening. He was going from house to house, playing his flute and begging for alms. The entire city was beside itself with excitement at his presence.

25

Ranjha in Rangpur

IT WAS MID-MORNING WHEN the sounds of the flute wafted over the hum and buzz of the street below and carried to Heer's room. She was lying listlessly upon her cot, half sleeping, barely aware of the maid sitting at her head and fanning her to keep her cool. Her eyelids flickered rapidly and the next minute she had sprung upright and was sitting on the edge of her bed, her feet on the floor, her face flushed with excitement.

'He is here,' she shrieked.

I rushed into her room.

'Sehti, he is here. I would recognise that sound even from my grave,' she said excitedly.

'Hush, Heer!' I said. I wanted her to be careful in front of Rabel.

With my eyes I indicated to the maid that she should leave Heer to my care now. Heer was given to muttering and shouting inexplicable things. I hoped Rabel would not think this was anything out of the ordinary.

'Hush,' I said again, seating myself by her side and putting an arm around her.

'Sehti, get me my slippers, I can hear Ranjha's flute in the street below,' she urged. 'There is no time to waste. I must go to him instantly. I must catch him before he disappears again.'

'Hush, my dear sister, hush. Let me tell you the whole of it before you rush out into the street,' I said.

I told her of the rumours my Murad had gathered of how Ranjha had become a jogi. How he was an ascetic now, a naked fakir. I gave to her Rabel's description of the sadhu who had arrived yesterday.

'What is the problem, Sehti? If Ranjha is a jogi, then Heer shall become a jogan and go with him. If he can give up the world, so can his Heer. What is begging for food and sleeping on a bed of nails compared to a life without him?' she said. 'Bring me my slippers, get me my dupatta, let us not waste time talking like this.'

'Heer, calm down. Listen to me. You cannot run into the street and meet Ranjha in front of the whole city. You are a daughter-in-law of this house, if only in name. If word of it gets to my father, there will be hell to pay. Neither you nor the fakir will leave Rangpur alive,' I said. My father did not have an army at his command, like Heer's father and other feudal lords in the countryside. But he did employ a few strongmen who insured that no one in the market went back on payments or failed to pay their dues on time. They were a bunch of nasty characters who were not above killing if the need arose.

For a moment she was quiet, as if considering what I had said. But the music was drawing closer towards our house every minute, and as it came our way, Heer's restlessness increased.

'Sehti, I have waited and prayed for this moment for a year now and you expect me to sit calmly and behave as if nothing has happened? I cannot do it,' she exclaimed. 'I must meet him at once. Let your father kill us after that for all I care. Life and this world are nothing to me. I only wish to see Ranjha once again.'

'It is the easiest thing in the world to die for love and leave the bards to sing sad songs about you. Laila-Majnoon, Sassi-Panoon, Sohni-Mahiwal, our land is full of stories of failed, tragic love. Heer Syal, I urge you in the name of what you once were, not to give up so easily. You were the bravest, brightest, most beautiful woman I had heard about while I was growing up. Girls all over this countryside idolised you for your valour. Is the corpse of yet another prematurely dead beauty to weep over the best you can give us? Heer, you owe it to all of us who have admired you to come out of this alive and triumphant,' I pleaded.

I saw her straightening her back, coming to attention, her neck lifting proudly. There was a steely glint of resolve in her eyes as she turned to me and arched her brows questioningly.

'What exactly are you suggesting?' she asked.

'We can run away together, Heer. Murad and I, you and Ranjha,' I answered. 'Start a new life with Murad's people.'

'Will your father not send his goons after us? Will we not be caught and brought back to be lynched in public?' she asked. 'Surely the Khera sense of honour will not take this double betrayal without retaliation?'

'I have an idea that will buy us time to make good our escape before anyone finds out we are gone. If we are able to do it, as I hope to, they won't know where or how we've vanished. Now let me go outside and engage your jogi in some conversation so that you can feast your eyes upon him for a while,' I said.

'Rabel,' I called to the maid. 'Stop that wandering minstrel from going ahead. Get some grains for me to put in his bowl.'

I wanted to be sure it was Ranjha before we made any further plans. By now the flute was playing right outside our house. Its music was sweet and beckoning. I wondered if Ranjha knew already that this was the compound of his beloved's in-laws. He could only be here in search of Heer. Why else would he have come to Rangpur? If his resolve to be an ascetic was firm, this was the last place on earth he would choose to visit. Could it be that Heer was mistaken, that this wasn't Ranjha at all, just a wandering jogi? Maybe her intense desire for Ranjha was deluding her into hearing his music in another's tunes.

'Wait,' I called out to the jogi, just as he was walking past our compound.

He turned around to face me. I knew it was Ranjha in that instant. His eyes had the same wounded intensity that I saw in Heer's, the same fierce burning for a lost idyll. His time-ravaged body was held tautly, its nervous tension making of his bare skin a living animal alive to the slightest twitch in the air around him. His face was too gaunt to qualify as beautiful any longer, but each bone in it spoke eloquently of the Creator's original intention to fashion a finely proportioned and exceedingly fetching visage. Large copper earrings shone on his torn ear, emphasising the hollows of his cheek and the line of his protruding collar-bone.

As our eyes met, I could tell that he knew he had arrived at his destination—that this was the compound of the Kheras.

I hurriedly put the coarse grains into his begging bowl. His eyes were looking past me, trying to catch a glimpse of the compound inside.

'I am tired and thirsty,' he said. 'May I come in and rest a while and have some water please?'

I was alarmed by his request. To call a near-naked fakir inside Father's compound and entertain him was unthinkable. My father had a vitriolic hatred of both mendicants and wandering holy men. They were all charlatans and thieves in his eyes.

Ranjha must have read the hesitation on my face.

'Ah, I see the size of your heart does not match the size of your large mansion. Why is it that the ones to whom the Almighty gives so generously guard their houses so meanly? If it costs you so much to give water to a thirsty man on a hot day, then here, keep this too,' he said, thrusting the begging bowl full of grains towards me.

Something in the way he spoke angered me. He had arrived suddenly, out of nowhere, throwing our lives into utter confusion. And now he stood arrogantly before our house, rejecting my small overture of friendship and instead, passing judgement on people whose circumstances and constraints he knew nothing of.

'What did you expect then?' I hissed at him, all of me seething. 'A bridegroom's welcome? Garlands of marigold? Fresh churi and sherbet made for you by the daughter-in-law of the house? An invitation to spend the night here? Silken sheets to sleep on?'

I roughly pushed his bowl back towards him. It tipped out of his hand and broke on the ground outside our house, the grain spilling in all directions.

There was a huge gasp behind me. Rabel came running from behind.

'Sehti, what have you done!' she exclaimed, gathering the broken pieces and the scattered grain as quickly as her hands could manage it, touching each broken shard to her forehead, as if begging its forgiveness. 'You have broken a beggar's bowl at the entrance to the house. Surely, bad luck will fall upon the family.'

'What has good luck ever done for us that bad luck can ruin?' I said to her shortly as I turned to go back inside the house.

I saw Ranjha's brows arch as I glanced at him before storming inside.

I only remembered that Heer would have been watching the whole scene that had unravelled below when I reached upstairs.

'I'm sorry …' I began.

'Did he annoy you with his superior ways?' she asked, smiling gaily at me. 'Never mind that for now, Sehti. You will grow to like him when you know him better. He is alive. He is here. Nothing else matters a whit.'

She was a changed person. The colour had come back to her cheeks, life to her eyes. Her body was held differently, no longer listlessly slumped inside her clothes. If it hadn't been only ten minutes since I left her, I would have sworn that she had put on a kilo or two of weight.

The plan I had in mind was risky, but with luck we could pull it off. My family had mango orchards about thirty miles out of Rangpur, in Kalabagh. There was a natural hot water spring nearby. Its waters were famous for their curative and restorative powers. Gardens had been laid out around the spring and people from far and wide visited. As children we had always stopped there for two or three days when journeying to my grandparents' place in Bawahalpur with my mother.

I proposed to my parents that I be allowed to take Heer to Kalabagh for a few days. The fresh air would do her good and the waters of the spring might work their magic on her health. The gossip in town over Heer's obvious illness and the possible reasons behind it were also getting intolerable. It would be good for us all to go away. I suggested that even Mother could come with us. The spring's waters had eased her joint pains in the past.

Mother declined to go with us. She was not feeling up to the journey, but she agreed that it was a good idea for Heer to go. A change of scene might help her forget the tragedy of her father's sudden death. Father, after giving some thought to the matter, said that we could go, provided Seida accompanied us. It was the fruiting season and he could usefully spend a few days there supervising the work, in addition to escorting us.

That was something of a setback to my plan. I had thought that Murad would bring Ranjha to Kalabagh and we would make good our escape before my family found out that we were no longer there. Still, it was better than being trapped at home with no prospect of making a getaway. We got ready to leave.

Meanwhile, Murad had been to see Ranjha. He had set up base on the bank of the river now and in the few days that he had been here, he had attracted something of a following. Colicky babies, injured children and animals and sick people were making their way towards him in a steady stream. His music, it was being said, had healing powers. He had also performed a few minor miracles—produced holy ashes and amulets out of thin air for followers to bring back home with them.

Hearing this, something of an idea began to form in my head.

I urged Murad to ask Ranjha to perform a few more of his flashy miracles. Everyone should get to hear of his powers. As per my plan, we would soon need the very best healer that could be found.

We set out early to avoid the mid-day sun. It was only half a day's ride. I had managed to persuade my parents that no attendants were necessary. They would only intrude upon our privacy and make it difficult for us to be relaxed with each other. I could see that both my parents were keen for Heer and Seida to spend time with each other. I played on that sentiment, promising to take care of all the mundane chores. The retainer's family living in the vicinity of our cottage would prepare our meals. With their help we would manage to take good care of ourselves for the fortnight that we expected to be away. With many such assurances, our little group finally left Rangpur.

We reached Kalabagh before noon. Even in the hot weather it was a soothing place, with its gently undulating hillocks. It had seemingly unending rows of round-topped, dark green trees with spreading branches, the entire canopy dense with softly rustling leaves and bowed with the weight of the fruit. The wafting breeze was sweet and heavy with the smell of ripening mangoes. There were birds chirping and trilling away as they flew from perch to perch. Parrots and cuckoo birds, mynahs and sparrows, crows and eagles all came to inspect us as we settled down in our little cottage. A peacock spread its wings out and danced on the tiled roof, its bejewelled emerald and sapphire fan tail juxtaposed against a clear blue sky

In no time at all, we had unloaded our few belongings and stocked drinking water in the empty earthen pots that had been left outside the one-room hut for our use. The simplicity of the place felt like a balm, the surrounding breeze like a benediction. Heer and I sat on the small raised platform outside, resting our back against the wall of the hut, watching Seida tend to the horses. Seida's presence had complicated the initial plan and I was now feeling nervous about our prospects.

'Why do you frown, sweet Sehti?' asked Heer, smiling happily at me. Since Ranjha's return, she had become unflappable. Nothing seemed to ruffle her calm or confidence. She seemed to think it was all already accomplished, that we were both united with our lovers, living free and happy.

'What if our plan fails? What if Seida suspects the truth or refuses to go back without us?' I asked.

So, my plan went like this. I intended to inflict a small injury on Heer's ankle, tie it up very tightly till the area became mottled and blue due to a lack of blood circulation, and then tell Seida that she had been bitten by a snake while we were strolling in the gardens. Heer was to feign that she had been severely poisoned and was on her deathbed. I was to persuade Seida to go back to Rangpur as soon as possible and fetch the jogi with magical healing powers while I tended to her here. Ranjha had been briefed by Murad on his role in the drama. He was to initially refuse and then agree after a lot of pleading on Seida's part, on the condition that he would be left alone with the patient. When Seida returned with Ranjha, I would insist on staying on to chaperone Heer while he returned home once again. Then Murad was to join us and we were to flee.

There were too many junctures at which the plan could go awry. I could not help but worry.

'Take Seida into our confidence. Everything will become easy,' said Heer nonchalantly.

I stared at her in horror. Did she realise the full import of what she was suggesting? I could not think of any reason why Seida would help his wife and sister elope. And once he knew of our plan, our fates would be sealed forever. I could not bear to think of what would happen if we failed in our endeavour or if Father came to know of it before we were out of the range of his influence.

'No, Heer, it will jeopardise everything,' I said firmly.

'As you see fit,' she shrugged.

Over the next three days, the realisation slowly dawned on me that there was something akin to friendship between Seida and Heer. It hurt to know that my brother, whom I had known all my life, stepped warily around me, our eyes scarcely meeting, while with Heer he was solicitous and direct. It was as if he was her brother and I was the stranger in the room.

They were tied by a shared secret. A shared enemy too, I suppose, in my overbearing father. They did not speak much to each other, but they were comfortable in each other's company, the way that two girls from the same village are in their in-laws' village. Neither of them knew that I knew Seida's secret too. It was such a personal matter that I did not even know how to tell them that they need not hide it from me.

It was the third evening of our stay in Kalabagh. The evening meal was over. I was in a pensive mood. We planned to fake Heer's snakebite early next morning. According to my plan, Seida needed to leave for Rangpur by noon. As I stared into the sky, my gaze fixed on the evening star just above the horizon, I felt a terrible ache in my heart. These were probably the last few hours I would be spending with my brother. And all there was between us was lies and deceit. I thought back to the friendship of our childhood and how one silly, childish act had jeopardised it forever. I felt tears starting up in my eyes.

'Seida, it was I who tattled to Baba about your friendship with Meru,' I heard myself say with a sob. 'I did not know Meru would die for that.'

There was a stunned look on Seida's face. Tears were gushing out of my eyes. Heer was looking from me to Seida, trying to understand what was going on.

'Your friend, the horse groom?' she asked Seida.

So they had talked about that too. Another stab of hurt went through me. What a fool I had been to let my brother drift so far away from me.

'I should have told you sooner, but I was scared. Scared you would hate me. Never talk to me again. Never love me,' I cried. 'Not that keeping quiet helped. We don't talk anymore, do we?'

'It was a long time ago, Sehti. Why are you telling me now?' asked Seida. His face was full of shadows, its expression hard to read, but I could tell that even after all these years he could not recall the incident without pain.

I stared back at him numbly. How could I tell him it was because I wanted my brother back, even if it was only for an evening?

'Knowing Heer has changed me, I think,' I said, after a long-drawn silence. 'However difficult the truth is, she never tells lies, she never pretends everything is alright if it isn't. I want to be strong like that too.'

'Oh, Sehti, you don't know how much that means to me,' said Heer. 'I have been so craven, so defeated these past months that I had begun to despise myself. That you could see strength in me is such a relief.'

She came closer to me and gave me a hug.

'Seida,' she said. 'Let your little sister out of her misery. Tell her she was only a child. She cannot carry the blame for your father's brutality.'

Seida was quiet for a minute. Then he looked at me and said, 'Forget about it, Sehti. You could not have known what would happen. It is senseless for you to carry the guilt of Meru's death on your conscience. You didn't have him killed. Father did. Let him answer his Maker on Judgment Day. And you are right about Heer. She gives me courage too. I am no longer as scared of Father as I once was. I would like to go and fetch her Ranjha for her, if you both can stay here for a day alone. We can help them escape.'

'You know where Ranjha is?' exclaimed Heer. 'You recognised him!'

'I could never forget such a handsome face on a man,' he said, his lips twisting in a bitter half-smile.

'Sehti, you had better tell him about Murad,' said Heer fixing her gaze on me sternly.

I felt the blood rush to my head in panic. To hear her take Murad's name so easily filled me with terror. I had kept him a secret from my family so carefully, and for so long, that to speak about him seemed unimaginable. I stared at them both, tongue-tied and lost for words.

Seida looked at me questioningly, waiting for me to say something.

'You tell him, please,' I begged her.

'Only since I owe you so many favours,' she laughed.

We sat outside the cottage in the mango orchard on a string cot, its jute strings thickly woven in a radial pattern fanning out from the centre, talking through the night. The stars hung so low that it seemed they were eavesdropping on our conversation. The trees emitted an occasional collective sigh, or a deep murmur of approval, as if they too were listening with deep interest. A few fireflies danced in the distance, flickering in and out of our line of vision.

The next day, around noon, Seida left for Rangpur to fetch Ranjha and Murad. He was eager to meet his future brother-in-law.

If only I could have had my mother's blessings, my happiness would have been complete.

X

THE EVER AFTERS

26

And Finally

WE WERE HEADED TOWARDS the Gomal Pass from Dera Ismail Khan, the point at which we had crossed the Sindh river. The landscape was rugged and sparse with steep, narrow stony paths through sun-scorched ridges and furrows, devoid of any vegetation except the occasional clump of gnarled olive trees. In the distant south-west loomed the Sulaiman range, with its imposing Kaiserbagh mountain frowning upon us from far, a five-o'clock shadow of chilgoza pines growing on it like a rough stubble darkening its chalky, limestone face.

We had been over a fortnight on the road. Murad and Sehti were on his camel. Heer and I on the two horses which had carried her and Sehti to Kalabagh. Just after crossing the river, we had joined a caravan of Baloch traders returning from Kabul and proceeding towards Kuhetta. My thoughts were with Seida Khera, a man I had hated in my imagination for so long, only to end up being in his debt for life. As I remembered our two evenings together at Kalabagh, I could not help but feel a deep sadness for him. The scene that Seida had described of his last meeting with Meru was branded into my mind forever, a deep scar destined to throb with pain every now and again in the smooth skin of my memories.

Behind the Khera's house, a short walk down a narrow footpath, beaten into a flat brown ribbon of earth, lie the stables, the astabal where the family's horses are lodged, groomed and fed. Seida went down this footpath every day to meet his friend Meru.

It was an afternoon in May. The day before Meru died, the two of them, aged seventeen and nineteen, raced each other towards the astabal, after their customary swim in the adjoining pond. Their thin kurtas were stuck against their chests and their hearts were galloping like truant horses with the exertion. The other grooms had finished the morning's feeding and left. The astabal was cool, the sweet smell of horse dung pervading it. Seida stood panting, trying to recover his breath. Meru shook the water from his hair and reached for a towel to dry his neck and face. Something in Meru's movements caught Seida's attention and he was struck breathless by the equine grace of the other. He swallowed quickly as he felt his body flush all over with an unfamiliar heat. Confused, he looked down and seeing a feeding trough at his feet, he picked up some horse-feed from it and showered it on the unsuspecting Meru. For a brief second Meru was taken aback and then bouncing back swiftly in retaliation, he took a bucket of water lying handy and doused Seida with it. Only, Seida was not doused but further enflamed, the blood rushing to his ears and his heart thudding audibly in the dark silence of the astabal.

They stood there staring at each other, one with chopped hay festooned in his hair and over his clothes and the other drenched in half a bucket of water, not knowing how to avert the next moment. It was not clear what happened next or who made the first move. Perhaps it was their intention to wrestle each other. But what they were wrestling with next, as they lay entangled with each other, their breathing short, alarmed and rasping, was a third. An emotion stronger than either of them, an emotion both languid and giddy at once, heavy with the sweet perfume of the dark horses who watched them silently on that hot May afternoon, light-headed with the thrill of being young and alive and touching each other.

The sound of approaching footsteps broke through the afternoon's haze. Seida looked up to see his father's livid face staring at both of them for a brief second. And then he had turned around on his heel and was gone. The next morning, the pond behind the stables rippled deep crimson and Meru's head floated upon it like a solitary, wilting lotus.

We had gotten away, Heer and I, Murad and Sehti, but Seida seemed trapped forever inside a life not of his choosing. My thoughts kept going towards him, wondering whether he had been strong enough to withstand the wrath of his father when he went back with the news of our elopement. How would he have explained his own position? How much scorn and blame must have rained down upon him? By now the Kheras must have sent out men to search for the runaways, but if all went according to plan, we had a good eight–ten day lead. Now that we had joined the Baloch tribesmen and their caravan, the Kheras were unlikely to find us.

Even as the thought that we were finally safe crossed my head, the caravan was brought to an abrupt halt. A troop of armed horsemen were barring the way.

'By the orders of Adali Raja, I bid you to stop and hand over the runaway bride of the Kheras and her paramour,' said the sipahadar, the captain of the troop.

I saw the chieftain of the clan, a venerable old tribesman with a flowing white beard and a matching white robe, long and fleeing, move up to parley with the captain. After a while, the chieftain made his way down to where Heer was seated on her horse, next to Sehti and a group of Baloch women. His face wore a grim expression.

'Is it true that you are the daughter-in-law of Ajju Khera of Rangpur?' he asked Heer.

'It is not true,' said Heer. 'As God is my witness, I am, I always was and always will be the wife of Deedho Ranjha, son of Mauju Chaudhary of Takht Hazara.'

'These men have been sent to summon you to the court of Adali Raja on the grounds of running away from your lawful husband,' he said. 'It is a grave accusation. If that is indeed the case, we cannot offer you both our protection. It is against the dictates of our conscience.'

'I can explain,' I said, stepping into the conversation. 'Heer Syal was my promised bride with the blessings of her father Mir Chuchak. We even pledged ourselves to each other at the cave shrine of Baba Farid, only a formal nikah was to take place after her father returned from Dilli. In Mir Chuchak's absence, she was given away, against her wishes, in marriage to Seida Khera by her uncle Kaido. I have brought her away with the full knowledge of Seida Khera, who acknowledges my prior rights and has willingly relinquished all claims on her.'

The sipahadar said this was a falsehood, as Adali Raja was acting at the behest of the Kheras, who had sent word to him that their bride had been stolen and must be returned to them.

The chieftain turned to Heer and me.

'This is quite clearly a disputed matter. Adali Raja is known for his keen dispensation of justice. Present yourself at his court and let him decide. If he rules in your favour, come back to us. We will be camping here for ten days, right up to the next full moon,' he said.

The sipahadar cleared his throat and spoke again.

'There is another matter. A Baloch by the name of Murad has run away with ...'

'Enough, captain,' snapped the chieftain. 'Tell the Kheras to be less careless with their daughters-in-law and leave us to look after ours. Please convey my regrets to Adali Raja. The bride of Murad the Baloch is ours to protect and take care of now. The Raja may be reassured that the Kheras' daughter is here of her own free will and happy in her new home. Let there be no further discussion on the matter, please.'

'We will wait here for you, brother. We will stay till you return,' said Murad as he hugged me to his chest and pressed his cheeks against mine in farewell.

We were handed over to Adali Raja's men and headed in the reverse direction once again. There was a sweet ache in crossing the now familiar milestones, the streams, the bridges, the rocks and passes that we had so recently associated in our hearts with freedom and happiness. The familiar landscape that had danced with hope only a few days ago now appeared bleak.

Heer and I scarcely spoke in the three days that it took to reach Fort Qubala, the high stone fortress on the hill in which we were to be locked into separate cells to await the great Adali Raja and his judgement. Guarded and watched closely by the soldiers, there was little opportunity for all but the most routine exchanges between us. As we rode across the green valley of the Sindh, my mind had become absolutely still. The words 'Alakh Niranjan' reverberated ceaselessly through my being. I kept reminding myself that though I was this limited Ranjha, once again being led by men of power, to be robbed of all I had loved and desired in this life, I was also unlimited, unbound by any form, the un-birthed and deathless spirit. Beyond mind, intelligence, ego and body I was the indestructible self.

As we dismounted from our horses, our hands were tied behind our backs and we were led towards our cells. I snapped out of my yogic trance and looked into Heer's eyes. They were ablaze with determination. In the Nath tradition it is the duty of the jogi never to let the dhuni, the sacred fire, die out. The fire in those eyes was the one I had been sent to keep alive at all costs. The time for feeling helpless was over, I told myself sternly. This was the moment to be so sure of what we desired that the universe had no choice but to bow to our will.

A week later, we were led to the king's courthouse. Our fame—or was it our supposed infamy?—was greater than I had anticipated. Hundreds of people filled the large hall, eager to watch the proceedings with their own eyes. The court was called to order. A clerk read out the application of Seida Khera, dictated on his behalf by his father Ajju Khera, for the restoration of his legally wed wife, Heer Syal, daughter of Mir Chuchak of Jhang.

Adali Raja's men had done due diligence on the matter. Testimonies of five ordinary people of Rangpur were presented, confirming that they had witnessed the wedding of Heer Syal with Seida Khera and further, had seen her living in the house of the Kheras for the past twelve months. Next, testimonies were presented from Jhang Syal. Heer's mother Malki, her brother Sultan, her uncle Kaido, the qazi and the head cook at the wedding feast had all affirmed that they were witness to the marriage. The nikah agreement and the terms of mehar that had been fixed were declared before the court.

'Heer Syal, daughter of Mir Chuchak, whom I had the privilege of knowing personally and held in great regard, what do you have to say in your defence?' asked Adali Raja.

Heer bowed to him formally.

'O Mighty King, friend of my esteemed father, I have grown up hearing tales of your sagacity, justice and fairness. I bow to you humbly and deeply and request to submit before you a question for your consideration,' she said.

'Go ahead,' said Adali Raja.

'Is it day or night at this moment?' she asked.

'It is day, of course,' he replied.

'If I say it is night, does it become night?' she asked.

'No.'

'So clearly, truth is independent of one individual's perception of it?' she asked.

'That is quite obvious, isn't it?' he replied.

'If a hundred people say it is night, does that change the verdict? If we suppose that this whole room full of people says it is night can we then call it night?' Heer asked.

'No, of course not,' said Adali Raja.

'So you concede, then, that truth does not belong to the majority, that it exists irrespective of the number of people in agreement or disagreement with it,' she said.

'Yes, carry on,' said Adali Raja.

'If you, as the most powerful ruler of this land, declare it to be night, then shall it become night?'

'No. Heer Syal, your argument is well taken. Now clearly say what you want to and get on with the matter,' ordered Adali Raja.

'I submit for your approval the contention that if the most powerful king in the land, or the most venerated qazi in the world, were to declare it to be night, day would still remain day. So truth does not belong to those in power or to heads of faith, even,' Heer averred. 'Truth is independent and exists in and of itself. So no matter how many testimonies are presented here and how powerful the people behind those testimonies may be, the good king must concede that the truth is not necessarily established by their mere presentation.'

A buzz went through the crowd. Her point had obviously generated a huge debate. My eyes were fixed on Adali Raja's face. Was he annoyed or impressed by Heer's arguments? It appeared he was deep in thought, his face clear of all expressions.

'Your argument is good, noble daughter of the Syals. However, night and day obey natural laws and are above man's jurisdiction. The matter before us relates to marriage, which is a social institution created by man and is subject to his laws,' said Adali Raja. 'By these laws and the evidence presented, it would seem that you were married to Seida Khera of Rangpur.'

'That is not true, O Great King. The laws of our land and the strictures of our faith require the bride's consent to her wedding. I stand before you declaring vehemently and repeatedly that Heer Syal did not, at any stage, agree to a marriage with Seida Khera,' said

Heer. 'I was already the wife of my Ranjha by then, for all intents and purposes.'

'Heer, for the purposes of this world, a marriage is more than a meeting of minds and bodies. It is a legal contract entered into by two parties, preferably in the presence of their families, and witnessed by God's representatives. A man and woman cannot simply declare themselves married. Their contract must be witnessed and sanctioned by society,' said Adali Raja.

'My father blessed our union and we exchanged our vows at the shrine of Shakarganj Baba, according to my father's wishes. Not all marriages are brokered on earth after weighing cash and jewels, matching property and status, fixing dowry and mehar. Some are made in heaven and are based on the true pairing of souls. Lovers are the Almighty's emissaries on earth. In every age, they are sent to demonstrate that the barriers of caste, class, country and creed are man-made and unreal. That all it takes is love to walk past them,' said Heer.

'Heer Syal, you take the moral high ground and leave us to struggle with the practical and the mundane. You invoke the name of the Panj Pir and the Almighty, but how do we know that these are not delusions of an impassioned mind, which seeks to justify your transgressions by imagining that they are divinely inspired?' asked Adali Raja. 'To admit your argument would be to allow all fornicators, adulterers and marriage breakers in future to claim sanction for their actions from saints and pirs.'

'To dismiss my argument means that the testimony of a qazi who commits perjury in full sight of a whole village counts for more in your dispensation than the letter and spirit of the Holy Book. If the Quran decrees clearly that the consent of the bride is mandatory to the solemnisation of the nikah, and if the bride stands before you declaring loudly and clearly that her consent was not given, then what scope is there for doubt?' asked Heer.

I looked at Adali Raja's face for some reaction. Surely, that was an irrefutable argument? But his face betrayed nothing.

'I have nothing more to say in my defence. It is for you to decide whether the laws and principles laid down in the Quran are sacred and inviolate or whether the qazis and the mullahs—these men who rule in the name of Allah—can overrule His word and are free to interpret and twist the law to suit their own purposes. But think, O King, what hope of justice would there be left in the world for the weak and the wronged if the powerful are allowed to manipulate the laws as per their own convenience?'

Her eyes were ablaze with anger.

'Heer Syal, you have posed a great conundrum before us and I would like to deliberate over the arguments on either side for one night before I declare my final verdict. I would not like to pronounce a judgment on this matter in haste,' said Adali Raja. 'This court is adjourned till noon tomorrow.'

Amid much palpable disappointment, the crowd began to vacate the courtroom. I had a chance to exchange a few words with Heer before the Raja's men locked us up again.

'Play your flute tonight, so I can hear you from my cell. Who knows how much longer we have together,' she said.

'What should we do if the verdict goes against us?' I asked her.

'Let us see what happens. I still carry a small dagger with me. However, I would rather kill a few with it than use it upon myself,' she said to me through gritted teeth. 'I would prefer to die a warrior's death than that of a helpless woman.'

I nodded back grimly. There had to be a better ending to our story than a suicide pact.

Why does love cause so much consternation in this world? Why can't a man and a woman who love each other simply be allowed to exist? Why do family and society align themselves into opposing them, why do councils and courts get dragged into the matter,

why are fatwas, feuds and killings unleashed to stop them? Would
it not be simpler to let lovers bear the consequences of their love,
let society go on with its business and let them get on with theirs?

I brooded over these questions long into the night in my solitary
cell.

At the crux of creation is love. In the mating of a man and a
woman lies the key to history. Every choice they make changes the
shape of the future. The rule-makers fear a dismantling of their
carefully constructed power structures, which are held up on the
fortified walls of caste and religion, class and country, language and
race. When lovers walk through these walls as if they are constructed
of air and signify nothing, the power brokers of the world begin to
shake. Perhaps, in each age, lovers are sent to challenge the status
quo and to expand the possibilities of life and creation. The marriage
of Sehti and Murad, I could see, would birth a new race, a new
language, new cuisines, new customs and rituals.

And the marriage of Heer and Ranjha? Would it outlast this
dark night?

I remembered Heer's plea to play for her.

The first few notes from my flute were hesitant and weak, unsure
of themselves. If this was the last time I was playing for her, what
did I wish to say and what would she wish to hear?

I began at the beginning, when the eagle of death swooped
down upon Takht Hazara and flew away into the unrelenting sky
with the morsel of Father's life held in its beak. I told the tale of a
boy's angry parting from his mother, brothers and sisters-in-law,
of dark animal eyes staring at him on lonesome nights spent in
the wilderness, of the cold stone floor and high minarets of an
unwelcoming mosque, of the turbulent crossing of a stormy, silver
river. My flute fell into a trance as it told of Heer and Ranjha's first
meeting on a boat, and how that boat rocked languorously with
our love-making and the waters of the Chanan blushed a rosy pink
in a slowly spreading suffusion. It recreated the trysts in the forest,

the swims in the river, and the fevered heat of the secret meetings in Mithi's hut. It spoke of an absent father and an unrelenting mother, of a cunning uncle and a conniving brother, and of a false wedding. Even as I played, I was transported into Heer's days of waiting for me on the rooftop of the Kheras, and I felt her agony in every cell of my being. And yet I played on and told the story of my own search for peace and salvation as I wandered the land separated from my Heer. The watchful eyes of a solitary crow on the neem tree, the helpless fluttering of pigeons in a dank, dirty loft, the woebegone eyes of a gentle goat ... all wound themselves into the sound of my music. As did riverbanks, meadows, high mountain passes and open blue skies.

Even as dawn broke in amber rays over the jagged, high stone walls of Kot Qubala, I fell into an exhausted stupor. I was indifferent now to whether we lived or died. Heer and I had lived and loved more intensely in our brief time together than many do over several lifetimes.

I awoke to the sound of my heavy cell door being unlocked and pushed open. From the sunlight that flooded in, it seemed to be close to noon. The sentries told me to get ready quickly. I had been summoned by Adali Raja.

When I reached the Raja's chambers, Heer was already there, facing him, sitting upright, her shoulders squared and her ankles crossed, her hands locked together upon her lap with the thumbs jutting out resolutely. The sentries bowed and left at a command from the king. We were alone with him.

'Yesterday, in the day, I heard Heer's arguments. Last night I could not sleep for the music that flowed out of Ranjha's flute,' he said. 'I do not need any further proof from you both that you belong together, no matter what the documents presented before me may say. To separate two human beings who are connected so deeply to each other is a sin I would not want upon my conscience.'

Heer and I looked at each other in relief.

'Yet, if I let you go free in court today, I cannot see this world of honour and shame, ego and entitlement, pride and possessiveness allowing you to live in peace. Sooner or later, you will be found and killed. If the Kheras don't get to you, the Syals will.'

It was a sobering thought. We were back where we had always been. The reason I had resisted the idea of an elopement to start with.

'If you will permit me to take the matter in my hands, there might still be a way out. In today's court I will pronounce the judgment that Heer is to return to the Kheras in Rangpur and that Ranjha will be our prisoner till such a time as we see fit,' he said. 'However, tonight, you will be released secretly and escorted back to the Baloch caravan. Later in the night, there will be a fire in the fort. All of Kot Qubula will see the flames from Heer and Ranjha's cells rise up into the sky. It will be understood that the lovers chose self-immolation over separation. Once you are believed to be dead, you can live together in peace. No search parties will be sent after you. You will be free to go wherever you wish.'

'So once more the world will be told that there is no place for lovers in it except the grave? That true love is truly doomed? That we lovers come, we love briefly and die, only our tragedies remain for people to gather around the fireside and weep over, so that they can mourn for the parts of themselves that they have allowed to be killed and buried unfulfilled?' asked Heer, a rebellious edge to her voice.

'Yes, Heer. Sometimes the only way to move forward is to take a few steps back and find another way. It is more important that you live than that you are seen to be alive. Forgive me, I can offer you only this compromise, but the other way seems doomed to failure,' said the raja. 'Why risk it?'

Still Heer looked at him with the last vestiges of doubt on her face.

I, who could find no fault with Heer, felt that for once she was being too inflexible, given the reality of our situation. I frowned at her warningly and stepped in.

'We are grateful for your kindness, O Mighty Raja. We will be in your debt forever,' I said.

We were getting a chance at love and life and it was enough for me. The world could tell itself any story about us that it wished, as long as we lived to truly have a story.

27

A Crow Signs Off

MY WHOLE LIFE FLASHES past my eyes as I breathe my last at the feet of the Great Balnath Jogi. From those early days of being a callow crow in the junior cacophony to this last, near impossible mission to Tilla Jogian to send Ranjha back to Heer, it has been a life well lived. I have no regrets.

28

The Pigeons' Postscript

SHE IS DEAD, DEAD, dead, dead, dead. Kaido Langra prevailed in the end. Heer and her cowherd died a terrible death, burnt to cinders at Fort Qubala. Some sentimental fools nevertheless built a grave outside Jhang Syal, in which Heer and her Ranjha are said to lie wrapped in each other's arms. Idiotic young women visit the grave and pray to Mai Heer to smile upon their love. No Syal will ever visit that grave. For ever after, Syal women will lower their eyes if anyone should take her name. Even hundreds of years later, the young men of Jhang will rise up in a mob and resort to street violence if any attempt is made to deify Heer's legend.

This is the fate of daughters who disobey. This is the legacy of the crippled man.

29

The Goat Says Goodbye

IT IS INEVITABLE THAT someone gets left out of the party. However happy the ending, someone is bound to get excluded. So, for me, this story ends with Eid in a place far away from home. For Seida Khera, too, it will be something like that. He will be a goat at the altar of marriage once again. When everyone around is happily celebrating Eid, who pays heed to the goat's strangulated cry?

30

The Other Story

I AM OTHER, THE TWICE-GIFTED CAMEL.

Murad first gifted me as a mate to his camel, Brother. And secondly, as a ride to his other new-found brother, Ranjha. There is much to tell about camels—bactrian and dromedary—our relationship with each other, and our long history with humans. Regretfully, there is no space for it in this narrative. However many stories get told, there are others that remain untold. It is the very nature of the narrative to be incomplete. To leave some trails for the curious to explore on their own.

Suffice it to say that the lovers are happy and safe. They are reunited with Murad's father's tribe. It is late summer in Kuhetta. The city is a natural fort surrounded by high mountains on all sides. From a distance you can see Lake Hanna, sitting like a turquoise jewel, guarded by steep mountains on all sides. Autumn will come soon in a splash of gold and a burst of red on the junipers. All of nature will don the colours of Murad and Sehti's nuptials, of Heer and Ranjha's reunion.

Ranjha has become somewhat drunk on music as he sits night and day with the Balochs, learning to play their saz and tar. Heer is back to her Razia-the-Queen days, teaching little girls to fight. Never forget you are one half of the human race, she tells them.

Not the better half or the worse, just an equal half. Ask to live your equal share of life.

New music is being birthed. And new valour.

In time, we will travel again. Heer, Ranjha and I. Across the Bolan Pass to see the many splendours of Persia. To the Mughal Darbar in Agra where Ranjha will enthral Mia Tansen with his music. Down, deep down south, past the Vindhyas to Kerala for Heer to learn new martial arts. As she will deepen her practice as a warrior, she will become more poised on the path of peace, for in the end, the way of the warrior and the path of the yogi meet.

Author's Note

THE STORY OF HEER and Ranjha has been told and retold many times in the last five–six hundred years. According to Annemarie Schimmel, a renowned scholar of oriental lore, the story has been written in over a hundred versions across Punjabi, Urdu, Sindhi and Persian. The first written version is attributed to Damodar Gulati, while the most popular version is probably Waris Shah's epic poem in Punjabi, written in 1766.

While the central characters, key dramatic elements and geographic location of the story remain the same, each version of Heer differs in its details. My rendering of the major events in the story follows Waris Shah's. However, the characterisation of Heer as a warrior, her clash with Noora of Sambhal, and her friendship with Hassi (and the character of Hassi) are taken from Damodar Gulati's version. The dialogues between Heer and Malki and Heer and the qazi owe their inspiration to two other popular versions of the tale—those by Kishan Singh Arif and Na'at. And many, many elements of the story in this telling are entirely the product of my own imagination. So, for readers who want to know how close this version is to the 'original' story of Heer-Ranjha, I can only say that Heer and Ranjha live on a continuum in our collective imagination. My rendering is one of many originals, no more, no less.

The story strikes a very deep emotional chord with the people of Punjab on both sides of the Indo-Pakistan border. What makes it so compelling, to my mind, are not the events of the tale, for it is the familiar and oft-told story of a boy and a girl in love, thwarted by familial opposition. It is the personas of Heer and Ranjha that come back to haunt us repeatedly. They symbolise the men and women we did not become and the social order we did not choose. Ranjha is the man who did not give the prevailing economic dispensation dominion over his soul, who rejected the idea that a man needed to own land and wealth or assert power over the woman in his life as a measure of his worth. Heer is the woman who took full responsibility for her life and body, asserting her rights, not just in the narrow sense of romantic or sexual agency, but in interacting with the outside world independently and fearlessly on every occasion. The lost social idyll these two represent for humanity is not just of a world that is more accepting of romantic love, but also one that is less dominating over nature, kinder to other species, and less consumerist in its orientation.

Select Bibliography

Charles Frederick Usborne, *The Adventures of Hir&Ranjha* (Karachi Lion Art Press, 1966).

RC Temple, *The Legends of the Panjab, Volumes I and II* (Kessinger Publishing, LLC, 2003).

Farina Mir, *The Social Space of Language: Vernacular Culture in British Colonial Punjab* (University of California Press, 2010).

Saba Imtiaz, 'Above Class and Clerics: The Saga of Heer Ranjha'.

Mushtaq Soofi, 'Ravi and Chenab: Demons and Lovers'.

Mushtaq Soofi, 'Damodar Gulati: Poet Who Immortalised Heer and Ranjha'.

Najam Hosain Syed, 'The Fakir as Hero: Ranjha'.

Najam Hosain Syed, 'The River and The Desert'.

Harjeet Singh Gill, 'The Cosmology of Heer'.

Salman Rashid, 'Hill of the Jogis'.

Salman Rashid, 'Monument of Wasted Labour'.

Made in United States
North Haven, CT
19 September 2024

57542262R00182